P9-BBV-672

BREATHERS

THIS IS NO LONGER THE
PROPERTY OF
KING COUNTY LIBRARY SYSTEM

MAR   2009

BREATHERS

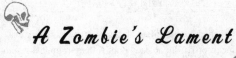 *A Zombie's Lament*

S. G. BROWNE

BROADWAY BOOKS
New York

BROADWAY

This book is a work of fiction. Names, characters, businesses,
organizations, places, events, and incidents either are the
product of the author's imagination or are used fictitiously.
Any resemblance to actual persons, living or dead, events,
or locales is entirely coincidental.

Copyright © 2009 by Scott Browne

All Rights Reserved

Published in the United States by Broadway Books,
an imprint of The Doubleday Publishing Group, a division
of Random House, Inc., New York.
www.broadwaybooks.com

BROADWAY BOOKS and its logo, a letter B bisected on the diagonal, are
trademarks of Random House, Inc.

Book design by Nicola Ferguson

Library of Congress Cataloging-in-Publication Data

Browne, S. G. (Scott G.)
Breathers : a zombie's lament / S.G. Browne. —1st ed.
p. cm.
1. Zombies—Fiction. I. Title.
PS3602.R7369B74 2008
813'.6—dc22
2008027080

ISBN 978-0-7679-3061-1

PRINTED IN THE UNITED STATES OF AMERICA

1 3 5 7 9 10 8 6 4 2

First Edition

For Shaka,
Thanks for giving me the opportunity
to discover what I wanted to do.

BREATHERS

Chapter 1

I wake up on the floor in darkness.

Faint artificial light filters in through a window, which doesn't make sense because there aren't any windows in the wine cellar. But I'm not able to deal with that question until I figure out why I'm on my back in a pool of liquid that's seeping into my clothes.

That and I can hear Sammy Davis Jr. singing "Jingle Bells."

When I sit up, something rolls off of my body and onto the floor with a hard, hollow *thunk*. It's a bottle. In the faint light coming in through the window, I watch the bottle roll away across the floor until it comes to rest against the wall with a *clang*. It's an empty bottle of wine. And the wall isn't a wall but the base of the Whirlpool oven.

I'm in the kitchen.

On the digital LED display at the top of the range, the clock changes from 12:47 to 12:48.

My head is pounding. I don't know how many bottles of wine I've consumed, but I know I started drinking before lunch. The impetus for my wine binge is as clear to me as the digital numbers of the oven clock, but I have no idea what happened to the last twelve hours.

Or how I ended up in the kitchen.

Or what I'm sitting in.

Part of me doesn't want to know. Part of me just wants to believe that it's nothing more than fermented grapes. That I somehow managed to get out of the wine cellar and into the kitchen and then passed out, dumping the contents of the bottle of wine onto the floor. Except the front of my clothes aren't wet, only the back, and since the bottle was on my chest when I woke up, I couldn't have spilled wine on the floor without soaking my shirt.

I put my hand down into the puddle, which is congealed and sticky, then bring my hand up to my nose. It smells sweet. At first I think it's yogurt or strawberry preserves, until I put my finger in my mouth.

It's Baskin-Robbins strawberries and cream ice cream. My father's favorite. He keeps at least two quarts of it in the freezer at all times. What I don't understand is what it's doing on the kitchen floor. Then I turn around and stagger to my feet and understand why.

Three quarts of Baskin-Robbins are smashed open, their contents melted and spreading out across the floor. Surrounding them are boxes of frozen vegetables, packages of frozen meats, containers of frozen juice concentrate, and half a dozen ice cube trays, their contents melted and mixed in with the ice cream, forming a pool of defrosted frozen items.

Oh shit, I think. *What the hell did I do?*

Not that it really matters. My parents are going to ship me off to a zoo when they get back from Palm Springs. Unless they wake up in the morning and my father is upset enough about what I've done to cancel their trip and ship me off to a research facility out of spite.

I don't know what I intended to accomplish by dumping the entire contents of the freezer onto the kitchen floor, but I figure it would probably be a good idea to try to put back what I can and clean up the rest of it before my parents wake up. But when I open the freezer, I discover there's not any room.

My parents are in the freezer. I can see hands and legs and feet and my father's face staring out at me from the second shelf. His head is in a large Ziploc freezer bag, as are the rest of my parents' body parts. Or most of them. When I open the refrigerator, my parents are in there, too.

All the wine I've drunk is suddenly trying to find its way back into the bottle and I barely make it to the sink before I throw up. Actually, it's more like reverse drinking. Just wine and a little stomach acid. But no chunks of Mom or Dad.

Our relationship wasn't always like this.

Sure, there were the standard growing pains and disagreements most parents and sons encounter.

Hormones.

Independence.

Latent Oedipal desires.

But when your only son reanimates from the dead, it creates an entirely new dynamic that your average parents just aren't prepared to handle.

After all, it's not like there's a handbook for dealing with spontaneous resurrection. That's the technical term for zombies you hear thrown around by experts on talk shows and news programs, as if they know what it's like to be a reanimated corpse. They have no idea of the emotional fallout from a rapidly digesting pancreas. Or how hard it is to keep your tissues from liquefying.

My father was a de facto expert. And by "de facto," I mean he was the only one who considered himself an expert on anything.

Plumbing.

Politics.

Personal hygiene.

"You know, Andrew, you can get rid of those blackheads by using olive oil and vinegar."

He actually believed this. Fortunately, he let Mom do the cooking. Otherwise, I would have been the only kid in my school eating arugula salad with sliced pears, Asiago cheese, and a benzoyl peroxide dressing.

Don't get me wrong. My dad wasn't an idiot. He just always thought he was right, even when he had no idea what he was talking about. He would have made a great politician.

However, I do have to give my father props for his choice in refrigerators. My mom wanted one of those Whirlpool side-by-side models, but my father insisted on an Amana bottom freezer. Said it was more energy efficient, drawing cold air down instead of up. He also claimed it provided better use of shelf space.

While my parents' heads and most of their limbs are tucked away inside the freezer, their bodies from hip to shoulder are stuffed into the refrigerator. Had it been a side-by-side model, I never would have been able to fit their torsos on the shelves. Thanks Dad.

On the CD player in the living room, Dean Martin is singing "Auld Lang Syne."

Staring at my parents stuffed into the Amana bottom freezer, their torsos crammed between the mayonnaise and the leftover Thanksgiving turkey, their heads sealed in Ziploc bags, I'm overcome with a surreal sense of disbelief. From the expression on my father's face, it appears he's just as surprised as me.

Maybe none of this would have come to pass had my father taken the time to understand what I was going through instead of treating me like a pariah.

Or maybe I'm just kidding myself.

Maybe everything that happened between the accident and now was inevitable.

Chapter 2

Two months before I find my parents in the Amana bottom freezer, I'm at the Soquel Community Center, sitting in a semicircle of chairs that's open toward a petite, fifty-two-year-old woman who looks like my third-grade teacher. Except my third-grade teacher never ended up on the wrong end of a twelve-gauge, pump-action Mossberg.

On the freestanding chalkboard behind her, written in block letters, is the proclamation:

YOU ARE NOT ALONE.

Upper- and lowercase letters probably would have softened the message, but the petite woman, the group moderator, a gunshot victim named Helen, is just trying to make us feel better.

"Rita, would you like to start tonight?" asks Helen.

Rita's face is a pale moon hovering in the black hood of her sweatshirt. She has on a black turtleneck and black pants. The only color she's wearing is on her lips, which are Eternal Red.

Rita slit her wrists and then her throat on her twenty-third birthday. That was less than a month ago. Most of the time she wears gloves and turtlenecks to hide the stitches. Sometimes she wears hooded sweatshirts. Other times she wears scarves. On bad days, she wears all three. Tonight she left the scarf at home, so at least she's not feeling morose.

Rita licks her lips—sucks on them, actually, removing most of her lipstick. From her pocket she produces a black cylinder and applies another coat, smacking her lips together. It's either an oral fetish or she needs a fix.

"I still feel alone most of the time," says Rita. "Once in a while, I can almost imagine none of this ever happened. Then I look in the mirror and the hopelessness comes flooding back."

Five other heads nod in understanding. Carl is the lone dissenter.

"You don't agree, Carl?" asks Helen.

Carl was stabbed seven times, twice in the face, by two teenagers who stole his wallet and used his credit cards to buy seven hundred dollars' worth of online pornography.

"No," says Carl. "I agree with her completely. She *is* hopeless."

"That's nice," says Naomi, lighting up a cigarette. Half African American, half Japanese, Naomi could still pass for a model if it weren't for her empty eye socket and the way the right side of her face sags. "Why don't you just rip open her stitches while you're at it?"

"I'll leave that to your husband," says Carl.

Naomi's husband came home after a bad day of golf and took out his frustrations on her with a Titleist four-iron.

"He's no longer my husband," says Naomi.

"Technically, no," says Carl. "But then technically, none of us should be here."

"And yet we are here," says Helen. "So why don't we focus on that."

In addition to Helen, Rita, Naomi, and Carl, the other members of the group include Tom, a thirty-eight-year-old dog trainer who nearly lost his right arm along with the left half of his face to a pair of Presa Canarios, and Jerry, a twenty-one-year-old car crash victim. Like me.

Because of our similar experiences, Jerry feels a connection with me, so he sits next to me at every meeting. I don't feel anything but lost, and Jerry, who listens to rap music and still wears his pants halfway down his ass, annoys me, so tonight I made sure to sit at the end of the semicircle next to Naomi.

"We're all survivors," says Helen, who then stands up and walks over to the chalkboard. "I want you all to remember that. I know it's hard dealing with the threats and the name-calling and the expired food products thrown at you, but you survived for a reason."

At times Helen reminds me of Mary Poppins—always cheerful and full of advice that works for characters who live in movies, fairy tales, or the Playboy Mansion. But I have to admit, without the support group I'd probably never leave my parents' wine cellar. Still, I think we need to come up with a name other than Undead Anonymous. After all, when you're undead, you're about as anonymous as a transvestite with a five o'clock shadow.

At least we don't get any support group imposters crashing our meetings, trying to pick up vulnerable women. That would be sick. Interesting, but sick.

Helen finishes writing another of her messages on the chalkboard and turns to face us. Beneath YOU ARE NOT ALONE, she's written the words:

I AM A SURVIVOR.

"Whenever you're feeling lost or hopeless, I want you all to say this out loud. 'I am a survivor.' Say it with me now."

By the time the meeting breaks up, it's dark outside. The end of October is more than two weeks away, but less than a month into autumn and it's already pitch black before *Jeopardy*.

I never liked autumn. Even before the accident I hated the weather growing cold and the changing of the leaves. Now it's a visual reminder of how my own life has grown cold. Lately I'm beginning to think there's just an endless autumn threatening an eternal winter.

I'm getting melancholy again.

Helen advocates the buddy system when we leave our meetings, though Carl says he doesn't need anyone to hold his hand and heads for home on his own. Jerry, Helen, Rita, and I all live in the same direction, so we head off one way while Naomi and Tom head the other. Most nights, Jerry buddies up with me and talks incessantly about his accident and how he needs to get laid and how he wonders what it would be like to be dead. I wonder about that, too. More so when I have to pair up with Jerry.

"Dude, that car was awesome," says Jerry. "Cherry red with a beast for an engine and a killer sound system. You should have seen it."

I know the story by heart. A fifth of Jack Daniel's, half a dozen bong hits, no seat belt, a utility pole, and bad judgment on a right-hand turn sent Jerry through the windshield of his cherry red 1974 Charger and skidding along River Street head first, scraping away a chunk of his scalp. I've heard the story so many times that I can almost believe it happened to me. Except my accident was worse. Jerry was alone in his car.

My wife was asleep in the passenger seat and, unlike me, she never woke up.

For the first two months after the accident, all I could think about was Rachel—the smell of her hair, the taste of her lips, the warmth of her body next to me at night. I wallowed in my suffering, consumed with anguish and self-pity. That and I had to deal with the smell of my decomposing scalp, the taste of formaldehyde in the back of my throat, and my own cold, decaying body. It was enough to make me want to take a gasoline shower and set myself on fire.

If you've never woken up from a car accident to discover that your wife is dead and you're an animated, rotting corpse, then you probably wouldn't understand.

Helen says that even though we've all lost more than our share, we need to keep our faith in the path that lies ahead of us. She says we need to let go of the past before we can embrace our future. I'm still working on that. Right now, the past is all I have and the future looks about as promising as the new fall lineup on CBS.

I used to wish Rachel would have reanimated with me so I wouldn't have to go through this alone, but eventually I realized she was better off dead. I'd thank God for small favors, but I doubted his existence before this happened and I haven't exactly changed my mind. Losing your wife in a car accident is enough to challenge the faith of even the most devout believer. But when you're a skeptic to begin with, being able to smell your own rotting flesh tends to put the kibosh on your belief in a divine power.

That's one of the biggest problems about coming back from the dead. The smell never quite goes away.

I reanimated within forty-eight hours after my death, before putrefaction and after I'd been embalmed. Upon reanimation, the process of decomposition slows down to a rate about half as slow as natural hair growth. However, for those of us who were fortunate enough to have been embalmed, formaldehyde is the magic elixir that slows decomposition down to an almost imperceptible pace, enabling the undead to maintain some sense of pride. The stigma of being a zombie is bad enough, but for those who reanimated prior to being embalmed, it's disheartening when your hair, nails, and teeth become detached. And it's downright embarrassing to be walking down the street and suddenly have one of your main body cavities burst open.

If you consume enough formaldehyde, you can keep the decomposition of your body and your internal organs at bay. Even if you can't get hold of the industrial-strength concentrated stuff, formaldehyde can be found in lipstick, makeup, fingernail polish, toothpaste, mouthwash, deodorant, antiperspirant, bubble bath, bath oil, shampoo, and soft drinks.

Rita gets most of her formaldehyde from lipstick and fingernail polish, while Jerry prefers his fix from a can of carbonated sugar. Personally, I try to stay away from the soda. Bad for the teeth. I get most of my supplements from shampoo and toothpaste. Occasionally, however, I like a helping of Alberto VO5 Conditioner.

". . . so then the next thing I know, I'm like, totally road surfing on my face," says Jerry. "Road rash city."

Jerry's been droning on about his accident the entire way home, while ahead of us, Rita and Helen walk in a blissful silence. It's times like this that make me wish I'd nearly lost both of my ears.

"Dude," says Jerry. "You wanna touch my brain?"

The last thing I want to do is touch Jerry's brain, but it's hard to write *No thanks* with one hand on a dry erase board hanging around your neck while you're shuffling along on a broken ankle. So I just shake my head and hope he doesn't start talking about his permanent erection.

The four of us make our way through empty parking lots, past stores closed up for the night and distant homes where warm lights glow behind curtained windows. A few of the houses have decorations up already, skeletons and ghosts and witches on broomsticks. Pumpkins not yet carved sit on doorsteps and porches. The cold breath of autumn whispers through the trees.

Halloween is coming, which seems more fitting than in years past. After all, it's not like I need a costume anymore.

Chapter 3

Highway 17 is a four-lane roller coaster of asphalt connecting Silicon Valley to the Pacific Ocean through the Santa Cruz Mountains. The highway is divided by a concrete barrier, with gaps that allow cars to make left turns onto secondary roads. On rare occasions, a vehicle veers into oncoming traffic through one of these gaps, causing a fatal head-on collision. On even rarer occasions, in the early hours of a star-filled July morning, a driver falls asleep on his way home from a dinner party and his 2001 VW Passat drifts through one of these gaps into the northbound lanes and hits an embankment on the opposite shoulder at just the right angle, launching the car nearly twenty feet off the ground and into the trunk of a three-hundred-year-old redwood tree at more than sixty miles per hour.

Even Hollywood couldn't re-create my accident and make it look unstaged. Of course in a movie, the lead actor would somehow manage to walk away from the car with his body intact.

Maybe not Mel Gibson or Bruce Willis, but Brad Pitt, definitely.

I don't remember the accident. I didn't see any bright light or hear any ethereal voices, but then this isn't exactly heaven. I just remember darkness, endless and close, like a membrane.

The next thing I know, I'm stumbling along the shoulder of Old San Jose Road, dragging my left foot behind me and wondering what day it is and where I'm coming from and why my left arm doesn't work. Then a pickup truck drives past and a rotten tomato explodes against the side of my face. Two teenagers are riding in the back of the truck. One of them has his pants pulled down and his bare ass pointed my way, while the second one throws another tomato at me and yells:

"Go back to your grave, you fuckin' freak!"

At first I think they're just being kids, throwing rotten tomatoes at people for kicks. Denial is one of the first hurdles zombies have to overcome. Then I stagger up to Bill's Groceries and catch a glimpse of myself in the front window.

My left ankle is twisted at an obscene angle. My left arm is useless—the bones pulverized from the shoulder to the elbow, ending in a twisted claw that used to be my left hand, while my left ear is mangled and my face looks like a jigsaw puzzle.

As I stare at my hazy reflection, dressed in a black suit and tie and looking like I just walked off the set of a George Romero film, a six-year-old girl walks out the door, drops her frozen fudge bar when she sees me, and runs off screaming.

Not exactly one of the top ten moments of my life.

Except this isn't life anymore. And it's not death, either. It's not even in between. It's more like a bad spin-off from a successful sitcom that the network refuses to cancel.

From my injuries, I figure I've been in a horrible accident and lost consciousness and wandered away without any recollection of what happened. Which isn't too far from the truth. Except I've lost consciousness for three days. And instead of wandering away from the accident, I've wandered away from my coffin less than twenty-four hours before my funeral.

I don't know any of this at the time. I just think I need help, so I go into Bill's Groceries to ask if I can use the phone. Before I can get more than one foot inside the door, Bill's wife comes at me with a broom and a spray can of Lysol disinfectant and shoos me away.

I wander off, confused, with rotten pieces of tomato clinging to my face as I stagger toward town, looking for help. A quarter mile away, I come to a park. There are two pay phones over by the restrooms, so I lurch my way up the sidewalk, dragging my left foot behind me, ignoring the screams of children as they scatter in front of me like the Red Sea parting for Moses. Though I suppose Lazarus would make a more appropriate biblical reference.

Still unaware that my injuries aren't causing me any discomfort, I reach the pay phone and remove the receiver, cradling it between my right ear and shoulder as I dial 9-1-1 with my right index finger. Seconds later, an operator is on the line asking me what my emergency is.

I don't know what I want to say or how I want to say it, so I just decide to open up my mouth and say the first thing that comes into my mind. Except there's one problem.

My mouth is sewn shut.

Frequently, prior to the embalming process, the mouth is sewn shut to keep it from dropping open. A curved needle enters the nostril, comes out behind the teeth, and then goes around and around until the jaws are sutured shut. But since I think I'm still among the living, I don't understand why I can't open my mouth. So I thrash my right arm around, make a lot of grunting noises, and stagger toward an old man and his wife who run away like Olympic sprinters.

When I hear the sirens and turn to see the Santa Cruz County Sheriff's car pull into the parking lot, I think I'm finally going to get some help. When I see the white Animal

Control van pull up moments later, it occurs to me that I might be in danger. Not from them, but mountain lion sightings are common in Santa Cruz County, so I turn around, my eyes wide, wondering when this bizarre nightmare I've awoken into will end.

Confused, scared, and overloaded, I don't hear the approaching footsteps behind me. The next thing I know, I have one snare around my arms and torso, another around both legs, and a third around my throat. The Animal Control officers guide me into the back of the van, while the sheriff's deputies assure the growing crowd of onlookers that everything is under control.

I spent two days in a cage at the SPCA until my parents finally came to pick me up. The stigma of claiming your undead son and bringing him home to live with you can wreak havoc on your social status, so I can't exactly blame them for not rushing out to claim me. But one more day and I might have been a crash test dummy.

The normal holding time for a stray zombie without identification is seventy-two hours. Seven days with ID. For stray cats and dogs, it's the reverse. But without regular formaldehyde fixes, most fresh zombies start to spoil within three days.

After the requisite holding period, unclaimed zombies get turned over to the county and salvaged for body parts or sold off for medical experiments. The SPCA is working to save more of us by soliciting zombie foster volunteers and implementing a companion zombie program, but those ideas haven't caught on yet. And since the majority of SPCA funding comes from private donations earmarked for animal programs, the accommodations for zombies at the shelter are pretty limited.

My stay at the SPCA wasn't as bad as you might think,

once I got over the initial shock. They gave me a bowl of fresh water and some kibble, along with my own litter box and a few squeaky toys to chew on. They even gave me a pair of dull children's scissors to cut out the mortician's stitches so I could open my mouth.

When we got home, my parents set me up with a mattress in the wine cellar. They didn't say much. Mom cried a lot and covered her nose and mouth with a towel to keep from gagging on the smell, while my father kept asking me why I couldn't have stayed dead like a normal son.

My mother spoke to me once, asked me what I wanted. I tried to answer, but the words came out in a croak and a screech. My vocal cords were so badly damaged in the accident that I can't talk, so I have to wear a dry erase board around my neck to communicate.

While my mother at least makes a pretense of understanding how difficult this has been for me, my father complains about the smell and the stigma and the expense of supporting a zombie. He even asked me once what I intend to do with myself.

As if I have some kind of an answer. It's not like I reanimated with a five-year plan. And no one exactly prepped me on How to Be a Zombie. It's a big adjustment, harder than you might imagine. After all, I still have the same basic hopes and desires I had when I was alive, but now they're unattainable. I may as well wish for wings.

On more than one occasion I've heard my parents discussing me, with my father suggesting that I find my own place to live. Some kind of zombie shelter. I've even heard him mention the idea of sending me to a zombie zoo. My mother tries to explain that I need support and that I'm just going through a period of adjustment.

"Like puberty," she says.

She assures me my father will come around and that if I believe in myself enough, everything will work itself out.

She says this with a straight face.

For a moment I believe her. Then I go to take a Pine-Sol bath and I look in the mirror and I see the jigsaw puzzle that was once my face and I wonder if my mother has lost her mind.

Either that or she's on Valium again.

Chapter **4**

"Andy?"

It's eight thirty in the morning and I'm drinking a bottle of 1998 Chateau Montelena Cabernet Sauvignon and watching *SpongeBob SquarePants* on Nickelodeon. Occasionally I flip the channel to the two cable PBS feeds and watch *Sesame Street* or *Barney and Friends*. I'd rather watch *Leave It to Beaver,* but we don't get TV Land.

"Andy?"

I feel like I'm six years old again, staying home from school and watching TV in bed while my mom makes me Cream of Wheat with sliced bananas and cinnamon toast. Except instead of comic book hero posters spread across my wall, I have bottles of wine.

And my mother isn't making me breakfast.

And my heart is no longer pumping blood through my veins.

"Andy?"

I've been living in my parents' wine cellar for nearly three months and my mother still calls out for me expecting an answer.

With a sigh, I turn off the television and get up from my

mattress. Dragging my left foot, I shuffle over to the stairs. At the top of the stairs, silhouetted by the light pouring in through the kitchen windows, stands my mother.

"Your father needs some help with the new disposal, honey," she says. "Can you come up for a few minutes and give him a hand?"

"I don't need any help, Lois," says my father from somewhere behind her. "Will you just let it be?"

"Oh nonsense," she says. "Andy would love to give you a hand. Wouldn't you, honey?"

I stare up at my mother and blink, wondering if she lost her mind when I died in the accident or when I showed up three days later at the SPCA needing room and board.

Behind her, my father reasserts that he doesn't need my assistance, adding that he would rather not have to breathe the stench of my rotting flesh.

"It's just for a few minutes," my mother whispers to my father, her head turned away from me. "It'll make him feel useful."

She says this like I can't hear her.

"Well don't just stand there dawdling," she says, turning back to me. "Come on up and help your father."

I could try to ignore her and just stay in my room watching TV, but she'll keep calling my name over and over and over, like a chant but in a high pitch that goes up one octave on the last syllable. Even turning up the television doesn't drown her out. I've tried it before. She's relentless.

It takes me nearly two minutes to climb the fifteen steps from the wine cellar to the house. The entire time, I hear my father grumbling about how other men have normal families.

Not every corpse that reanimates moves in with his or her

parents or has a friend or relative willing to take them in. Nearly half end up homeless or in shelters, with the less fortunate getting harvested for parts and sold to medical facilities or impact testing centers. And it's rare for a spouse to take the undead back into the fold, especially if there are any Breather children. I don't know about the other states, but California's Child Protective Services frowns upon single parents who allow a zombie to live at home. And when it comes to visitation rights, the undead have zero.

After the accident, my seven-year-old daughter, Annie, went to live with my wife's sister in Monterey. As far as Annie knows, I'm dead. But during the first few weeks after I reanimated, I would call my sister-in-law's place every day, hoping Annie would answer the phone just so I could hear her voice, until her aunt and uncle got an unlisted phone number.

I wrote several letters to Annie but the letters never made it out of the house. Mom and Dad confiscated and destroyed the first letter when I asked for a stamp. The second letter vanished from under my mattress while I was soaking in Pine-Sol. The rest got intercepted at different points along the path to Annie before ever getting stamped with a postmark.

After a couple of months, I gave up. Eventually, I decided my parents were probably acting in the best interests of my daughter. As much as I miss Annie and wish I could see her again, I don't think it'd be a good idea. Knowing that her father is a zombie might not be something she's ready or able to accept. Besides, I don't want her to remember me this way. And I don't exactly think she'd want to take me to any father-daughter picnics.

Show and tell, maybe.

When I reach the top of the stairs and step into the kitchen, my mother sprays me with a can of Glade Neutralizer fragrance, circling around and covering me from head to toe, emptying the last of the can in my hair. My parents buy Glade in bulk. Mom prefers the Neutralizer fragrance because it works directly toward the source of the odor. I'm partial to Lilac Spring, though Tropical Mist has a nice, fruity scent.

My father is on his back under the kitchen sink, his head and upper torso inside the cabinet. Several wrenches, screwdrivers, a can of WD-40, and assorted tools lay on the floor around him. A brand new garbage disposal sits on the counter next to the sink.

"Harry," my mother says. "Andy's here to help."

"I don't need any goddamned help," he says, straining to loosen a bolt on the old garbage disposal.

"Oh nonsense," says my mother. "You've been under that sink for over an hour already. Of course you need help."

My father could probably pay a plumber and have the disposal fixed in under an hour. Instead, he'd rather spend three hours growing frustrated and swearing at inanimate objects so he can save one hundred and twenty dollars. After all, he is a de facto expert.

"Lois," my father says, going after the bolt again. "I'm going to say this one last time. I don't . . . need . . . any . . . help."

The wrench slips and my father's hand smashes against something hard and metal.

My father slides out from under the sink, holding his right hand and reeling off a string of profanities that would make me blush if I still had any blood in my cheeks. He storms out of the kitchen, making sure to give me a wide berth and holding his breath while avoiding eye contact.

"Don't mind your father," my mother says, walking over to the oven as the timer goes off. "He's just in a mood."

My father's been in a mood ever since I came home.

My mother removes a cookie sheet filled with Pillsbury cinnamon rolls from the oven and sets it on the counter, then grabs a knife and starts to slather the cinnamon rolls with the prepackaged icing.

There are a lot of things I miss about being alive:

Going out to the movies with Rachel.

Watching Annie play soccer.

Sitting around a beach bonfire without having to wonder if someone's going to try to throw me into it.

And sometimes, I miss food.

It's not that I don't eat. I eat all the time. But one of the major drawbacks of being a zombie, aside from the decomposing flesh and the absence of civil rights and the children who scream at the sight of you, is that food has lost most of its flavor. Everything tastes unseasoned, unsweetened, watered down. Even the wine I drink I can't appreciate. And I don't get drunk. You need a functioning circulatory system for that. So mostly I eat out of habit or boredom, with perfunctory pleasure and no definitive memory of how anything is supposed to taste.

But as I watch my mother spread icing across the cinnamon rolls, I'm overcome with nostalgia. It's like thirty years have been wiped away in an instant and I'm sitting at the breakfast table, my stockinged feet dangling above the floor, a mug of steaming hot chocolate in front of me as I wait in anticipation for my mother to finish icing the cinnamon rolls.

I want to tell my mother that I love her but I can't. I want to give her a hug but I don't because I'm afraid she might scream. Or else open up another can of Glade on me.

Sometimes I feel guilty about what I've put my parents through, but it's not like I've done this on purpose. Still, I appreciate what they've done for me, all that they've sacrificed.

They could have left me at the SPCA. I guess that just proves that you never stop being a parent, even after your son comes back from the dead.

"Here you go, honey." My mother hands me a plate with a hot, steaming, freshly iced cinnamon roll. I smile and go to sit down at the kitchen table.

"Oh, Andy, could you take it downstairs?" she says. "We have company coming over."

Chapter 5

I go to a therapist twice a month.

His name is Ted. He and Helen used to work together, so he sees me as a personal favor to her. If you can call charging twice his hourly rate a favor.

I've been meeting with Ted for six weeks. Several other members of the group have seen Ted on one or more occasions, but I'm the only regular. Naomi went once and said she didn't get anything out of the session that she couldn't get from watching *Oprah*. Tom's been in three times but canceled his last two appointments due to conflicts with the League Championship Series between the Giants and the Cubs. Neither Carl nor Jerry thinks they need therapy. And Rita isn't ready to talk to anyone outside of the group.

I don't think Ted really helps me much, if at all, but it gets me out of my room two nights a month and Wednesday nights have a dearth of quality TV programming.

"How are you feeling today, Andrew?"

That's the first thing Ted always asks me, a smile plastered on his face like someone's taking his picture and he's supposed to look happy about it.

Ted is fifty-five going on thirty. Over the last five years

he's had a facelift, necklift, chin tuck, and cosmetic muscle enhancement. He works out in a gym five days a week, has a wardrobe that comes exclusively from The Gap and Eddie Bauer, and he has a full head of his own hair that he dyes dark brown because he's going gray. He also wears a twenty-four-carat gold hoop in his left ear, which he had pierced for his fiftieth birthday.

I know most of this because Ted has told me all about himself during our previous five sessions. I guess he feels comfortable with me. Either that or he figures one of us has to do the talking.

He stares at me, still wearing that fake plastic smile, waiting for an answer to his question. I scribble the word *Peachy* on my dry erase board, which is resting in my lap and elevated at an angle against my bent knees. Ted sits just behind me and off to my right, so he can read my responses. I can see him out of the corner of my eye. Even after six weeks, I still catch him staring.

"Do I detect a hint of sarcasm?" asks Ted.

I scribble *You think?* beneath my first response.

In the corner above us, a timed air freshener releases the scent of lilac into the room with a hiss. The air freshener wasn't there on my first visit.

"Then why don't you tell me how you're honestly feeling."

I glance at Ted over my shoulder. He smiles at me with a strained expression. No teeth.

How am I honestly feeling? I'm resented by my parents, abandoned by my friends, and discriminated against by a community that no longer considers me human. That's how I feel.

But I can't say this to Ted. He wouldn't understand. And even if he did, he wouldn't care. So I erase the other words on my dry erase board and scribble down the word:

Abhorred.

"Good," says Ted. "What else?"

Discarded.

"Yes," he says. "Is that all?"

Frustrated.

Demoralized.

Bereft.

Anxious.

Insignificant.

I hesitate, then erase everything and scrawl out the word *Tired.*

I wait, expecting a response, but receive only silence.

I know Ted hasn't snuck away because I see him over my shoulder. I know he hasn't fallen asleep because his eyes are open. And I know he isn't dead because I hear him breathing.

On the wall above Ted's framed diplomas and certificates and letters of achievement, there's a digital clock that shows the hours, minutes, and seconds in a red LED display. I sit and watch the silence stretch out one second at a time.

. . . thirteen . . . fourteen . . . fifteen . . .

We have moments like this at every session. Ted sits there with absolutely no idea of how to help me and I sit there watching the seconds tick off one by one in monochrome. It's like watching the clock count down to the New Year, only in reverse. And the ultimate moment never comes.

. . . twenty-five . . . twenty-six . . . twenty-seven . . .

"When you say tired," says Ted, "do you mean physically, emotionally, or spiritually?"

Chapter 6

Rita, Helen, Jerry, and I are on the way home from another meeting with a new group member, a forty-five-year-old surfer named Walter who wiped out and hit his head on his surfboard and drowned. They actually never recovered the body until Walter walked out of the surf in his wetsuit at the Santa Cruz Beach and Boardwalk two days later—his lungs filled with salt water and his hair tangled with kelp.

"Dude," says Jerry. "So what was it like being under water for two days?"

"Don't know, dude," says Walter, his voice a water-logged gurgle. "I just woke up in a kelp forest and couldn't figure out how I'd fallen inside my waterbed. Except I was wearing my wetsuit and I never wear my wetsuit to bed."

If I didn't know any better, I'd swear Walter and Jerry were related.

"At first I figured I was dreaming," says Walter. "Until I felt something sliding down the back of my wetsuit."

"What was it?" asks Jerry.

"Sea slug, dude," says Walter. "It was gnarly."

"Dude."

"Totally."

It's not like I can just walk away from them. At least if I keep them on my left I don't hear them as well through my disfigured clump of an ear, but somehow one of them always seems to end up on my right-hand side.

We cross a parking lot and head down an alley, doing the Robert Frost thing and taking the road less traveled. Not from any desire for adventure, but because we're less likely to disturb any Breathers this way. It's one of the Undead Commandments:

You will not disturb the living.

You will not be out after curfew.

You will not commit necrophilia.

You will not covet your neighbor's flesh.

There are a few more about honoring your host guardians and refraining from acts of civil disobedience, but for the most part they're just a bunch of rules we have to follow in order to coexist with the living. Breathers, on the other hand, don't have to follow any rules regarding the undead. Except for the necrophilia part. But that's just common sense.

The alley runs behind several blocks of light industrial complexes, all of which are closed for the night. Helen and Rita walk ahead of us, probably sharing a nice conversation about something meaningful while I'm stuck in purgatory.

"Dude, you wanna touch my scalp?" asks Jerry, removing his baseball cap. "It's, like, totally cool."

Helen suddenly stops and holds her hand up like a crossing guard.

"Dude," says Walter, running his fingers across Jerry's glistening brain. "That's awesome."

"Shush," whispers Helen.

At the end of the alley, in the darkness behind us, car doors open and close. Male voices echo through the alley along with laughter and the sound of a bottle breaking. Then silence.

"What's going on?" asks Rita.

"Breathers," whispers Helen. "By the sound of it, my guess is fraternity boys."

Rednecks mostly just scream insults and break bottles over your head and terrorize you until they get bored. Teenagers are more dangerous because of all the raging hormones, though they lack imagination. Bowling leagues are typically single-minded, using the tools of their trade to inflict their damage after a night of drinking. But frat boys dismember, beat, mutilate, torture, carve, and flambé. And they never seem to get tired of it.

That's what I hear, anyway. I've never actually encountered any fraternity members, bowling leagues, or rednecks. And other than the teenagers who hit me with tomatoes to christen my new existence, most of the abuse I've encountered has been verbal.

After a few minutes, another bottle breaks. More laughter, followed by a single voice:

"Zombies, come out and play-ayyy!"

"Uh oh," says Jerry.

Uh oh is right.

At the end of the alley behind us, more than two blocks away, five or six figures materialize out of the darkness carrying various objects of destruction.

"Run," says Helen.

That's easy to say when both of your legs work. But when your left ankle is a surrealistic piece of art, running isn't really an option.

"I'll help Andy," says Rita, slipping over to my left side. "You three go."

Walter and Jerry don't have to be told twice and take off. Helen hesitates a moment, then follows, her short legs pumping faster than I would have imagined a fifty-two-year-old zombie could run.

Rita puts one arm around my waist, draping my left arm around her neck. "Ready?"

I want to be brave and tell her to leave me here. But I'm glad I can't talk because it's comforting to be touched by Rita, to have her arm around me and her body pressed up against mine. And it's so much better than getting dismembered all alone. So I just nod.

It's slow going at first, but by the time Jerry, Walter, and Helen reach the end of the alley up ahead, we've got a rhythm going and it feels like we're making good time. Then I glance back and see the frat boys barely a block behind us.

"Gaack," I say to warn Rita.

Hoots and hollers echo along the alley as the steady threat of footsteps running on asphalt grows closer. Rita and I keep stumbling toward the end of the alley, like the last contestants in a three-legged race trying to cross the finish line. Except we're not laughing.

And no one's cheering us on.

And if we fall down we'll get attacked and mutilated.

We're past the last building and I'm hoping we can find someplace to hide, some way to ditch our pursuers, when a figure appears in front of us.

"Come on!" says Jerry, helping to escort me around the side of the building to a Dumpster. "Let's get him inside. Hurry!"

Together, Rita and Jerry help me up and over the edge until I'm falling face first into something soft and sticky that seems to split open on impact.

"Stay there," says Jerry. "We'll come back to get you."

Like I have a choice.

I listen to Jerry and Rita run off, and then make myself comfortable in the warm, gooey substance spreading across my face. It feels like glue but smells more like motor oil. Not exactly the way I envisioned spending my Tuesday night.

Less than ten seconds later, footsteps come around the corner of the building, approach the Dumpster, and continue past, racing off in the direction of Jerry and Rita. At least most of the footsteps race past. One of the fraternity members stops right outside the Dumpster.

When your heart's not pounding and adrenaline isn't pumping through your system, you feel oddly at ease during moments of duress. Still, that doesn't mean I'm not afraid of being found. I just don't experience the physiological effects of fear the way I used to. It's more like a memory. And right now, my memory is telling me I'm pretty much screwed.

Helen suggests that each of us find a creative way to deal with our feelings of hopelessness, a sort of artistic therapy to cope with the challenges of being one of the undead—like painting or sculpting or writing poetry. The idea is to create something beautiful that transcends our less-than-glamorous existence.

I used to pen an occasional haiku just to give the right side of my brain some exercise. I don't know if it matters anymore, considering my brain is gradually liquefying, but old habits don't die even when you do.

So as I'm lying in the Dumpster coated with industrial goo, thinking about immolation and dismemberment and toxic waste, this is the thing of transcendent beauty I come up with:

shattered life dangles
a severed voice screams in grief
i'm rotting inside

After several minutes of hearing nothing, I finally roll to one side and wipe some of the goo from my eyes so I can look out the open lid. At first all I see is darkness, then I make out the silhouette of what looks like a face peering down into the Dumpster.

"Randy!"

I don't know who jumps more—me or Randy. But the silhouette disappears beyond the edge of the Dumpster.

"What are you doing?" asks the approaching voice.

"Nothing," says Randy. "I was just . . ."

He must whisper because I can't hear the rest. Seconds later, two silhouettes are looking down at me. One of them raises a long, thin object and then plunges it into the Dumpster.

"Over there," says Randy, pointing.

The probe comes down again, closer this time, barely missing my arm. I think it's a steel rod, or maybe a piece of rebar. Whatever it is, it's going to do some damage if it strikes home.

When it comes down again, it plunges into my side, tearing through my clothes and flesh and snapping one of my ribs.

Definitely rebar. Three-eighths inch. Sharpened by the feel of it.

It comes down again, catching me in the thigh. The next one misses me, but the one after that pierces my palm and I wonder if this is how Christ felt on the cross.

While there's no pain, the sensation isn't pleasant. It's more invasive than uncomfortable, with a hint of humiliation.

If you've never been in a Dumpster coated with industrial waste while someone stabs you with a piece of sharpened rebar, then you probably wouldn't understand.

Part of me wants to just let them find me, to let this be done with so this existence can come to an end and I can be free of the memories that still tuck me into bed at night and greet me at dawn, sitting on my chest like a weight that never leaves. Except even in undeath, when faced with your potential demise, there's a self-preservation instinct that kicks in, that compels you to fight for your survival, that won't allow you to just give up. Besides, if I'm going to be destroyed, it's not going to be at the hands of a bunch of drunk college boys.

The next stab lands inches from my head. Just as the rod raises again for another go, a voice in the distance shouts out, "We got one!"

The silhouettes turn and vanish, their footsteps racing away. I lay there a moment, oddly thankful to still be undead, then pull myself up to the edge of the Dumpster and peer out into the night, hoping that whoever they found isn't Rita.

In the wash of a parking lot light more than a hundred yards away, several figures are moving in rapid motion, swinging objects, beating on another figure struggling to get away. At first I think it's Jerry and I'm surprised to discover how much that thought depresses me. Then the figure shouts out with a voice that sounds like a water bong.

"Help! Somebody help!"

The frat boys pounce on Walter, drive him to the ground, and beat on him. One of his arms is ripped away. Then the other. Within minutes, he's dismembered and dragged off to the fading hoots and hollers of drunk fraternity boys. No one comes to his aid. Not the police. Not the animal control. Not any other Breather who might happen to be passing by. And certainly not a fellow zombie with one useless arm and one useless leg.

I drop back down into the Dumpster and listen to the shouts drift away until I'm alone with the silence and my feelings of inadequacy. But when you spend most of your existence in your parents' wine cellar drinking bottle after bottle of wine and watching reruns of *Joanie Loves Chachi* while you gradually decompose, feelings of inadequacy are part of the room and board.

Problem is, even if I would have tried to help Walter, even if I *could have* helped, it wouldn't have mattered. Presuming I wouldn't have been dismembered along with him, any form of aggression by zombies against humans is considered grounds for immediate destruction. Even if it's in self-defense. And as I've suddenly discovered, I'm more interested in self-preservation than I thought.

It's times like this that make you question the values of a society that allows this to happen. That permits the random mutilation and dismemberment of someone who used to be a living, breathing person without consequences. I know it's no one's fault that I reanimated, that any of us came back from the dead, but someone should have to be held accountable for what happened to Walter.

I wait in the Dumpster for the return of Rita, Jerry, and Helen, wondering how long it will be before they come back for me, hoping they show up before the Waste Management truck, thinking about Walter. You hear about things like this happening all the time to other zombies who live in another town or another state or another country. But when it happens to you, to someone you know, it becomes something personal.

Something that affects you.

Something that inspires you.

Something that makes you want to take some action.

Chapter 7

I'm sitting on the front lawn of my parents' house next to a homemade sign that says:

ZOMBIES AGAINST MUTILATION.

I'm the only non-Breather in the vicinity, so technically it should read ZOMBIE AGAINST MUTILATION, but I thought the message would carry more weight if it was written in the plural.

The sign is on poster board attached to a four-foot wooden tree stake that's stuck in the lawn. Mom helped me make the sign and attach it to the stake. I don't think she had any idea what I planned to use it for. Just thought it was something cute I wanted to do and she was always eager to help me with projects when I was in school, so she dove right in. Of course, she screamed when I tried to hug her and she nearly vomited after I sneezed and a piece of my brain came out my nose, but it's what passes for quality time around here lately.

It's a nice afternoon to be protesting. The sun is out, the sky is blue, and the abuse is flowing.

A car drives past filled with teenagers who yell derogatory comments laced with expletives, like Fucking Decomposing Freak and Abortion-Sucking, Brain-Dead Fuckstick. I just smile and wave with my right hand as if their words don't bother me, but you can't help but take it personally when someone says you're brain dead.

So far I've been out here for nearly an hour and have seen about half-a-dozen cars drive down the street. While most of the Breathers ignore me, some of them actually take the time to stop and take pictures with their camera phones or shower me with slurs and zombie epithets and whatever garbage they have handy. Granted, I'm only getting my message out to the people who live on my parents' street and in their neighborhood, but even zombies who make themselves a public nuisance are jeopardizing their existence. This way, by staying on my parents' property, I can make a social statement without taking too much of a risk. I don't know if it will change anyone's mind, but considering everything we're up against, you have to start somewhere.

In addition to getting mutilated and dismembered, zombies are used as crash dummies for impact tests, get farmed for donor organs and spare body parts, and are left out to rot in various conditions to help with the research of criminal forensics. As if that isn't enough, we can't vote, get a driver's license, apply for credit, or run for public office. We're not allowed in grocery stores, restaurants, movie theaters, or any other public venue where we might disturb the living. No one will hire us, we can't apply for unemployment, and we can't collect food stamps. Even homeless shelters turn us away.

I don't really understand it. I mean, it's not like we're any different than we were before we died. We crave security, companionship, and love. We laugh and cry and feel emotional pain. We enjoy listening to Top 40 music and watching reality television. Sure, there's the whole eating-of-human-flesh stigma, but that's so George Romero. Outside of Hollywood, the undead typically don't eat the living.

Once in a while, you hear about a rogue zombie or a couple of delinquent zombies who devoured a homeless person or a neighbor or a U.S. postal mail carrier, which is actually a federal offense. Not like it matters. You eat any Breather, even if they don't work for a government agency, and the next thing you know, your head is in a disposable aluminum chicken roasting pan at a face-lift refresher course for plastic surgeons.

Across the street, at a house with a For Sale sign in the front yard, a neighbor comes out to get his mail. When he sees me, he picks up several rocks from his immaculately landscaped yard and hurls them at me, hitting me twice in the chest and once in the head, shouting in triumph each time.

I don't understand why Breathers get so bent out of shape when the dead come back. I know we bring down the property values and that the living, in general, find us repulsive, but it's not like they haven't had a chance to get used to the idea of us.

Zombies have been around for decades, blending in with the local homeless population of just about every town in the country since the Great Depression—though the majority migrated to the coasts and to the cities where they were less likely to get noticed.

New York City has the most zombies per capita in the nation, while California boasts the largest zombie population of any state. In general, states along the West Coast are more tolerant and progressive when it comes to the undead. You don't find many zombies in the southern states, since heat tends to speed up decomposition. That and when you're a zombie in a region that has a reputation of prejudice against minorities and outsiders, you tend to stick out like good taste in a country-western bar.

While there are no official records of zombies in the United

States prior to the 1930s, you can find historical eyewitness accounts of resurrections as far back as the Civil War. But for the most part, society didn't begin to address the growing zombie population until the last couple of decades. With Undead Anonymous chapters popping up all over the country and creating local communities for zombies that never existed before, we've become a more accepted part of society—if you can call being denied basic human rights being *accepted*.

A woman comes down the sidewalk taking her standard poodle for a late afternoon walk. The street isn't heavily traveled and the dog is apparently well trained, so it's not on a leash and comes running up to sniff me. With only one working hand, I can't do more than try to push the dog away. Before the woman can reach us, the poodle has started rolling on me.

This isn't exactly the kind of exposure I was looking for.

"Camille, no!" shouts the woman. "Bad girl! Bad . . ."

When the woman realizes I'm a zombie, she backs away in revulsion. I try to tell her that I'm not going to hurt her, but sometimes I forget that I speak in grunts and menacing gasps that tend to freak Breathers out.

The woman screams and runs off. A moment later, Camille stops rolling on me, gets up, pisses on my lap, then runs off after her owner.

So much for making a statement.

Chapter 8

F riday's meeting is somewhat subdued, what with Walter's dismemberment and the emotional residue from his attack. The first real rain of the season doesn't improve the mood. That and Carl didn't show up for the meeting.

Carl's missed meetings before. We all have. Except tonight is Halloween, so we're a little paranoid. It's bad enough that we've all been transformed into the ghoulish archetypes that children use to frighten themselves and each other with on the spookiest day of the year, but then you hear stories about Breathers driving around on Halloween, dismembering stray zombies or stuffing firecrackers into their orifices.

Still, that hasn't prevented everyone from observing the occasion. Putting on a costume can be therapeutic and empowering by pretending to be someone or something you're not. It's also good camouflage. Who expects zombies to get dressed up for Halloween?

Helen is dressed like a fairy godmother, complete with blue hair, wings, and a tiara. On the chalkboard behind her, beneath HAPPY HALLOWEEN! and a couple of cartoon bats is:

HOPE IS NOT A FOUR-LETTER WORD.

"Continue to breathe deeply," says Helen, leading our

guided meditation. "With each exhale, let go of all of your fears and concerns."

Jerry has fallen asleep in the chair next to me. His costume is nothing but red sweatpants, a red long-sleeved T-shirt, a red knit beanie, and a pair of devil horns held on with elastic. He's painted his face red, but it's hard to tell where the paint starts and the road rash ends.

"Empty your mind of all thoughts," says Helen as she walks around the room, her voice a soft, maddening whisper. "Imagine nothing but a blank screen or a canvas devoid of images."

We're supposed to keep our eyes closed during meditation to help us focus. I keep opening one eye to see what everyone else is doing. It's not that I don't respect what Helen is trying to do, but all I can focus on is the rain drumming against the roof of the community center and the sound of Jerry snoring.

Rita is sitting directly across from me. She's wearing a black one-piece bathing suit, bunny ears, and Satin Red lipstick—most of which she's consumed during the meditation. A white dog collar and leather wrist cuffs conceal her scars. She looks just like a Playboy Bunny.

Once the meditation has ended, Helen rings a little bell and I nudge Jerry to wake him up.

"Would anyone like to share how they feel about what happened to Walter?" asks Helen.

"It sucked," says Jerry. "I say we go kick some fraternity butt."

Naomi, who is dressed like a pirate with a head scarf, a black-and-white striped shirt, and a patch over her empty eye socket, nods her head in vigorous agreement. "Right on."

"Really?" says Tom.

Tom is painted white with a toga draped over his shoulders

and a laurel wreath around his head. When he sits or stands completely still, he looks like a Roman sculpture.

"No, not really," says Helen. "As soon as someone spotted you, they'd call the Sheriff's Department and the next thing you know, you're all in restraints in the back of a van on your way to the SPCA."

"Or Dr. Frankenstein's," says Rita.

That would be appropriate, since I'm dressed up like Frankenstein's monster. Mom bought an old suit from the thrift store and even did my makeup. I'm pretty convincing, which doesn't exactly thrill me considering the monster gets torched by a mob of angry townspeople.

We spend the next thirty minutes trying to lift one another's spirits while discussing what action we can take and how we can help one another deal with the loss of one of our own. Though this isn't the first time we've lost a member. We had a burn victim in the group, a young guy named Spencer, who got drunk one night when he was still alive and thought it would be fun to try his hand at pyrotechnics with a lighter and a can of Raid. Nearly burned his entire face off. He hasn't shown up to the meetings in a couple of months and no one knows what happened to him. Naturally, we all think the worst.

Although zombies can't technically die, contrary to the popular urban myths, we are not immortal.

It's true we can't bleed to death, since our hearts are no longer pumping blood through our arteries, but we can gradually decompose until we're not much more than a skeleton. At that point, your existence pretty much comes to an end. Not exactly a pleasant way to go.

If you've never been staked down on the side of a hill and left out to rot at a research facility for human decay, then you probably wouldn't understand.

So theoretically, we can be killed, which is a bit misleading since we're already dead. Destroyed would be a more appropriate description, though Helen prefers to use terms like "dispatched" or "removed" or "permanently processed" because she's fond of euphemisms.

Destroying a zombie isn't easy. Bullets, knives, poisons—none of these have any adverse effect. You can't smother us, drown us, or beat us. Disemboweling or dismembering us just empties our body cavities or turns us into undead quadriplegics. Decapitation would probably do the trick. As would immolation, though you'd have to use gasoline or a good quality lighter fluid. Without a decent accelerant, zombies tend to burn like wet firewood, smoldering for hours.

"I know we're all saddened by the loss of Walter," says Helen, "and that we all have our own problems to contend with, but there are others like us out there, some of them worse off than we are, and they need help. So I want each of you to find another survivor to bring to our Friday meeting in three weeks."

"You mean, like homework?" asks Jerry.

"Yes," says Helen. "You could call it that."

"Oh man," grumbles Jerry. "I fuckin' hate homework."

"Now, does anyone else want to share about how they're personally coping with the attack on Walter?" asks Helen.

Everyone looks around at each other and no one says anything. I consider raising my hand, but every other time I've tried to communicate at the meetings it's been laborious and most of my attempts have turned into frustrating games of Charades, so I decide to keep my failed protest to myself. Besides, in addition to getting pissed on by a poodle, when my father came home from work and saw me sitting in front of the house, he didn't say a word but just turned on the outdoor hose and sprayed me with the power nozzle until I got up and went inside. Either he wasn't happy with me or he just wanted to water the lawn.

At least I didn't have to take a bath.

The rest of the meeting sort of sputters to an end, with no one in much of a mood to talk about what happened to Walter and everyone struggling to stay positive, though I do get to pair up with Rita for the honest emotional contact, so the evening isn't a total loss.

I've never paired up with Rita before, and the sensation of having her this close to me, of having this level of intimacy, would bring me to tears if my tear ducts were still functioning. I don't think I realized how much I needed the comfort of a woman's embrace until now.

I still miss and love my wife, but any heterosexual man, alive or undead, would rather get hugged for ten minutes by an attractive, twenty-three-year-old zombie in a Playboy Bunny outfit instead of being hugged by the likes of Tom or Jerry. The best part about being so close to Rita is that she doesn't have an overwhelming odor of death. That's hard to pull off. Even the most heavy-duty perfumes and disinfectants can't completely cover the smell of decomposing flesh.

I know I can't smell good. Even in life I had a fairly strong natural body odor. And lately I smell anything but natural. But Rita doesn't seem to mind. Instead, she holds me close enough and tight enough to make me feel self-conscious, so I try to distract my thoughts by making up haikus. None of them work. I keep getting the number of syllables wrong. Finally, I come up with one that I call "Recipe for the Undead":

reanimate flesh
simmer organs in decay
formaldehyde stew

When we're done, Helen gives us each a bag of Halloween candy and reminds us all about bringing another survivor to the meeting next month, then she casts a fairy godmother spell over us before getting a ride home from her sister, leaving the rest of us to walk home together in the rain.

I never cared much for the rain when I was alive. Didn't like driving in it and hated getting wet. Kind of like a cat. Or the Wicked Witch of the West. Now, the rain provides a protection that even a heavy police presence doesn't. As a general rule, Breathers are less likely to cause themselves physical discomfort in order to give the undead any grief. On a rainy Halloween, they're more likely to be at a party or in a bar than out hunting a Playboy Bunny, the devil, and Frankenstein's monster.

At least that's what you tell yourself.

"Hey," says Jerry, after we part with Naomi and Tom and are walking along the back streets to avoid the traffic. "Do either of you have someone to bring to the meeting next month?"

"No," says Rita, adjusting her bunny ears.

I shake my head and grunt.

"You wanna see if we can find someone tonight?" he asks.

"Sure," says Rita, pulling out her lipstick and applying another coat. "Why not?"

Jerry puts one arm around me. "How about you, Andy old pal?"

After what happened to Walter, I should probably play it safe and go home. But if I do that, then I'm just giving up. Plus I can't really go out and find someone on my own, and other than *Halloween, Halloween II,* and *Halloween III,* there's not much on TV tonight, so I give Jerry the thumbs up. Or in my case, the thumb up.

There's not a lot of traffic and once you get out of the Soquel Village there aren't any storefronts, but we still have to be careful, even with the rain and our costumes, so we keep to the shadows and hide whenever a car comes by.

Jerry seems to find the idea of ducking into shadows to hide from Breathers entertaining. It's like a game. Even when there aren't any cars around, he hides behind garbage cans or trees or telephone poles, darting from one to the other, then pressing himself against a wall or a fence before diving for cover behind some hedges. He's like a demon with ADD.

The most likely place to find other zombies at night is a cemetery and the closest haunt is the Soquel Cemetery, about a mile up Old San Jose Road. That's where Rachel is buried. I used to visit her grave several times a week but I haven't stopped by in a while. Almost two weeks. I think I should feel guilty, but for some reason I don't. Maybe it's a natural progression of the grieving process. Maybe I'm learning how to move on with my undeath. Or maybe I've been distracted by a certain twenty-three-year-old zombie.

"Hey, Andy," says Rita, slowing down to keep pace with me as Jerry races from one side of the road to the other ahead of us in the rain. "Do you ever think about God?"

This is the first time in the three weeks we've known each other that Rita has asked me a question directly. Even if I could talk, I would probably stumble over my own words trying to come up with a reply.

Instead, I just shake my head. I was a borderline atheist before I came back from the dead, so I can't blame God for what happened to me and I'm not about to thank him because as far as I'm concerned, this isn't exactly a divine miracle.

"I think about him," says Rita. "I think about him sitting in his La-Z-Boy recliner, drinking ambrosia or mead or a pint

of Guinness, watching us on his widescreen television, waiting to see what happens next. Like an experiment."

As if in response, thunder rumbles across the black sky. I
glance at Rita. Her hair is drenched and her bunny ears are
drooping, but she doesn't seem to mind.

"Sometimes I wonder if this whole planet isn't one big experiment, one big maze, and we're the mice trying to find the
cheese."

She turns to look at me and I'm transfixed. Her dark eyes
pierce me as the rain drips down her pale face. In the diffused
glow from a street lamp half a block away, she looks almost
ethereal. Like a zombie Playboy angel.

"Or do you think I'm just full of shit?" she says.

I shake my head, a little too eagerly, and Rita laughs, her
eyes holding mine, the rain a distant nuisance. When she
smiles at me, for the first time in months, it feels like my
heart is glowing.

Up ahead, Jerry dives headlong over a bush and slams into
a telephone pole.

Rita hooks her left arm through my right. "Come on," she
says. "Let's catch up with the secret agent."

Jerry is on his back next to the telephone pole, his mouth
open to catch the rain. His red beanie and devil horns are on
the ground next to him and his brain is getting wet. Just past
him is a yellow traffic warning sign with a black arrow indi-
cating a reverse curve.

"It's a good thing I'm already dead," says Jerry, smiling.
"Otherwise, that would have hurt like a bitch."

"You're not dead," says Rita, reaching down with her right
hand to help Jerry to his feet. "You're undead."

"Whatever," says Jerry. "You live in your world, I'll live in
mine."

I watch the two of them converse with envy. I want to say something clever. Or witty. Or profound. I want to say anything at all just to be a part of the conversation instead of a silent bystander. I can't even pull out my dry erase board because I left it at home. So all I can do is stand and watch and smile until I want to scream.

So I scream.

Jerry and Rita look at me, startled into silence. For a few beats we all stare at each other and I feel like an unruly child waiting to be rebuked by my parents. Then Jerry starts to laugh, which gets Rita going. Before I realize what's happening, I'm laughing, too. I sound kind of like a sick sea lion, but it's the first time I've laughed in over three months and it dawns on me that I'm having a good time.

"Hey!" a voice shouts.

The three of us turn and see a figure coming toward us across the field on the other side of the street. In the darkness behind him, two other human forms follow his lead.

Thunder booms above us like special effects in a B-horror film.

"Let's get out of here," says Jerry.

"Good idea," says Rita, taking my arm and pulling me back toward town.

"Hold on there!" the man shouts.

There are no houses nearby. No bars or restaurants or businesses of any kind. But then, they wouldn't exactly be places where we could seek refuge.

We're halfway to the cemetery and, other than the field, a vineyard, and an abandoned stone granary, there's nothing out here. Just a single streetlight, darkness, and rain.

The man's running now, almost to the road, and his friends aren't far behind. He shouts out something else but it gets lost in another round of thunder.

Jerry is running ahead of us, saying "come on, come on, come on," as if we're not aware of the urgency. Rita is holding on to me, looking back over her shoulder, trying to get me to move just a little bit faster, but I'm going as fast as I can.

I glance back and see the man crossing the road, not fifty feet behind us. He's dressed in cowboy boots and jeans and a brown leather jacket. Just past the field, headlights flash around the reverse curve and a car appears, fishtailing as it accelerates out of the turn.

At the sound of the approaching car, the man turns and slips on the wet asphalt and falls to the ground. Before he can scramble to his feet and get out of the way, the car slams into him, sending him through the air, limbs flailing, until he hits the shoulder of the road and tumbles head-over-heels three times, finally coming to a stop on his back less than ten feet from us.

The car, a beat-up Chevy Nova filled with drunk high school kids, flies past without stopping. Seconds later the car is gone, its one working red taillight disappearing around another turn, and all we hear is the rain on the asphalt and the sound of approaching footsteps.

Rita and I back slowly away from the lifeless body lying on the shoulder of the road as the other two figures cross the street and come toward us. Without warning, Jerry appears behind Rita and me, causing both of us to jump and yelp and grab on to each other.

Jerry looks down at the corpse and says, "Is he dead?"

The corpse sits up, raising himself on his forearms, and shakes his head like a dog after a bath. "Nope. And I aim to stay that way. So why don't we all get the hell out of here before any more Breathers show up."

This is how we meet Ray Cooper.

Chapter 9

Nearly three stories tall and made of stone, the granary on Old San Jose Road has been abandoned for more than thirty years. Most of the roof is gone, as are any other signs of the farming operation that existed before the winery took over the land across the road and replaced the wheat with grapes. A faded assortment of graffiti covers the granary's circular walls, while weeds and wildflowers have overgrown the land surrounding it.

Ray has lived in the granary since September, when his wife kicked him out because she couldn't put up with the stench. His wife must be overly sensitive to odors because other than Rita, Ray is the only zombie I've met who doesn't have the telltale underlying smell of roadkill.

"Welcome to my humble abode," says Ray with a twang that smacks of overalls and cow pies.

Ray leads us through the back door of the granary. Jerry goes first, followed by Rita, then me. Behind us come the other two zombies who were with Ray in the field—Zack and Luke, adult twin brothers who died from neck and skull injuries when they dared each other to dive head-first from a railroad trestle into the San Lorenzo River. They did this in the summer when the river was two feet deep.

Ray told us their story. Zack and Luke haven't offered up more than grins, nods, and a couple of "Howdy's." They're kind of creepy. But then, who am I to judge?

Inside, Ray turns on a propane lantern, the light from the flame flickering off the stone walls. The interior walls cut in about four feet from the curved exterior walls, creating what would have been storage areas for the threshed wheat. A square sliding door in each wall sits at about shoulder level, while iron ladders attached to the walls climb up to the top of the granary.

A single door leads from the back to the front, where another door large enough to accommodate a vehicle is boarded up from the inside. Other than the six of us, a couple pieces of charred wood, and an old, dirty tennis shoe discarded in one corner, the granary is empty.

Behind me, Luke whispers something to Zack, who giggles.

The rain has stopped, which is nice since most of the roof is gone. The remaining portion of the roof covers one of the grain storage areas, which Ray has converted into his own personal sleeping space and pantry—complete with shelves lined with canned goods and Mason jars and bottles of Budweiser.

Just because we're the undead doesn't mean we don't like creature comforts.

Ray also has firewood, matches, and old issues of *Playboy*. He pulls out several pieces of wood, some kindling, and one of the *Playboy*s, which he hands to Jerry. "Just tear out the articles, ads, and interviews," says Ray. "Anything with nudie pictures stays."

While Jerry alternately peruses the contents of the *Playboy* and tears out pages for Ray to use to start the fire, I glance over at Rita to see if she's uncomfortable about any of this and find her flipping through an old *Playboy* with Charlize Theron on the cover.

Within minutes, Ray has a fire crackling in the middle of the floor, the smoke drifting up and out through the open roof. In the darkness of night, it's doubtful any Breathers can see the smoke rising from the granary.

"Anyone hungry?" asks Ray.

Zack and Luke raise their arms fast and rigid like Hitler youth. Rita voices her desire while I grunt.

"How about you, Jerry?" asks Ray.

Jerry is sitting cross-legged on the ground near the fire with a *Playboy* in his lap and a stack of magazines next to him. "I'm good," he says, not looking up.

From inside the storage area, Ray pulls out a couple of Mason jars, two forks, a sealed plastic Baggie, and five bottles of Budweiser. He hands one of the jars to Rita and another to Luke, who takes it like an eager child accepting chocolate. Luke opens the jar, the lid unscrewing with the *hiss* of a vacuum seal, and seconds later he and Zack are taking turns shoveling hunks of meat out of the jar and into their mouths.

I'm sitting next to Rita, who is looking at the contents of the Mason jar in the light from the fire. "What's in here?" she asks.

"Venison," says Ray, opening up the Baggie and pulling out a piece of jerky. "I used to shoot deer a lot. Not always legally, of course, but I was good with a rifle, so I had to can a lot of what I killed. It's a little gamey," he says, taking a bite of the jerky, "but it's still fresh."

Rita unscrews the lid, which hisses open, then reaches in

and digs out a forkful of venison. She holds the fork up to her nose, sniffs it, then puts the fork into her mouth.

"Wow," she says, her jaws working. "That's good. It actually tastes like meat."

"The food of the gods," says Ray, his mouth full of deer jerky. He cracks open a bottle of Budweiser and takes a swallow.

Rita takes another bite, then holds the jar out and hands the fork to me. In spite of the fact that Rita has already given it her approval, I hesitate, mostly because I've never eaten deer and never had much of a palate for game meat. That and I have a hard time believing it tastes like anything other than marinated tofu.

Across the fire from me, Zack and Luke have already finished their venison and are wiping the inside of the jar with their fingers.

"Try it," says Rita. "It's good."

Now I'm not one to look for religious symbolism in simple gestures or unexplained events, but as Rita sits there in her Playboy Bunny costume holding the venison out to me, I'm reminded of Eve holding the apple out to Adam. Then again, this isn't exactly the Garden of Eden. And if there is a paradise, then we've already been kicked out. So I take the apple.

Rita's right. The first bite actually has more flavor than I would have expected, considering I haven't tasted much of anything since the accident. The second bite tastes even better. I take four bites before I realize that I'm supposed to be sharing with Rita.

"You sure you don't want any, Jerry?" asks Rita.

"Not hungry," says Jerry. He's pulled away a little from the fire, his back against the wall, a bottle of Budweiser and the propane lantern on the floor next to him, his nose buried in a centerfold.

While we eat venison and drink beer, Ray asks us how we all ended up in our current condition. Since I don't have my dry erase board, and with Jerry preoccupied, Rita does all the talking—explaining how each of us died and how we all meet twice a week with a support group. Ray, in turn, explains that he met his living end hunting deer nearly one year ago. He trespassed on private property and the land owner claimed he was simply firing back in self-defense.

"Self-defense my ass," says Ray. "My gun was leaning up against the tree next to me."

"What were you doing when he shot you?" asks Rita.

"Taking a leak," says Ray. "Son of a bitch plugged me with my pants down."

I take another bite of venison and grunt.

By the time we finish eating, Zack and Luke are asleep, curled up against each other like cats, the empty Mason jar and two bottles of Budweiser on the ground next to them. Jerry is still lost in a world of soft-core pornography.

"So tell me about this group of yours," says Ray, putting another log on the fire and cracking open another beer.

Rita gives a quick rundown of the group, its members, and its purpose, one of which is to expand our numbers by bringing other survivors into the fold.

"Survivors?" says Ray. "Sounds like a pretty way of saying 'screwed over' to me."

"Helen is kind of New Age," says Rita. "She likes to help us feel better about ourselves."

I nod and say "exactly" but it comes out sounding like a sneeze combined with a dry heave.

"Well, you've gotta admire someone for trying to help others," says Ray. "But eventually, you've got to help yourself. Isn't that right, Mr. Hefner?"

Jerry glances up from the *Playboy* with a glazed expression and his mouth slightly ajar. I think he's drooling.

"Personally, I'm not ashamed of what I am," says Ray. "And you shouldn't be, neither. The point is to make the most with what you have. And if you don't have as much as you need, then take it. Or find a way to make it yours."

Basically, Ray is saying the same things Helen's been telling us for the past three months, only coming from him, the words seem to make a lot more sense.

"Would you come to our meeting?" asks Rita. "I'm sure the others would like to meet you."

"Well, I can't speak for these two," says Ray, pointing to the twins asleep next to the fire, "but I'm not much for self-help groups. Still, I guess it wouldn't hurt to stop by for a visit."

Rita gives Ray the details about the meeting and asks him to bring the twins along. He says he'll do his best, then offers each of us another beer.

"We should probably get going," says Rita, checking her watch. "It's getting late."

There's a midnight curfew for zombies to prevent the undead from gathering unchecked in large groups. And other than UA meetings and cemeteries, zombies aren't allowed to congregate in public places at all. We've even been restricted from cyberspace, as Breathers don't want us surfing the Internet. Maybe they're afraid we'll create zombie pornography. Or lure unsuspecting Breathers into online romances. Or develop a political community that would petition for social change. Although that's possible, it's more likely we'd petition for the right to develop zombie hygiene products.

Rita and I thank Ray for his hospitality, which he continues by giving each of us another jar of venison for the road. Jerry stands up, a stack of *Playboy*s in his arms, and says, "Dude, can I borrow some of these, instead?"

When we leave, I glance back at the granary, watching it recede into the darkness, feeling like I've discovered something that's been missing. I can't put my finger on why, but for the first time since I woke up into a world that has discarded my humanity, I feel almost human. For the first time, I feel like I have value.

For the first time, I feel like I matter.

Chapter 10

Sunday morning when I wake up, the pervasive feeling of impotence, of resigned monotony that has defined my existence for the past three and a half months, is overwhelmed by a sense of restlessness. Of agitation. Of feeling like an adolescent who can't stop fidgeting.

"What, you got ants in your pants?" my father used to say to me.

I don't know about ants in my pants, but it feels like something's crawling under my skin.

That and my parents have invited friends over to watch the 49ers game with mimosas and pupus. I can hear them and their guests upstairs, laughing and cheering, shouting at the television, while the walls of the wine cellar surround me with ennui.

I feel like a prisoner.

I try subduing my anxiety with reruns of *The Nanny* and *The Golden Girls*. I try subduing it with a bottle of 1985 Chateau Cheval Blanc. I try subduing it with the extra jar of venison Ray gave me. All I accomplish is to discover that the Lifetime Channel, expensive French wine, and preserved game meat aren't good remedies for combating restlessness.

I need to get out.

To ensure that I don't make an unexpected appearance and ruin their first hosted party since I took up residence in the wine cellar, my parents have locked the door at the top of the stairs. Fortunately, the wine cellar has an exterior entrance through a storm door in the back of the house, which is how I come and go. It's more convenient than using the front door and there aren't as many stairs, but mostly it saves my parents the embarrassment of having to explain me to their company.

The recent rain has left behind sullen skies with pregnant clouds, so I throw on a black hooded rain slicker, grab my dry erase board, and head out the rear exit into the backyard, closing the storm door behind me. Through one of the rear windows I can see my father sitting in his favorite chair in front of the television—a beer in one hand and a handful of chips in the other, laughing it up with the Putnams and the Dolucas while my mother walks in smiling and carrying a tray of mimosas.

Everybody's having a good time.

I consider staggering in through the front door and letting out a wail or a screech just to see the looks on their faces, but it's not worth the familial fallout, so I lurch away from the window and around the side of the house, where a narrow path cuts between our house and the next, leading to a small creek that runs through a gulch behind our street. On the other side of the gulch are some industrial buildings that are generally silent on weekends. No one to hassle me. No one to hear me scream if someone decides to have some fun at my expense.

Generally, it's not a good idea for zombies to walk around without a chaperone. Helen always says there's strength in numbers, but I don't want company. I just want to take a walk. I don't think that's asking too much. To be able to take a walk without having to explain myself. Without having to look over my shoulder.

The great thing about having to wear a dry erase board around your neck to communicate is that it doubles as a picket sign.

I remove the dry erase board and set it on a tree stump at the edge of the gully. I think for a moment, considering my options, then decide to take the clear and simple approach. Using my black erasable marker, I write

> *I have*
> *the right*
> *to walk*

then I slip the dry erase board back over my head and continue on my way.

The gully is wet and muddy, making the going a little more challenging, but I manage to get through without falling down, which is a first for me. I stand at the top of the opposite embankment looking down at the thirty-foot drop and imagine that climbers who scale Mount Everest must experience this when they reach the summit—a feeling of total satisfaction and accomplishment. Or maybe I need some perspective.

As expected on a Sunday, the industrial complexes are silent, except for a radio somewhere playing "Sweet Home Alabama." Even though Confederate flags and gun racks are rare in Santa Cruz County, I figure it's a good idea to steer clear of anyone listening to southern-fried rock and roll, so I head across the street, past Elaine's Dance Studio, and down an alley behind Pet Pals before I come to a stop in front of an empty building that used to be the Berge-Pappas Funeral Home.

I stop and look through the front window, drawn by a morbid fascination to the mortuary even though it's been empty for years. I've never been inside but still I feel a connection with the place, as though I'm attuned to its energy.

I spend a lot of time thinking about death.

Not Death, as in the Grim Reaper, skulking around in his dated Goth robe and carrying that ridiculous scythe. What a poser. No. I'm talking about the experience and how it affects and consumes the body and the mind.

When the heart stops pumping blood, tissues and cells are deprived of oxygen. Carbon dioxide levels increase and wastes accumulate, poisoning the cells, which begin to dissolve from the inside out, rupturing and releasing fluids that make their way throughout the body. Brain and liver cells tend to go first, while skin cells can be taken from a corpse twenty-four hours after death and still grow in a laboratory culture.

I have a lot of time on my hands.

Maybe I can't stop thinking about death because it's on my list of things to do:

Take a Pine-Sol bath.
Watch *Grosse Pointe Blank* on TNT.
Think about death.

The rate of decomposition of a human body above ground is twice as fast as when the body is under water and four times as fast as when it's buried. Corpses tend to last longer when buried deeper, providing the soil isn't saturated with water, while a corpse left to rot outside is rapidly consumed by insects and animals—such as carrion fly maggots, beetles, ants, and wasps. In tropical climates, a corpse can become a riotous rave of maggots in under twenty-four hours.

These are the comforting thoughts that help me relax when I'm having trouble falling asleep.

Maybe I'm preoccupied with death because I got cheated out of it. My wife won an all-expenses-paid ticket from the Afterlife Travel Agency while I was left standing at the gate with my luggage. Except I don't really have any luggage. Nothing from my life followed me into my undeath. No suitcases. No keepsakes. No personal effects. Nothing but the suit I was wearing when I staggered out of cold storage. Everything else we had, all the material things that connected me to Annie and Rachel in life, were claimed, sold, donated, or thrown away. Sometimes it seems as though Annie and Rachel never existed anywhere but inside my head.

Helen always encourages us not to dwell on the past, to let go of the life we used to know and all its accompanying baggage. While I have to admit that the group has helped me to stop feeling sorry for myself, that doesn't change the fact that I miss my wife and daughter. Even though my heart has stopped beating, it still aches.

Before I turn to leave the mortuary, I notice my reflection in the glass. As a rule I tend to stay away from mirrors or anything that casts a solid reflection. It's hard enough trying not to dwell on the past without having a visual reminder of what I look like now. Maybe it's the hazy reflection or the soft lighting or Ray telling us that we shouldn't be ashamed of what we are, but this morning my scars and stitches don't look quite so horrifying.

Filled with a confidence I haven't felt in months, I make my way out to Soquel Drive, cross the street, and stagger along the opposite shoulder toward Soquel Village. It's the same route I take to get to the Community Center, but this is the cloud-filtered light of late morning instead of the shadowy twilight of early evening and I'm alone—hunched forward and limping, the quintessential, stereotypical zombie wearing a black rain poncho and a sign of protest around my neck. So even with my hood pulled up, I stand out like a vegetarian at a Texas barbecue.

Less than two minutes on the street and cars are honking at me. The shouts and insults come next. I have to admit, some of the comments are at least inventive.

"Hey zombie, it's the time of the season for rotting."

"George Romero called and you didn't get the part."

But most of what I get is your basic gutter variety abuse, the lowest common denominator of insults.

"Zombie go home."

"Dead guys suck."

And my personal favorite:

"Eat this!" (accompanied by the extended middle finger).

I wonder how many of these people go to church.

Not all Breathers are nasty and venomous toward us, but sometimes I'm embarrassed to think that I used to be one of them.

In spite of the abuse, I'm compelled to continue toward the village. I don't know if it's the restlessness I've felt the past few days or the self-righteousness of standing up for what I believe in or the sign of protest around my neck that has emboldened me, but I've given in to the impulse. It's as if nothing else matters.

A black Nissan Sentra passes me and a woman leans out the window and calls me a freak. A silver Dodge Plymouth slows down so a black guy with dreadlocks and a goatee can spit on me. A kid in the backseat of a white BMW launches a half-eaten sandwich that hits me in the chest, splattering mayonnaise and tuna across my sign and my rain poncho. I hear his laughter, followed by his mother's praise as the car passes.

"Good one, Steven."

Just past Safeway and Round Table Pizza, the road descends into Soquel Village. By the time I reach the sign that says Soquel—Founded 1852, I've been hit with coffee, potato salad, raw eggs, orange juice, and a bucket of Kentucky Fried Chicken. Original recipe.

Not all zombies suffer through the same indignities as me. A lot do. Some suffer worse. But I'm the epitome of a zombie, the poster child for the undead, lurching along, dragging one foot behind me, my face a quilt of flesh and stitches. I may as well have a sign stapled to my back that says *Abuse Me*.

At the official boundary of the village, the shoulder turns into a sidewalk and stores appear along the road on either side. I stop in front of Crawford's Antiques, which is closed on Sundays. In the front window I see my reflection again, partially obscured by the curving letters of the store's name but clear enough to see what I look like, covered in discarded food, and this time I wonder what the hell I'm doing.

I don't belong here. I'm not a Breather. The world of the living no longer belongs to me, no matter how much I want it or miss it or think I can just stroll through it without consequences. And I don't want consequences. I just want to be left alone, given some space, provided the freedom to be what I choose to be and to do what I choose to do. But I'm not allowed to do that. I'm a nonhuman, soulless freak. I may as well not even exist.

I stand there staring at my reflection and realize coming here was a huge mistake. Whatever impetus has driven me this far is gone. Now I just want to get home before people start throwing something at me that will do more damage than a bucket of KFC.

Before I turn from the window to make my way back home, another reflection appears next to mine. For an instant

I freeze, stuck in a moment I wasn't expecting, with no idea what to do next. All I can think of is that I'm glad I went for a walk.

The reflection smiles at me, runs a finger across my poncho, puts her finger in her mouth, and says, "Needs more salt."

My own reflection smiles, then turns away from me as I face Rita.

She's wearing a royal blue V-neck sweater over a black T-shirt with blue jeans and black boots. Her lips are Juicy Pink. They look like they're coated with bubble gum.

She's not wearing a scarf. Nor any gloves. The stitches across her throat and her wrists are on display, black against her pale skin for everyone to see. She looks stunning.

We smile at each other, neither of us saying anything. Rather, Rita doesn't say anything and I don't grunt or groan, but we recognize that we both came here because some intangible notion compelled us. Why both of us? Why today? It doesn't matter. What matters is that we've come this far. What matters is that we're not afraid.

Taking my right hand in her left, Rita leads me away from Crawford's and down into the village. I'm wearing a constant smile. It's like I'm on a first date that I can't believe is real. I'm nervous and excited and filled with a confidence I haven't had since before I died. I'm all that and more. But mostly I'm smiling. I glance at Rita and notice she's smiling, too.

We remain silent as we walk down the street, keeping to ourselves, doing nothing to create a scene, yet we're magnets for attention. It's like we're walking down the red carpet at the Academy Awards, except we're not exactly Tom Cruise and Katie Holmes.

Gasps of surprise and horror follow us like applause. Insults explode like flashbulbs. Someone throws a Styrofoam drink container, splattering me with root beer. Someone else throws a jelly doughnut. Another person is on a cell phone, calling the police. In the distance I hear sirens, growing louder. Moments later, the Animal Control van comes squealing around the corner, headed our way.

This is the greatest day of my existence.

Chapter 11

All zombies are expected to register with the County Department of Resurrection, at which time we're issued an identification number. A license. Like the type you'd get for a dog or a cat. My license has my name, address, phone, and ID number, which is 1037. That means I'm the one-thousand-and-thirty-seventh member of the undead in Santa Cruz County to be issued a license.

Typically, the license is worn on a chain, like a dog tag, which I'm sure is an insult to military personnel and dogs alike. Some zombies wear ID bracelets, while other, more anarchist zombies refuse to wear an ID tag. After all, in addition to providing a convenient way for zombies to be identified and returned to their homes, the ID tag helps to track troublemakers. Not every zombie wants to be found. Not every zombie has a home to return to. Not every zombie has parents as understanding as mine.

"Two hundred dollars!" my father shouts from behind the steering wheel as he drives my mother and me home, his face red with rage. "Two hundred dollars!"

That's how much it cost to bail me out of the SPCA.

My initial trip to the shelter was a freebie, since I'd reanimated without my parents' knowledge. Any subsequent visits, however, require a fine to help pay for my accommodations and for the Animal Control shuttle. Tip and tax included.

"Do you have any idea how much you embarrassed me today?" says my father, looking at me in the rearview mirror as he pulls to a stop at the signal. "Did you think about that before you left the house?"

"I don't think he meant to embarrass us, Harry," says my mother, turning to look at me from the front passenger seat, smiling like June Cleaver. "Did you, honey?"

To be honest, I don't know the answer. Maybe some part of me did want to embarrass my father. Ever since I've come home he's done nothing but denounce me. He's offered no support. No sympathy. No parental love. Maybe I'm like the ignored child who screams for attention, only instead of screaming I get captured by Animal Control and thrown into a cage at the SPCA.

I almost nod in response to my mother's question, then I shake my head and smile. There must be something unsettling or mischievous about my smile because my mother's own smile falters, then becomes strained before she turns her attention to the traffic crossing the intersection ahead of us.

In the car next to us, a young boy is staring at me through the back window, his eyes wide and his mouth open. I stick my tongue out at him and he starts to scream.

"Just what the hell were you doing in the village, anyway?" asks my father as he accelerates through the green light.

My dry erase board is on the seat next to me. I put it on my lap, pull out the black marker, and write *Taking a walk*, then pick up the board and turn it toward my parents.

"Taking a walk?" says my father. "You can't just take a walk whenever you want. On Sunday, of all days. Jesus Christ, it stinks in here."

"Harry, don't be so hard on him," says my mother. "He's had a rough day."

"I don't care," says my father, rolling down the window. "That doesn't give him the right to go gallivanting all over town and costing us money. Not unless he wants to get shipped off to a research facility."

My father's been threatening to get rid of me ever since I came home.

"Maybe he was just bored," says my mother. "After all, he spends most of his time cooped up in the wine cellar watching television. I'd get bored, too."

"Too bad," says my father. "He has a place in society and he better learn to accept it if he wants to continue to stay in my house."

More often than not, my parents discuss me as if I were in another room. But today it doesn't frustrate me or make me want to wave my good arm and shriek. I'm still feeling high from the rush of getting snared with Rita while being assaulted with obscenities and disparaging remarks. I can still hear Rita's laughter as we were loaded into the Animal Control van. The laughter wasn't nervous or contemptuous, but full and free—the way someone would laugh on a roller coaster when they forgot their fear and realized it was much more fun to enjoy the ride.

At the SPCA, Rita and I were given separate holding cages across from one another. Kind of like Charlton Heston and Linda Harrison in the original *Planet of the Apes*. As we stood at the front of our cages, holding on to the bars with our faces pressed against the metal, both of us smiling and not saying a word, I half expected a uniformed gorilla to walk past and beat us back into our cages.

Rita's mother came to get her not long after we arrived. Before she left, Rita came over to my cage and asked me if I was okay. I nodded and gave her a thumb up. Then she motioned me forward, leaned up to the bars, and kissed me on the lips.

"I'll see you soon, Andy," she said, and then sauntered away like a goddess.

When I smile at that memory, there's no sense of the mischief my mother saw in my previous smile. But neither Mom nor Dad notice. They're too busy talking about me in the third person.

Chapter 12

. . . thirty-two . . . thirty-three . . . thirty-four . . .

I'm sitting in my therapist's office, watching the red numbers on the digital clock tick off the silence again second by second. Nearly five minutes have elapsed since I sat down in the chair and Ted just sits there over my right shoulder, tapping his pen on his notepad, making little faces. He has fewer wrinkles than last time, which means he had another Botox injection.

The air freshener in the corner hisses, releasing a breath of lilac into the room.

"How are you feeling today, Andrew?"

I think a moment, then scribble my answer on my dry erase board:

Anxious.

Another two minutes go by. I hope we're not going to sit here for the entire session like this. Otherwise, I could have stayed home and watched *Mystic Pizza* on FX.

. . . seventeen . . . eighteen . . . nineteen . . .

"You felt anxious last time as well, didn't you?" he says.

At least I know Ted's taking notes. Either that or he's projecting his own anxiety onto me. After all, he is sitting in a room alone with a zombie.

"Perhaps we should explore the source of your anxiety," says Ted.

I sigh. It doesn't take much exploration to determine that someone who's been made an outcast from society and spends most of his days watching cable television and drinking wine and coveting freedoms prohibited by law might suffer from occasional anxiety. I've done my best to accept my situation and all of the trials it entails. One of Helen's favorite sayings is:

ACCEPT YOUR REALITY.

So I try. But ever since Halloween, I've had a harder time accepting mine. I thought the feeling would go away but, if anything, it's grown more pronounced. Over the past few days I've found myself venturing out after my parents have gone to bed, wandering through the gully, barely making it back to the wine cellar before curfew. It's as though I'm searching for something and I can't figure out what it is.

Ideally, that's what a therapist is supposed to help you with. Understanding yourself and your behaviors. Your motives. Your desires. I'm thinking most Breathers who need that kind of help don't end up sitting in an office with an artificially preserved, self-absorbed therapist whose idea of personal growth is reconstructive surgery.

Ted's tapping his pen on his notepad again and making faces. I glance up once more at the digital clock, at the seconds counting away the minutes, at the minutes consuming the hour, and I wonder if Ted is ever going to get around to exploring the source of my anxiety.

"What was your childhood like?" he asks.

I roll my eyes and wonder how many of Ted's patients commit suicide.

I consider giving him the stock answer, the always bland and perfunctory *Fine* or *Normal*. Which it was. Dad worked. Mom kept the house clean and cooked meals. Andy went to school and played sports and got into the bare minimum of trouble. Nothing spectacular. Nothing catastrophic. Nothing horrible. But instead of sticking to the script, I write:

I was abused.

"Really?" says Ted.

No, not really. But why not?

"Were you abused sexually or emotionally?" he asks.

Both.

Ted scribbles something down, then starts tapping his pen again.

The air freshener releases another hiss of lilac. Personally, I would have chosen lavender. Or maybe gardenia.

"How is it living with your parents now?" he asks.

Wonderful.

"Wonderful?" he says, his brow furrowing.

It's hard to keep a straight face, but this is the most fun I've had in a while with a Breather.

"There are no feelings of resentment or animosity?"

None, I write.

"Fascinating," says Ted, scribbling down more useless notes.

. . . forty-two . . . forty-three . . . forty-four . . .

"How do you and your parents spend your time together?" he asks.

We play Parcheesi.

"Parcheesi?" he says, as though he's never heard the word before. "You and your parents play Parcheesi?"

And Twister.

Chapter 13

The first Friday night of every month is a social event of sorts for the group. A rotating field trip.

Jerry calls it the World Death Tour.

We all meet at a local graveyard to pay our respects to a relative or a friend of the group and to remind ourselves that although we're no longer alive, neither are we dead. It's supposed to make us appreciate the opportunity we have to do something with our new existence, to realize how special we are. For me, it just reinforces the idea that I have no social life. Or is it social death? Or social undeath? Whatever. It makes me feel about as special as mayonnaise.

Tonight we're meeting at Oakwood Memorial Cemetery, which is located right across the street from Dominican Hospital. That must be a comforting thought. I wonder if they put the terminally ill patients and the elderly in the south wing with a window overlooking the cemetery so they can get used to the view.

A few days removed from the new moon, the cemetery sits in near complete darkness, save for the ambient light from the hospital parking lot. Zombies don't see all that well to begin with, which makes wandering around a graveyard at night a bit of an adventure. Even if you died with twenty-twenty vision, your eyesight begins to deteriorate almost immediately upon reanimation. The longer you're among the undead, the worse your vision gets. It's not uncommon to see zombies who've been around for a while wearing glasses.

Up ahead, Tom trips and falls into a tombstone with a grunt.

Maybe it's just me, but a bunch of reanimated corpses wandering around a graveyard after ten o'clock on a Friday night isn't exactly the best way to break the zombie stereotype.

While some West African and Caribbean cultures believe that zombies are created by voodoo spells or by the transmission of a virus, the most widely held opinion is that zombies are flesh-eating monsters—a stereotype perpetuated by Hollywood and horror writers that doesn't help us in our ever-losing battle to change our public image. Then again, it's kind of hard to hire a good publicist when you don't have a budget to rival Twentieth Century Fox or Random House. And when most publicists probably believe you want to eat their brains.

If you ask me, the media is as much to blame as anyone for the proliferation of anti-zombie sentiments. With twenty-four-hour news available up and down the channel guide and a public that demands the sensational and fear-inducing over the humble and uplifting, zombies get more bad publicity than the president and Congress and O. J. Simpson put together.

Anytime a zombie does something wrong, even if he was provoked into attacking, it makes national news and is played to death, saturating the airwaves with opinions and eyewitness accounts and calls for our wholesale destruction. But instead of covering stories that show the undead holding meetings or toy drives or bake sales, the media focuses on a minority of our population and spreads fear with their misleading reports. After all, just because some Asians don't know how to drive doesn't mean they're all bad drivers. Okay. Bad example. But you get my point. Breathers are going to believe what they want to believe, regardless of the facts.

Other media-induced zombie myths:

We are slow-moving.
We have almost zero intelligence.
We can see electromagnetic pulses.
We have superhuman strength.
We are related to vampires.
We go deaf within a few weeks of reanimation.

And, although our olfactory nerves are still functioning, contrary to popular belief, we are not able to smell Breathers from several miles away.

One of the few characteristics the media got right about zombies is that we are insensitive to physical pain. However, we can still get our feelings hurt.

"Here we are," says Tom, once we reach the burial plot for his sister, who was mauled to death by a pit bull. I guess it runs in the family.

We all gather around in a circle.

"This is Donna," says Tom. "Donna, this is everyone."

A murmuring of "Hi, Donna" from everyone and a "What up?" from Jerry. I just wave.

"How old was your sister when she died?" asks Naomi as she lights up a cigarette.

"She was only fourteen," says Tom, the torn, exposed flesh beneath his left eye a black, consuming birthmark in the flicker of Naomi's lighter. "She's actually the reason I became a dog trainer. Thought I could help prevent the same thing from happening to someone else."

"Whoops," says Carl.

Jerry snickers and Rita giggles, her laugh infectious. I can't help but smile.

Tonight, Rita is wearing an ankle-length black skirt with a black wool cardigan and a white turtleneck that's just a shade lighter than her skin. In the darkness, she almost appears to be naked beneath her cardigan.

This is the first time I've seen Rita since our Sunday stroll and good-bye kiss at the SPCA and I'm feeling a little awkward. I'm not sure how to act or what to grunt. That and there's the guilt factor. Being in a cemetery reminds me of Rachel. Not exactly the way I want to be reminded of my wife, but there you have it. But when Rita glances my way and smiles, the guilt just sort of dissolves.

Once we've finished paying our respects to Tom's sister, we follow Helen to her mother's grave. Tom stumbles again and falls into another headstone, tearing the stitches in his right shoulder and knocking his arm loose. Jerry and Rita can't stop laughing and have to fight to stifle their giggles through the moment of silence Helen asks we observe for her mother, who died of a heart attack while sitting on the toilet at Macy's.

After we finish up with Helen's mother, we spend the next forty-five minutes visiting the recently deceased, not to pay our respects, but to make sure they're still dead.

It stands to reason that there are undead who reanimate after they're buried or entombed, so one of our purposes on the World Death Tour is to find those newly laid to rest and listen for any indications that they might not be resting so peacefully. Telltale signs include pounding, screaming, crying, and hysterical laughter.

It's not always easy to hear them, considering we're dealing with six-foot barriers of earth and twelve-inch layers of marble and concrete, not to mention a hardwood casket. But we undead are on the same spiritual wavelength, which allows us to hear what the living choose to ignore.

Breathers typically aren't as attuned to the undead, so they don't hear their cries for help. Even if they could, it's doubtful they'd do anything. It costs a lot of money to disinter a corpse. Not to mention the social embarrassment and the stigma of bringing the undead back into your life.

Tonight we don't find any buried or entombed undead, which isn't surprising. On average, only one out of every two hundred corpses reanimates each year. With more than forty-three hundred annual deaths in Santa Cruz County, that comes to around two dozen zombies per year. And most of those reanimate before funeral services are completed. On rare occasions, someone actually reanimates during their funeral.

Which is what happened with Jerry.

A friend of his videotaped the whole thing and sold it to *America's Funniest Zombie Videos.* Jerry taped the episode and brought a copy of the video to one of the meetings so everyone could watch.

It was a typical funeral. The father standing up at the podium, speaking with conviction through his choked emotion. The sound of people crying. The casket, surrounded by photographs, closed and draped in flowers. Then one of the arrangements slides off the casket as the lid slowly opens and you hear people gasping and screaming as chairs are turned over and horrified faces blur past the camera and the father stumbles back from the podium and shouts, "Dear God!" Then Jerry sits up in his coffin, pulls the eyecaps and cotton out from beneath his eyelids, and glances around the room, his eyes blinking.

The camera moves in closer, a full frame shot of Jerry with

his cheeks raw and red and his head wrapped in gauze as his father wails off camera. Jerry blinks and shakes his head, looks once more around the room and down at his casket, then turns and stares straight into the lens and says, "Dude, is that my video camera?"

Since the service was closed casket, the mortician opted not to sew Jerry's mouth shut. I should have been so lucky. My mortician was a stickler for details. A real by-the-book kind of guy. Packed my external body cavities with cotton soaked in autopsy gel and dressed me in a skin-tight plastic body suit under my clothes to control the leakage of any body fluids. I had a hell of a time getting out of that damn thing.

"Okay," says Helen, once we've all gathered behind the main mausoleum. "I want everyone to spend the next ten minutes on your own. Empty your minds of all negative thoughts, all preconceived notions of who you are, and connect with the universe. Let your minds drift. Don't force it. Allow yourselves to feel the moment and just be."

Sometimes I wonder how much acid Helen's mother took while she was pregnant with her.

Everyone wanders off in different directions while Helen remains at the mausoleum, watching all of us like a yard duty volunteer at lunch recess. Within moments, everyone is consumed by the darkness, though I can spot the embers of Naomi's cigarette floating off to my right.

I try to follow Helen's advice, focusing on nothing, attempting to clear my mind. It doesn't work. All I can think about is Rita and Rachel. Rachel and Rita. One who shared ten years of my life, the other who shared ten minutes with me in an Animal Control van. One who smelled of lavender soap and White Linen, the other who smells faintly of decomposing flesh. One who is dead and cold, the other who is undead and hot.

Not exactly the type of relationship dilemma I thought I'd ever be having.

While part of me acknowledges the commitment I shared with Rachel and the grief that still overwhelms me at times, another part realizes that we've been separated by something more than just death. We've been separated by culture. By class. By the difference that exists between the living and the undead. Even if Rachel had survived, we wouldn't have been able to remain a couple. The issues with raising our daughter aside, Breathers don't tend to reconcile with their undead spouses. At least this way, it's easier. This way, no one's feelings have to get hurt. This way, there's no choice that has to be made.

Except I realize, that's not entirely true. I do have to make a choice. My wife is dead and buried beneath six feet of dirt while Rita is right here, undead and not breathing. One of me. And as one of the undead, my options for romance are pretty limited. I haven't been to any of the zombie singles' mixers, but I hear they're a regular maggot-fest.

Some nights when I'm having trouble falling asleep, I can still hear my mother's voice, shaky and high-pitched, as she stood in the doorway to the wine cellar the day they brought me home, a towel held over her mouth and nose.

"What . . . what do you want, Andy?"

I want my life back, that's what I want. I want everything I used to have that's been taken away. I want everything I'm not allowed to do anymore. But mostly, I want someone I can share this with. Someone who can understand me. Someone who can hold me and comfort me late at night when the emptiness and the loss and the grief surround me like the walls of a coffin. Someone like Rita.

Before I can continue to justify my romantic interest in someone other than my dead wife, a woman screams.

When a Breather screams, there's not much to it other than throat and lungs. The primal force has been diluted. It's like a tea kettle at the end of its life. The scream of a zombie, on the other hand, sounds like the shriek of a raccoon mating, except the raccoon is on crack and weighs about 150 pounds.

This was a zombie scream.

The scream came from in front of me and to my left. I'd seen Naomi's lighter flare up off to my right a few minutes earlier and Helen stayed back at the mausoleum, which left Rita.

Another scream, followed by the sound of Rita struggling and Breathers laughing, then Tom's voice, loud and demanding, traveling through the darkness.

"Hey, leave her alone."

I move as fast as I can toward Tom and Rita, but I'm still getting lapped by banana slugs. As I shuffle past the headstones, accompanied by the approaching voices of the other members of the group, Tom shouts out again, this time in despair.

"Get off him!" yells Rita. "Get off . . . !"

Her words are cut short by the sound of impact, of wood against flesh.

By the time I reach them, Tom is on the ground getting attacked by two young male Breathers in sweatshirts and jeans. A third Breather is keeping lookout while holding Rita at bay with a baseball bat and a pair of suture removers.

I want to help Rita and Tom, but there's not much I can do with a bum arm and a broken ankle. If I were a superhero, my name would be something like the Undead Gimp. Or Useless Zombie.

All I can think to do is let out a shriek.

"Hurry up, you guys!" says the lookout, his voice full of adrenaline as he brandishes the suture remover at me.

Tom lets out a final, struggling shout as one of the Breathers pulls his right arm free and slaps Tom in the face with his own disembodied hand. Then the three Breathers are scrambling away, whooping and laughing, waving Tom's right arm at us as they run off.

Carl and Jerry race past and chase after the Breathers. If not for my broken ankle, I'd be running alongside them. Instead, I shuffle over to see how Rita is as Naomi and Helen arrive.

"What happened?" asks Naomi, helping Tom to his feet.

"I heard Rita scream and saw these three Breathers pin her to the ground," says Tom. "I tried to scare them off and the next thing I know, they're on top of me cutting at my stitches."

"Fraternity boys," says Rita. Her hair is tousled, thick strands hanging over her face. Otherwise, she appears unharmed. "I got this off one of their sweatshirts."

She holds out her hand, revealing a silver pin of the Greek letters ΣΧ.

"I've heard of this," says Helen. "It's some kind of pledge initiation. They have to steal a body part from the living dead."

"They weren't trying to steal any body parts from me," says Rita, the insinuation in her voice unmistakable.

This time, instead of a shriek, I let out a growl.

"Breathers are so disgusting," says Naomi as she puts out her cigarette in her empty eye socket.

A few minutes later, Carl and Jerry return empty-handed.

Carl leans against a headstone. "They had a car waiting," he says. "We couldn't reach them in time."

Tom sighs and sits down, his left hand over his face.

"Sorry about your arm, dude," says Jerry.

"Did you get a license plate number?" asks Naomi.

Carl shakes his head. "It was too dark."

"What does it matter?" says Rita. "It's not like anyone's going to help us."

She's right. The police would want to know what we were doing in the cemetery. The college would take the side of the fraternity. And the executive council for Sigma Chi would protect its members. If we presented the pledge pin as evidence, we would likely be accused of stealing it. No lawyer would take our case. No witnesses would back our claim. No court of public opinion would be in our favor. Even Amnesty International wouldn't intervene. After all, technically, we're not human.

Since we're no longer alive, any crimes committed against us are misdemeanors at worst. Most of the time, they're not even considered crimes. So we have no legal protection. No public advocate. No recourse for the abuse and humiliation that we endure from a society that reviles us.

If you've never seen someone get his arm torn out of his socket by a gang of drunk college fraternity boys who slapped him in the face with his own hand, then you probably wouldn't understand.

'm sitting home, in my wine cellar studio, writing a letter to my representative.

It's a petition, really. A sort of a cease-and-desist request. Nothing outlandish. Nothing unreasonable. I'm simply asking the government to give the undead back their unalienable rights, not the least of which is the right to not get dismembered and to not have your arm stolen as part of a fraternity initiation.

I think that's in the Constitution somewhere, right after the amendment repealing Prohibition.

For the first few months after reanimating, I led a fairly sheltered zombie existence in my parents' wine cellar. Sure, I've been verbally abused by everyone from prepubescents to octogenarians, and I've heard horror stories about the atrocities committed against zombies. I've even been threatened with zombie zoos and medical research labs and Cadaver College (all by my father). But I hadn't experienced the dangers of being one of the undead until I witnessed the attacks on Walter and Tom.

While the dismemberment of Walter opened my eyes, the stealing of Tom's arm hit me on a more personal level. Maybe it's because I was standing right there and looked into the eyes of the Breathers who attacked him. Maybe it's because they attacked Rita, as well. Or maybe it's because Tom is my friend and I know how embarrassing this is for him.

You have to understand about Tom.

First of all, he lives with his mother. Sure, so do I, but Tom was living with his mother *before* the pair of Presa Canarios tore into him like Mike Tyson going after Evander Holyfield's earlobe.

Second, Tom is what Jerry would call a Magoo. A doofus. Sweet and naive. The kind of person others would have made fun of even when he was a Breather. Chances are pretty good that Tom was the kid in your high school who wore corduroy and plaid, who ate lunch by himself, and who routinely had his clothes stolen from his gym locker. The phrase *atomic wedgie* comes to mind.

Third, even among zombies, Tom is self-conscious. Sure, we all finger our stitches and our wounds or play with little knobs of exposed bone, but Tom obsesses with his loose flaps of skin as though he either can't get used to the idea that they're real or he thinks he can somehow make them go away.

Now his right arm is gone. Stolen. As a prank. Without any regard to his feelings or his sense of equilibrium. And that's just not right. Something has to change. Something has to be done. To paraphrase George Herbert Walker Bush: *This aggression will not stand.*

So I'm writing my letter. My petition. My Constitutional request. Specifically, I'm addressing the First Section of the Fourteenth Amendment, which more or less says: *No State shall enforce any law which abridges the privileges of its citizens, nor deprive any person of life, liberty, or property without due process, nor deny any person equal protection of the law.*

The problem I'm running into involves the definition of

citizens or *persons,* which is the language in which the Fourteenth Amendment and the rest of the Constitution is written. It's a little jargony and difficult to follow at times, with vague references to persons and no mention of zombies. The whole life, liberty, and the pursuit of happiness thing? The self-evident truth that all men are created equal, even if they're undead men? That's in the Declaration of Independence, which doesn't really stand up to Constitutional interpretation. It's a nice idea, though. Just not realistic when actually put into practice. More of a guideline than a truth.

What is self-evident is that nothing's going to change for us unless we do something to affect our nonhuman status. Unless we can change the way we're perceived by Breathers. It's not as though zombies are a social issue that just popped up overnight. It's not like we haven't been a recognized part of the culture for most of the past century.

During the Great Depression, we blended in with the homeless and stood in bread lines with the unemployed—which didn't go over well, since we were taking handouts from the living. The only thing more unpopular than zombies in the early 1930s was Herbert Hoover.

World War II provided us with the chance to contribute to society as most of the male zombie population enlisted to serve our country. But our participation was kept secret by the government and our contributions edited from history. Breathers don't want to know that the first troops to land at Normandy were the American undead.

While the 1950s brought the beginning of the civil rights movement for African Americans, zombies became increasingly targeted for discrimination and violence. Public lynchings were common, and you didn't have to be a card-carrying member of the KKK to enjoy one. *Happy Days* my ass.

During the 1960s, some of us escaped to either Vietnam or

Haight-Ashbury. But once the war and the acid trips ended, we returned to the same reality we'd left behind. Except for the public lynchings. And disco.

Thirty years later, nothing much has changed.

I think it's about time we remedy that.

Chapter 15

I
t's amazing how much perfectly good food Breathers waste.

Milkshakes. Big Gulps. Double lattes.

Bagels. Vegetable soup. Ham and cheese croissants.

Whoppers. Big Macs. Jumbo Jacks.

You'd think they'd care more about actually eating their food than throwing it at a defenseless zombie who's picketing back and forth on Soquel Avenue in front of an abandoned mortuary like an arcade shooting-gallery target, carrying a sign that says:

ZOMBIES FOR CITIZENSHIP.

And I'm not even counting the health-conscious Breathers who stopped by to unload a bag full of organic produce, cage-free eggs, and silken tofu on me.

I've been out here for less than an hour and already I look like a movie screen at a fraternity rush selection meeting. I'm surprised no one's called Animal Control yet, but I guess they're all having too much fun throwing their uneaten fast food and coffee at me to worry about protocol. Besides, even though I look like the archetypal zombie, I'm not particularly threatening. I mean, how menacing can I be covered in Slurpee and bean curd and seasoned curly fries?

A pair of crows have started circling me, scavenging the splattered fast food detritus, the supermarket smorgasbord dripping from me onto the abandoned mortuary lawn. I'm not sure what made me pick this location—the public exposure, the absence of Breather foot traffic, or the fact that corpses used to call this place home—but the crows kind of add a nice touch, being harbingers of death and all. The problem is, I'm not sure if the crows are more interested in the food that's collected at my feet or if they're more interested in me.

"Freak!" comes the shout from a passing Ford Mustang, followed by a Reuben sandwich from Erik's Deli that nails me on the side of the head in an explosion of sauerkraut and corned beef. As an afterthought, a cup of Texas Jailhouse Chili hits me in the crotch.

Next time, I won't bother to eat lunch first.

With the variety of fare that I've been hit with, it makes me wonder if the Breathers who drive past are throwing random food they just happen to have in their cars or if they're zipping over to 7-Eleven or Burger King or Safeway just to get something to throw at me. Considering most of the food that's been cast my way is uneaten, and that more than a few of the same vehicles have returned with fresh supplies, I get the feeling it's not just a spur-of-the-moment thing.

In a way, I'm encouraged that they would go to the trouble of making a special trip just for me, though I'm concerned my message of protest might get lost in the excitement of Pelt the Zombie. At least I hope I'm making an impact. Kind of like one of those television commercials you can't stand but you just can't seem to forget.

"Zombies suck!" yells another motorist, who unleashes a Taco Bell burrito that hits my sign with a *splat* and then slides off.

I glance down at the burrito, partially dressed in its wrapper, a few bites taken out of it, beans and salsa spilling out onto the grass. Like I'm impressed. Maybe if he'd thrown a Gordita Supreme or an Enchirito. But a partially eaten, seventy-nine-cent bean burrito? Please.

Right now, I'm not concerned about getting attacked by gangs of teenagers or frat boys or rednecks. During the day, Breathers tend to shy away from blatant acts of zombie violence. Most of the mob mentality takes place after sunset, when courage is fed by beer and whiskey and the cover of night. Breathers are like that. They don't want to have to confront the unpleasant realities of their nature beneath the glaring light of the sun. They'd rather deal with them after dark, where they're harder to see and easier to ignore.

In the middle of a Monday afternoon, my physical safety isn't much of an issue. I'm not going to get dismembered or torched. Pretty much all I have to worry about are food projectiles and incendiary comments. Of course, eventually some tattling Breather will get on a cell phone and call Animal Control.

When I first hear the sirens I don't think anything of it. The Dominican Hospital is less than a mile away, so ambulances and emergency vehicles pass by here every day. But as the sirens grow louder and the flashing lights appear around the curve and the crows abandon their supper in a flurry of wings, I realize the emergency is me.

I don't even bother to try to escape. What's the point? It's not like I can outrun anyone. And it would just make things worse. So instead I set down my sign, pull some stray sauerkraut out of my hair, and walk toward the sirens to display my cooperation. If I'm going to get taken away in an anti-zombie harness, at least I can do it with dignity.

Just before the Animal Control van screeches to a stop in front of the mortuary, someone launches an original size Jamba Juice that hits me in the chest and erupts, coating my face and hair with Matcha Green Tea Blast.

Chapter 16

Why are we here?" asks Helen.

Helen used to counsel other zombies in her private practice before she became one herself. Her prior experience is the main reason she was allowed to head up the local chapter of Undead Anonymous.

While most UA chapters are run by zombie moderators, we're not completely autonomous. Helen has to report any new group members to the County Department of Resurrection, and once a month a Breather liaison stops by to make sure we're decomposing on schedule and behaving like good little zombies. But they usually don't stick around very long.

I think it has something to do with the smell.

Or the way Carl fingers the knife wounds in his face.

We're halfway through our ninety minutes, most of which we spent discussing the theft of Tom's right arm and what we can do to get it back. But our options are pretty much what they were with Walter. Which means we either accept what happened and move on, or we risk more than just losing a limb. Or at least more than getting stoned with fast food and chauffeured off to the SPCA.

This evening's message on the chalkboard shouts:

WHY ARE WE HERE?

Jerry leans over to me. "Dude, I'm here because I drank a bottle of Jack and smoked three huge bowls."

Tell me something I don't know.

"Jerry, do you want to share with the group?" asks Helen.

Jerry's cheeks are raw from his road rash, so he looks like he's constantly blushing. "I was just saying that I wouldn't be here if I would have been wearing my seat belt."

"Maybe," says Helen. "Maybe not. But that's not why we're here."

I almost didn't make it to the meeting. After my "stupid little stunt," as he called it, my father threatened to leave me at the SPCA for a week, which is the maximum time they'll hold on to a zombie with guardian hosts before turning me over to the county. From there, it's just a short trip to having my head in a roasting pan for some fledgling plastic surgeon's midterm.

Mom didn't offer up any arguments in my defense, but just stood back while my father berated me through the bars of my kennel. Eventually my father backed down on his threat, but only because it would have cost him an extra fifty bucks a day to keep me there.

I'm glad I didn't have to stay a week at the SPCA. The accommodations aren't all that bad and there's not much difference in taste between dry cat food and Mom's meat loaf, but I would have missed being able to see Rita.

Tonight she's sitting across from me, wearing the ΣX pledge pin in her left earlobe and a white sweater with a red silk scarf that looks like a river of blood beneath her pallid face. She's not wearing any gloves. Instead, she has her hands in her lap as she applies red nail polish to the fingernails on her left hand. Before the polish can dry, she raises her hand to her lips and licks each fingernail clean.

I suddenly wonder what it would be like to be her finger-nails.

"We all survived for a reason," says Helen. "Can anyone tell me why?"

Silence answers her as each of us looks around the room at the faces of our fellow survivors. Even Carl manages to keep from making a snide comment.

Next to Rita, Tom raises his remaining arm and waves his fingers in the air.

I have to admire Tom for showing up to the meeting. It's not only demeaning and embarrassing to have one of your arms stolen, but psychologically painful. Even though Tom didn't have the use of that arm and can't feel the physical pain of its absence, he has the empty socket as a constant reminder of what he's lost. That and it's hard to keep your balance.

"You don't have to raise your hand, Tom," says Helen.

"Oh, yeah. Right," he says, lowering his arm. "Well, I fig-ure we're here because we're not supposed to be dead."

"Brilliant," says Carl, snorting out laughter. "Leave it to the vegetarian to come up with a wacko answer."

"Why do you insist on being such an ass?" asks Naomi. When she talks, the right side of her mouth hangs limp be-neath her empty eye socket.

"Oh, I don't know," says Carl. "Maybe it's because the ex-tent of my social calendar is sitting in this room with all of you twice a week instead of feeling like I can go to the movies or take a walk on the beach or play a round of golf."

Carl used to be a member of the Seascape Resort, where he played tennis and golf and attended weekly dinners and hob-nobbed with the social elite of Santa Cruz County.

Naomi takes a drag on her cigarette and purposely blows the smoke at Carl. "Just because you're bitter doesn't mean you have the right to take out your frustration on the rest of us. It doesn't serve any purpose."

"What a wonderful transition," says Helen. "Thank you, Naomi."

Helen gets up and walks over to the chalkboard. I glance at Rita, who is licking the fingernails of her right hand now. Her tongue is red. I wonder if it tastes like Revlon or Estée Lauder.

Helen turns back to us and sits down. On the chalkboard, under WHY ARE WE HERE? she's written the words:

FIND YOUR PURPOSE.

"Tom, you said you thought we were here because we're not supposed to be dead," says Helen.

Tom nods and looks around, his left hand massaging the empty socket where his right arm used to be.

"Would you like to elaborate on that?" she says.

"Sure," says Tom. "You see, when I became a vegetarian, it wasn't really a conscious choice."

"That's not surprising," says Carl.

"Anyway," says Tom. "I didn't become vegetarian for any causes or for health reasons. I just stopped craving meat. I didn't ask for it. It just felt like a random thing that happened to me, and so I went with it."

"So what?" says Jerry. His lips have turned purple from the diet grape soda he's drinking. "We're all, like, not dead because we're supposed to stop eating Big Macs?"

"No. My point is that this feels different for me," says Tom. "I didn't ask for this, either, but I feel like I survived not because of some random thing, but for a specific reason."

"A purpose," says Helen.

Tom nods.

I glance around the room. At Carl, picking at the knife

wounds on his face. At Tom, with his empty arm socket and half of his face gone. At Rita, licking her fingernails. At Jerry, grinning like an idiot, his cheeks red and his lips purple. At Naomi, her eye socket a dark, ragged hole.

"No one knows for sure why we survived while others have not," says Helen. "But I agree with Tom. We're all here for a purpose, and each of us needs to find out what that purpose is."

"If you ask me," says Jerry, "my purpose is to introduce all of the ladies to a new definition of *stiffy*."

Jerry is the only one who laughs at his joke, with a snort and a head bob and all of his teeth showing like medals.

The fact that Jerry's the only one laughing apparently amuses Rita, so she starts laughing. Then Tom joins in, followed by Naomi, and pretty soon everyone's laughing and the moment reminds me of a dream I had the other night.

We're all in a limousine, a super stretch job, like one of those Hummer limos. Jerry has a bottle of his beloved Jack Daniel's, which he pours directly onto his exposed brain so he can get drunk faster. Tom keeps removing his right arm and then popping it back into place like a magic trick, while Helen laughs and lifts up the back of her shirt to show off her exit wounds. Naomi is on a cell phone talking to someone and drinking champagne, a tiny, hand-painted Vacancy sign sticking out of her eyebrow above her empty eye socket. Carl is tending a barbecue grill, the smoke drifting up and out through the limo's sunroof. He cuts into a steak, then reinserts the knife into one of the wounds on his face. Rita is sitting directly across from me, no hoods, no turtlenecks, no scarves, just a black evening dress with spaghetti straps and a knee-length hem. Her exposed flesh is alabaster and covered with scars. And they are magnificent.

I didn't know what to make of this dream, but I came away

from it with a good feeling, a definite positive vibe. Maybe it was a false hope, but I couldn't deny the atmosphere inside that limousine.

We were all happy.

For the next half an hour, Helen forgos the regular meeting structure and we all talk about what we'd do if we could do anything we wanted without having to worry about what we were or how we looked or what anyone thought. That is, everyone else talks. I write on the chalkboard and make grunting sounds, with an occasional shriek that gets everyone laughing again. Even Carl joins in and manages to contribute constructively. He's still an ass, but he's the kind of ass you'd like to have around because he knows he's being an ass, not because he thinks his behavior is acceptable.

"Okay," says Helen, looking at her watch. "Before we finish up, I want to remind everyone that next Friday is our Bring a Survivor Meeting."

This excites me I think more than the others. I haven't told anyone about my petition yet because I plan to bring it to the next meeting, when our numbers will be doubled and I can get twice as many signatures. I don't know if that will matter, considering that legally they're all worth about as much as a politician's promise, but I'd rather send off my petition with as many signatures as I can possibly get.

I'm also excited to see Ray and the twins again. At least Ray. Maybe he'll bring along some jars of venison for the group.

"Now," says Helen. "For the remainder of our time, I want everyone to pair up with another survivor and practice giving and receiving honest, emotional contact."

Tom, who is sitting next to Rita, pairs up with her before I can make my move, while Jerry bolts over to Naomi, leaving me and Carl sitting at opposite ends of the semicircle, staring at each other.

"Oh for Christ's sake," Carl grumbles, then stands up and walks over to me. "Come on, Andy. We might as well get this over with."

I stand up and more or less embrace Carl, face-to-face, though I'm four inches taller, so I'm looking at the top of Carl's head. His hair is graying and matted, his scalp dry and flaky. He needs to shampoo more often. He also needs a stronger deodorant or body fragrance. But I can't exactly complain.

Hugging is meant to give us the feeling of acceptance, of emotional and physical comfort, to remind us that we're still human beings. So far, all I've felt is awkward. I'm not homophobic, nor am I in a constant state of arousal like Jerry. But I don't think the exercise is providing anything but the opportunity to remind me that my left arm is as useless as a deflated basketball.

"Focus on how this makes you feel," says Helen, walking around the room, speaking with a soft, gentle voice. "Don't think about how this relates to a prior memory or to a feeling you want to recapture. Remember, we're not here to dwell on your past. The past was your existence before this."

She's said this to us before, at almost every meeting, and told us to reinforce the idea with positive visualization that focuses on *now.* So what you're supposed to do is start with your first memory after the accident or the shooting or the dog mauling. This is what matters. This is where your new existence began.

Chapter 17

When asked about their first memory, most Breathers recall breast feeding, riding a tricycle, being afraid of the dark, getting dressed for bed, discovering their bellybutton, playing with bugs, their first day of school, their first stuffed animal, or their first Christmas.

No one remembers their birth.

Getting evicted from the womb and squeezed out through the vaginal canal. Your skin covered in amniotic fluid and placental blood. Emerging into a noisy world with strange smells and blinding lights. Someone with a white mask and gloves grabbing your soft, malleable head with a pair of forceps.

No wonder newborn babies cry.

My new existence, my zombie birth, began with the realization that little girls would drop their ice cream and run away screaming at the sight of me.

How's that for a first memory?

I guess it could have been worse. I could have reanimated while the mortician was packing my body cavities with autopsy gel.

In addition to memories we'd like to repress and self-image complexes, the undead suffer from a host of afflictions that would challenge even the most compassionate and skilled therapist. Of course, most of these afflictions are caused by Breathers.

I'm thinking about Annie.

I'm thinking about how I'm not allowed to see her. Or talk to her. Or write letters or e-mails or communicate with her in any way. I just want to know how she's doing, to know that she's okay, to know that she's coping.

To simply know that she *is*.

When your life is ripped away and you're reborn into an existence of undeath, nothing seems real. Not what's happening to you now. Not what the future holds. Not what you remember of your past. Now is too surreal, the future too bleak, and the past has been inherited and sold and donated and auctioned and stored in a place where you can't be reminded of everything you've lost.

It's even more unreal when the wife and daughter who shared your life are gone. Poof. Like a magic trick. One moment you're in a car driving home from a party and the next, you're a zombie staggering home on the side of the road. Except you have no home. You have no wife. You have no daughter. They've been erased from your existence. No good-bye letters. No keepsakes. No pictures. Nothing to let you know they ever existed. Sometimes you wonder if they ever did. Sometimes you wonder if it was just a dream you were having until you woke up into your present nightmare.

I never saw Rachel's body and I missed her funeral, so I have to take my parents' word for it that she's buried beneath her headstone under six feet of prime real estate in the Soquel Cemetery. But at least I have a headstone. A marker. Some kind of tangible proof that Rachel existed, that this is what happened to her while I was temporarily dead.

With Annie, there's no proof. Nothing tangible. Nothing I

can point to and say for certain that I know what happened to her. That she's still alive. That she ever existed.

I'm thinking about this as I'm watching a young girl about Annie's age who is staring at me with big, blue O's, her curiosity framed by blond pigtails like the ones Annie used to wear. She's wearing pink pants and pink boots and a pink zip-up sweatshirt with an undeployed hood. All around and behind the little girl, in the periphery that extends a good thirty feet from the park bench where I'm sitting, more than a dozen adults are yelling and screaming, horrified at my presence. Not the little girl. She's less than ten feet away and as calm as the Dalai Lama.

And why shouldn't she be? I'm not hurting anyone. I'm not threatening anyone. I'm just sitting on a park bench with my dry erase board around my neck with the words *Zombies Are People Too* written on it in bold, black letters.

A few of the adults yell at me from their safety zone, threatening me with bodily harm if I so much as touch the little girl. Funny how none of them are brave enough to approach the inner circle and actually rescue the little cutie from the big, bad zombie.

The little girl looks at my face, glances down at my sign, then back up at my face as if she's trying to figure something out. Finally, she points at my chest, at my proclamation of equality, and says, "Is it true?"

I nod.

Before the little girl can ask me another question, her mother sprints in like a rugby player, scoops up her daughter, and carries the little girl away, leaving me alone in my thirty-foot radius of Breather buffer.

Given more time before her mother showed up, I wonder how much progress we could have made. I wonder if the little girl would have sat down next to me. I wonder if I could have answered more questions. I wonder if it would have made a difference.

I'm sure the little girl will ask her mother and father about the zombie she saw in the park today and the sign he was wearing around his neck, and she'll ask them if it's true. Are zombies people, too? I'm sure her parents will explain to her that zombies are not people. Zombies are dirty, disgusting creatures and she shouldn't ever touch or trust them. And I'm sure that, as time passes, she'll grow to believe it.

But I'm hoping she'll ignore her parents and think for herself. I'm hoping she'll persuade her friends to think the same way. I'm hoping that eventually I'll be able to sit on a bench in the park without a thirty-foot boundary of fear.

I'm still hoping this when the Animal Control van pulls up.

Chapter 18

I'm sitting in my room Wednesday night, eating Oreo cookies and drinking a $350 bottle of 1982 Chateau La Tour Haut-Brion, watching *Jaws* on Bravo and wishing I had some truffles.

Upstairs I hear my parents moving around, arguing. I can't make out what my mother's saying, but my father keeps shouting phrases like, "Goddamned sideshow freak" and "What's so wrong about donating him to science?" I turn up the volume on the television to drown them out when someone knocks on the back entrance to the wine cellar.

I'm not expecting company.

My Breather friends have all developed a convenient case of amnesia that wiped away all traces of the friendships we shared before my reanimation. Occasionally I see them on my way to the meetings. If they're wearing smiles, the smiles vanish when they see me. And though they never shout out slurs or derisions or join in with the laughter of other Breathers, they always look away.

None of the other survivors from the group have ever come by to visit and it's not like I've ever invited them over. I'm sure my parents would love that—a room full of zombies sitting on the furniture and stinking up the house, playing Trivial Pursuit and listening to Green Day or Bachman Turner Overdrive.

I wonder if Mom would serve mimosas.

The knocking comes again, more insistent this time. Maybe it's Rita, stopping by to see if I want to take an evening stroll. But I don't let myself believe this, otherwise I'll be disappointed if it's not her. Whoever it is, I hope they don't mind Oreo cookie backwash in their Bordeaux.

When I open the door, Jerry is standing there in the darkness with a backpack slung over one shoulder, his Oakland A's hat on sideways, and a big *surprise* grin on his face. Next to him, Tom wears a less enthusiastic expression, though he does raise his remaining arm to give a halfhearted, salutatory wave.

"Andy my man," says Jerry. "What's shakin'?"

I motion toward the television, where Robert Shaw is sliding down the deck of his ship to his impending death, then I take a swig of Bordeaux and offer Tom a taste. He declines. Jerry doesn't wait for the offer. He reaches for the bottle and turns it nearly upside down into his upturned mouth, reminding me of a nestling about to receive a regurgitated meal. Which isn't too far from the truth.

Seconds later, Jerry's road rash face contorts and he pulls the bottle away before spraying a mouthful of red wine onto the floor.

"Dude!" he says, spitting. "What the hell is in that stuff?"

I reach into the pockets of my sweatpants and pull out two Oreo cookies.

"Oh man," he says, continuing to spit out wine, saliva, and soggy Oreo cookie onto my floor. "That's gross."

Tom reaches his left hand toward the cookies. "Can I have one of those?"

I hand him both, which he consumes without a trace of joy, then I take the wine back from Jerry before he drops the bottle and wastes any more wine. From the looks of it, there's already about $37.50 worth of Chateau La Tour Haut-Brion on the floor.

"Forget the wine and cookies," says Jerry, with one final spit. "Put on your shoes. It's boys' night out."

It sounds tempting, but it's after 9:00 p.m. After my most recent trip to the SPCA, my father is about one more protest from dismembering me himself, so even without the midnight curfew, I'm reluctant to take an unchaperoned excursion. Then Jerry says the magic words.

"We're going to Ray's."

In less than two minutes we're out the door and around the back of the house on our way toward the gully. Jerry explains how he thought a visit to Ray might help to cheer up Tom, give him a chance to stop freaking out about his arm. Maybe there's some truth to Jerry's motives, but I have a feeling Tom was more likely corralled so Jerry could look through more of Ray's *Playboy* collection.

Tom has a tough time negotiating the gully with his right arm missing. Even Jerry slips a couple of times and lands hard on his tailbone, letting out a curse and hitching his pants back up. Maybe it's because I'm excited to visit Ray. Maybe it's because I've made this trip dozens of times. But for some reason, I don't have any trouble at all. Not a slip or a stumble. It's as if I've finally figured out how my new body works.

We stick to the side streets and undeveloped land as much as possible, avoiding the heart of the Soquel Village altogether, coming out onto Old San Jose Road just before the field where we first saw Ray and the twins. A couple of cars pass by, but other than a belated honk and a shout of "Freaks," we arrive at the granary without incident.

"Animal Control," announces Jerry as he opens the back door and steps inside.

Tom follows Jerry and I bring up the rear. Light is flickering off the granary's stone walls. Even before I see Ray, I hear his voice.

"Come on in," he says with his farm-boy twang that makes me think we'll find him milking a cow. Instead, he's sitting behind the fire facing us, a bottle of beer in one hand and a half-empty Mason jar of deer meat next to him. The twins are nowhere to be seen.

Ray takes a swig of beer and nods at us. "I see you've brought a new friend."

"This is Tom," says Jerry.

Tom hasn't spoken a single word since asking me for the Oreo cookies. Apparently he's hungry because he points to the Mason jar on the ground next to Ray and says, "What's that?"

"Ray's Resplendent Rapture," says Ray, scooping out a piece with a fork. "Venison. Freshly preserved. You're welcome to a jar if you're hungry."

"I'm vegetarian," says Tom, with a trace of reluctance.

"To each his own," says Ray. "But believe me when I say that you don't know what you're missing."

Tom may not know what he's missing, but I do, so I drag myself over to the fire and sit down next to Ray, who provides me with a jar and a fork.

Jerry isn't interested in food. "I brought these back," he says, pulling a stack of *Playboys* from his backpack with the reverence of an archaeologist unearthing ancient manuscripts. "Could I borrow some more?"

"Sure you don't want to keep those a little longer?" asks Ray.

"Nah," says Jerry. "I scanned all the pictures into my computer and printed them up. I almost have enough to cover my bedroom ceiling."

Jerry says this with a sense of pride.

If Jerry were a Breather, he could just log on to Playboy .com and download the pictures directly to his computer. But since the undead are prohibited from using the Internet, Jerry has to do it the old-fashioned way.

"Take your pick," says Ray, motioning to the storage area behind me. "And help yourself to a jar if you're so inclined."

While Jerry switches out his issues of *Playboy*, I dig into my jar of deer meat like a kid digging into an ice-cream sundae. It tastes kind of like chicken, but with a gamier quality that makes me think of moving stealthily through a forest in search of a meal. I never went hunting for deer or duck or anything that didn't already come prepackaged in the refrigerated section of Safeway. Never even cast a fishing line. But sitting here by the fire, shoveling preserved deer meat between my lips with the juices running down my chin, I feel almost primal.

Tom is still standing a few feet from the fire, rubbing his empty right arm socket and looking like the last kid waiting to be picked for kickball.

"Don't just stand there," says Ray. "Pull up a beer."

Tom considers this, then nods and sits down while Ray grabs four bottles of Budweiser from his storage. After handing one to each of us, he takes a seat across the fire from Tom.

"Here's to new friends and old habits," says Ray, raising his bottle.

"And to pictures of naked women," says Jerry, sitting down with half a dozen *Playboys*.

Tom and I say nothing—Tom because he's obviously self-conscious and me because I can't. And I'm too busy shoveling deer meat into my mouth.

For several minutes there's nothing but the sounds of eating, drinking, and the turning of magazine pages, accompanied by an occasional "Oh my God!" from Jerry.

"So Tom," says Ray, "what's your story?"

Tom takes a sip of beer and says, "I was mauled by a pair of Presa Canarios."

"Ouch," says Ray. "That had to hurt."

"Yeah," says Tom, fingering the flaps of flesh on his face. "I probably should have stuck to poodles."

"You part of the 'survivor' group?" asks Ray.

"Hey, Tom," says Jerry before Tom can respond. Jerry holds up one of the magazines to display Miss September 1997. "You want to look through one of these?"

Tom stares at the centerfold for several moments before shaking his head. Like me, I think he's more self-conscious than uninterested. What man wouldn't be curious to see more when he's looking at a two-foot, full-body, glossy image of a twenty-year-old blonde in high heels and strategically displaced lace undergarments? But when you have only one arm, it's tough to turn the pages of a magazine and drink a beer. Trying to eat venison out of a jar is hard enough. I have to wedge the jar in the crook of my right leg to keep the jar from falling over.

"So," says Ray, "did the dog take your arm, too?"

Tom looks around, as if waiting for someone else to answer, until he realizes the question has been directed at him.

"No," says Tom, looking down into his beer. "It was stolen."

"Stolen?" says Ray.

Reluctantly, Tom recounts the stolen arm fiasco in the Oakwood Memorial Cemetery.

"Do you know where these frat boys live?" asks Ray.

"They belong to Sigmund Chai," says Jerry.

"Sigma Chi," says Tom.

"Whatever."

Jerry has pulled a jar of Ray's Resplendent Rapture over to him and is unscrewing the lid as he continues to flip through the September 1997 issue.

"Have you tried to get your arm back?" asks Ray.

Tom shakes his head. "We talked about it, but decided it was too much trouble."

"It's too much trouble to take back something that belongs to you?" asks Ray.

We hadn't looked at it like that before, but since he put it that way . . .

"Hey," says Jerry, licking his fingers, his mouth half full of venison. "This stuff is pretty good. You should try some, Tom."

"I'm vegetarian."

"That's bullshit," says Jerry. "You told me you eat fish."

"That's not the same," says Tom. "There's a difference between meat and fish."

"Whatever," says Jerry, displaying the universal gesture for masturbation.

"I've got some tuna if you want some," says Ray, getting up. "Anyone want another beer?"

Both Jerry and I raise a hand.

"You have tuna?" says Tom in disbelief.

"Freshly caught and jarred," says Ray, climbing into his storage area. "Though I can't take credit for catching it myself."

"Who caught it?" asks Tom.

"Friend of mine," says Ray, appearing with a jar and three more beers. He hands a bottle to Jerry and me, then presents the jar of tuna and a fork to Tom.

From where I'm sitting, the stuff in the jar looks just like venison, but then my vision isn't what it used to be.

Tom holds the jar up to the light of the fire, then secures the jar between his feet, unscrews the lid, and lifts the jar to sniff the contents.

"It doesn't smell like tuna," says Tom.

"Let me know what you think," says Ray. "I haven't sampled it myself yet."

With his fork, Tom removes a sliver of the tuna and places it on his tongue. An expression that looks like doubt furrows his brow, but he takes another sample, using all three tines this time, and his eyebrows do a little dance above his partially devoured face.

"It's good," he says, plunging his fork in again and removing a chunk of tuna, the juices glistening in the flicker of the fire as he slides the tuna off the fork and into his mouth. "It's really good."

For the next few minutes the conversation stops as Tom devours the contents of his jar and Jerry returns to the hedonism of his magazines. Before I've finished my second beer, Tom has emptied the jar and is using his finger to clean out the remaining residue.

"If you want, I'd be happy to send you home with some more," says Ray.

"Thanks," says Tom, licking his fingers. "That would be great."

"In fact, you're all welcome to take home a jar," says Ray. "In return, all I ask is your help with something I'd like to remedy."

"Sure," says Tom.

"What is it?" asks Jerry.

"Gaack," I say.

Chapter 19

We're riding in a 2001 Chevy Lumina with Ray behind the wheel and Jerry riding shotgun. I'm behind Jerry while Tom sits to my left, looking nervous and uncomfortable. With my dead left arm and Tom's missing right arm, I feel like we're conjoined twins adjusting to our recent separation.

Ray has the Lumina's radio tuned to KPIG 107.5, a local central-coast station that plays a mix of country, folk, and classic rock and roll. As we drive north along the frontage road of Highway 1 on our way toward downtown Santa Cruz, the interior of the Lumina is filled with The Who's "Magic Bus."

I've heard the song dozens of times, but coming out of the speakers behind me are unfamiliar background vocals, slightly off-key, but in harmony with one another. Still, I can barely make them out over Jerry's falsetto butchering of the lyrics.

I stare out the window as Ray turns the Lumina away from the highway and drives through some residential streets, skirting the main thoroughfares. I probably shouldn't be here, considering my father is one hydrogen sulphide fart away from sending me off to a zombie zoo, but what am I supposed to do?

Sit in my room all the time channel surfing from reality TV to unimaginative sitcoms to movies edited for television with two hundred commercial breaks trying to sell me products I'm not allowed to purchase and can't use?

If I'm going to slowly rot away, I don't want to do it watching *Wife Swap*.

"Magic Bus" fades out and a Stevie Ray Vaughan tune comes on. I recognize the song but not enough to remember the name. The weird thing is, those unfamiliar background vocals from The Who are now singing along with Stevie Ray.

"So, do you really think this will work?" asks Tom.

I look at Tom, at his bloodshot eyes staring out at me from his shadowed, torn-up face, looking hopeful yet with an expression that will drop into his lap if I don't tell him what he wants to hear.

To be honest, I don't know if this is going to work. I don't know if we'll all come out of this intact. I don't know if this is a good idea, considering what happened to Walter.

For an instant I hesitate. I want to reassure Tom in spite of any doubts I might have but I don't want to give him any false hope. But then I look at the empty space where Tom's right arm should be and I realize that, for us, false hope is probably the brass ring.

Tom is still staring at me, the expression of hope straining to remain on his face. I raise my right hand and extend my thumb like Roger Ebert and say, "Aur splroch."

Tom has no idea what I said, but it doesn't matter. His ruined face splits open in a smile.

Five minutes later, we pull to a stop on a residential street three doors down from Sigma Chi.

Most of the UC Santa Cruz fraternities are located off campus, which is a bonus for us because it means we won't have to worry about campus security. But with the hour approaching eleven we're pushing the curfew envelope. Then again, we're about to invade a house full of Breathers who belong to a registered living group of the University of California school system, so being concerned that we'll get caught for breaking curfew would be like robbing a bank and worrying that we'll get a parking ticket.

"So what's the plan?" asks Jerry.

"The way I see it," says Ray, "one of us needs to create a diversion while the rest of us do a little recon to find Tom's arm."

"Sounds easy enough," says Jerry.

Tom nods in earnest, the loose skin on his cheeks flapping up and down, making his face look like it's trying to fly away.

"Now, seeing as how Tom and Andy aren't in any shape to help with recon and retrieval," says Ray, "they'll have to create enough of a diversion so that someone has time to get in, grab Tom's arm, and get out."

We all look at Jerry, who nods for several seconds before his eyes grow wide with realization. "Me? Why me?"

"I have to stick around to make sure nothing happens to our appendage-challenged friends," says Ray.

Jerry opens his mouth to say something, then closes it and mutters, "Fuck."

Tom groans and puts his remaining hand over his eyes.

"Don't bust your stitches," says Ray. "You'll have help."

"Help?" says Jerry, looking from Ray to Tom to me. "What help?"

"Never underestimate the resourcefulness of Ray," says Ray, who pushes a button on the center console, popping the trunk.

The Lumina shifts back and forth as the trunk lid opens behind us. Ten seconds later, Zack and Luke appear, one on either side of the car like zombie bookends.

That explains the extra background vocals on "Magic Bus."

Chapter 20

I'm standing in the shadows with Tom across from Sigma Chi, glancing down the street at the Lumina parked half a block away. In the glow of the street lamp, the car is a safe haven that beckons to my common sense as I experience the second thoughts that often follow a decision to take action based on a self-perceived righteousness. Think Jesus on the cross but without the pain or the Romans or the all-expenses-paid trip to Heaven.

Midnight is fast approaching and I've got one good arm and one good leg and I'm about to use myself as bait to try to get Tom's right arm back. But my common sense is countered by a growing need for justice, for the retrieval of Tom's appendage and retribution against those who took it. Still, that doesn't prevent me from hearing my internal clock ticking toward curfew.

"Do you see anything yet?" asks Tom.

I shake my head, not knowing whether he can see me. Tom's vision is worse than mine and I can't make out the street sign at the end of the block two houses away, let alone see a hand signal from Ray to let us know we're on.

When Ray gives us the signal, Tom and I are supposed to

stagger across the street and onto the front porch of Sigma Chi, acting like Hollywood zombies to draw the fraternity members outside. Ray, who looks less like a zombie than the rest of us and can pass for a Breather in subdued light among drunk college kids, will intervene as our chaperone and apologize for letting us get loose before anyone beats on us with aluminum bats or sets us on fire. While the fraternity members have their attention on the three of us, Zack, Luke, and Jerry will sneak into the fraternity through the back door and find Tom's arm.

If Plan A doesn't work, Plan B is to storm the house, freak everyone out, and hope we can find Tom's arm before the Animal Control van shows up.

What the hell. You're only undead once.

Though I'm not sure what we're supposed to do if anything goes wrong. Tom might at least be able to run away, but I don't have that luxury, which means I'll have to stand and fight. If it comes to that, I hope I can at least take one of them down with me.

Tom is whispering something to my left. After a few moments I realize he's repeating one of Helen's euphemisms.

"I am a survivor . . . I am a survivor . . . I am a survivor . . ."

Across the street at Sigma Chi there's no activity and no sign of Ray. The anticipation is unnerving, which isn't surprising except that I realize I'm feeling anxious. Not just the memory of anxiety but the physical sensations that accompany it. For the first time since I died, I'm experiencing something that feels strangely like an adrenaline rush.

Before I can explore this any further, shouts erupt from inside the fraternity. Seconds later, an upstairs window explodes outward in a shower of glass as a body flies through the window, tumbles across the roof, then falls over the edge and lands facedown on the front lawn.

"Is that the signal?" asks Tom.

The shouting escalates inside the fraternity, the noise spilling out through the broken window as Ray comes running around from the back of the fraternity house shouting, "Plan B! Plan B!"

Tom and I watch Ray run out to the sidewalk, then down the street toward the Lumina as front porch lights start to go on at the neighboring houses, including the one behind us.

On the front lawn of Sigma Chi, the body that fell from the roof gets to its feet, then starts running toward us and raises three arms in the air.

"Got it, dude!" yells Jerry, waving Tom's arm in triumph.

Beside me, Tom lets out a sob of joy.

Bedlam has engulfed the fraternity. People are shouting and screaming as shapes and shadows move past the windows like phantoms. The front door opens and two Breathers come running out, chased by either Zack or Luke, I can't tell which, but he's laughing.

As Tom and I hurry across the street to Jerry, Ray pulls up in the Lumina and gets out, leaving the car running.

"Take the car," he says, running past us toward Sigma Chi.

"What about you?" shouts Tom.

"Just get out of here!" yells Ray before he vanishes around the back of the fraternity.

I don't have to be told twice. I can hear the sirens off in the distance and the thought of taking a ride in the back of the Animal Control van doesn't have any of the justified glory that previously accompanied this mission.

Jerry tosses the arm across the car to Tom, who catches it

with one hand like a star NFL receiver and then slides into the front passenger seat as I fall in the backseat behind him and pull the door shut. Before I have a chance to get my seat belt fastened, Jerry floors the accelerator and the Lumina races off down the street to the opening strains of Steppenwolf's "Magic Carpet Ride."

I glance out the back window as the sirens grow louder and neighbors began to come out onto the street, grateful that I'm leaving this scene behind.

"Wooo hooo!" screams Jerry, taking the first turn fast and tight, sending me sliding across the backseat into the passenger door, my face smashing against the window. "Hold on to your nuts, boys. You're in for a treat."

Before Jerry can make another turn, I pull the shoulder strap across my body and buckle myself in.

"Slow down!" says Tom, cradling his arm as Jerry makes a hard left, the tires squealing and the rear of the Lumina drifting to the right. "Slow down, slow down!"

The only thing worse than being a backseat driver is wanting to be a backseat driver without the ability to talk. So all I can do is voice my concerns by screaming.

There's not much traffic on the streets but what cars there are Jerry swerves around, driving in the opposite lane to pass. We're safely away from the scene of the crime, so the last thing we want to do is draw attention to ourselves, but Jerry is still a twenty-one-year-old showoff and he's not about to listen to reason.

"Hey," says Tom, studying his reclaimed appendage. "This isn't my arm."

"It's not?" says Jerry.

"No," says Tom.

"Are you sure?"

"Yes, I'm sure!" says Tom, his voice rising. "Look!" With

his left hand he holds the arm up by the wrist. Even from the backseat I can see that the arm is at least two inches shorter than Tom's left arm. And it's covered with thick, black hair.

Jerry passes a Volkswagen Vanagon and glances over at Tom. "Oops."

"Oops?" says Tom. "Oops?"

"Dude, there were like, dozens of them and I couldn't grab them all, so I picked out the one that I thought looked like yours."

"Does this look like mine?" says Tom, brandishing the arm at Jerry.

"Dude, I said I was sorry."

"Well, what am I supposed to do with this?" he says, tossing the arm onto the dashboard.

"Try it on," says Jerry.

"Try it on?" says Tom. "What am I? Frankenstein's monster?"

Jerry glances over at him. "Now that you mention it . . ."

There's a red light up ahead and Jerry's doing fifty in a thirty-five zone. I let out a warning shriek that only makes Jerry drive faster. If I could break out in a cold sweat, I would.

"Red light, red light, red light!" shouts Tom, his right arm momentarily forgotten, his left hand pointing at the windshield.

Jerry starts humming the theme to *Mission: Impossible* and floors the accelerator as Tom and I both let out identical screams of "Noooooooo!" An instant before we reach the intersection, the light turns green.

"Relax Grandmas," says Jerry. "I've got it under control."

Tom is slumped down in the front seat, his left hand covering his eyes. I'm sitting behind Jerry, alert and focused. If I were alive, my heart would be racing and my palms would be sweating. The absence of these physical symptoms makes me feel oddly at ease. That and I can't get over the realization that I actually screamed something intelligible. Apparently, neither Tom nor Jerry noticed. Or if they did, it didn't register, but I clearly shouted "Nooooooooo." At least I think I did. I want to see if I can say it a second time, or if I can say something else, but I'm a little anxious and self-conscious, so I try it under my breath, singing along to Steppenwolf:

> *Why don't you come with me little girl*
> *On a magic carpet ride?*

Most of the words still sound like gibberish, but a few come out right, or nearly so, and I wonder if there's some kind of strange, cosmic connection between the songs that played on the radio tonight and my newfound ability to utter intelligible sounds.

Is this a magic bus? Will I still be able to speak when the magic carpet ride comes to an end? Or is this just the beginning? It doesn't really matter. All I know is that the last couple of weeks have been exhilarating and I can't wait to see what happens tomorrow. Provided, of course, that Jerry doesn't destroy us in a fiery crash.

Jerry's whooping it up as he races down Chestnut Street toward Highway 1, running stop signs and breaking the speed limit while Tom sits sullen and brooding in the passenger seat. Jerry glances at me in the rearview mirror and I smile back, give him the thumb up, and whoop along with him.

Chapter 21

Sometimes I give myself the creeps.

Usually this happens in the middle of the night, when I wake up and forget why my left arm doesn't work or that I'm gradually decomposing and I wonder what that smell is.

Other times, I catch my reflection in a mirror and nearly scream before I recognize the look of horror on my own face.

On rare occasions, I sit in the wine cellar on my mattress watching the thirty-two-inch television my parents bought for me, my attention drifting to the bottles that line the walls, imagining that each bottle is filled with a magic elixir that will heal a different portion of my body.

The 1986 Grgich Hills Cabernet Sauvignon restores my left arm, the Beringer Founder's Estate 2000 Merlot my left ankle, the Castello Di Brolio 1995 Chianti my face, and the Monticello 1999 Pinot Noir my voice. My father has Chardonnays, Sauvignon Blancs, Chenin Blancs, and Rieslings down here, too, but I never had much use for white wine. It's like drinking a Corona instead of a Guinness. I just never saw the point.

This morning, I'm watching *Back to the 80s* music videos on VH1 while I gargle with the 1999 Monticello Pinot Noir.

It's probably just my imagination, but the wine seems to have more flavor this morning.

Between each round of gargling, I swallow my magic elixir and test out my singing voice. Not that I'm belting out lyrics at the top of my lungs. I don't know all of the words to most of the videos, and most of the words I do know come out as muttered gibberish, as if I'm afraid to discover that I'm deluding myself into thinking my power of speech is actually returning. But when "Bohemian Rhapsody" by Queen comes on, I crank the TV up loud enough to drown out my own screeching. Maybe a little too loud. My father starts pounding on the wine cellar door, telling me to "turn that damn thing down!"

I pretend I can't hear him.

I still don't know all of the words. But with the volume turned up, it doesn't matter. I'm butchering the song, croaking out unintelligible words that sound like a duck trying to learn how to speak Dutch. Except every now and then, I quack out something that sounds vaguely familiar, a grunt or a screech that approximates speech. Words like "too" and "no" and "eye." Sure, they're just baby steps. But what am I, if not an infant?

Born into a world of decay.

Relearning how to walk and talk.

Suckling from the bosom of hope.

I don't understand how it's physiologically possible for my speech to be returning. Maybe it's not. Maybe I'm just learning how to create sounds that mimic words. Either way, it's something new. And when most of the newness of your existence tends to involve a new odor or a recent loss of a body part or a fresh crop of maggots, anything that seems to point in the opposite direction is a definite improvement.

When the song ends and the station goes to commercial

break, I turn down the volume, take a celebratory gargle of the Pinot, and listen to my father curse me from behind the door upstairs. Normally, when my father denounces my existence, it tends to darken my mood. It's kind of hard to think happy thoughts when one of your parents suggests that you would better serve mankind by feeding yourself into a wood chipper.

This time, his contempt amuses me and I start to laugh, spraying Pinot out my nose and across my bedding, which only makes me laugh harder. Pretty soon, I'm laughing so hard I could almost choke to death if that were possible. And suddenly, I wish I had someone to share the moment with. Someone who would laugh with me. Someone who would appreciate the changes I'm going through. Someone who would understand how I feel.

On the television, a man and a woman walk hand in hand along the street, drawing the attention of everyone they pass—their smiles radiant, their faces perfect. I don't know what they're advertising but it reminds me of Rita and the walk we took through the village and I find myself wishing we were like the couple on television.

I reach up and touch my own face, my fingers running across the patchwork of stitches, and I wonder if my voice is the only aspect of my zombieness I can improve. I wonder if there's anything I can do to make myself look less corpse-like. I wonder if there's any way I can be as happy as the people in the commercial.

Until I realize it's an ad for life insurance.

Chapter 22

T he trick," says my mother, as I spread the makeup with a soft applicator sponge, "is to blend outward and not get it too cakey or thick. Otherwise, you end up emphasizing the blemishes instead of hiding them."

My mother's choice of concealer is Yves Saint Laurent Ivory Beige, which works well with her complexion. I need something more like Ivory Paste. And my skin is so dry that it seems to suck all of the moisture out of the makeup.

"You should clean and moisturize your face before applying the concealer," she says. "It'll make your skin smoother and more receptive. You might even want to try a nice exfoliant."

When I asked my mother if she had anything that might help to hide the stitches on my face, I was just hoping for a jar of cream or something simple that I could experiment with on my own. Instead, she grabbed her entire makeup kit along with her lighted vanity mirror and sat me down at the kitchen table.

"Now, the concealer doesn't exactly match your skin color," she says, without a trace of sarcasm, "so what we'll want to do is use a lighter-colored foundation and blend it in."

When my mother says "we" she means me. In spite of her enthusiasm in wanting to help me hide my stitches and make me look more human, as she so tactfully put it, my mother still refuses to touch me. She just points and gives me direction and slides the tube or bottle or jar I need within reach. I don't think she realizes how repulsed she is by the thought of physical contact with her son, but at least we're spending some quality time together.

The liquid foundation looks and feels like whole wheat pancake batter as I spread it across my cheeks with a tiny damp sponge. Just because I'm curious and I know it won't hurt to try, I take a swig of the foundation to see if it tastes like pancakes. It doesn't.

"Andrew!" scolds my mother. "That's thirty-five dollars a bottle."

You'd be amazed at how much formaldehyde you can consume from a single bottle of liquid foundation. Cover Girl is especially nourishing.

Once I have the foundation spread across my cheeks and forehead and chin, it's time for the contouring powder, which has the appearance and consistency of ready-to-mix chocolate cocoa. I'm tempted to give it a taste, just to see, but my mother is watching me so instead I apply it to my face with a brush.

"Make sure to brush in a downward motion, honey," says my mother. "That way the hairs on your face won't stick up."

After the contouring powder comes a translucent finishing powder. I can't really tell the difference, except the finishing powder seems finer and gets patted on with a cosmetic sponge rather than a brush. My mother tries to persuade me to put on some blush as a finishing touch, but somehow I don't think having a rosy glow to my cheeks will create a natural appearance. Then again, after the concealer, foundation, and powder, *natural* isn't the word I'd use to describe how I look.

My mother comes around the table, stands two feet behind me, and leans down to look over my shoulder. "I think it's perfect," she says, smiling at me in the mirror. "What do you think, honey?"

I think I need a second opinion.

Just then my father walks in and sees me sitting there wearing a smock with my hair drawn back from my makeup-encrusted face with hairpins, and says, "Jesus H. Christ," then turns around and walks back out of the kitchen.

Chapter 23

I wake up in the middle of the night and I can't get back to sleep.

I'm restless. Agitated. My mind won't shut down.

That and the mask of foundation and concealer my mother helped me to apply has my skin so tight that my face feels like it's been pumped full of formaldehyde.

While it's true that being embalmed can get rid of crow's feet and laugh lines and take fifteen years off your obituary, it can also leave your face as hard and as fake looking as a porn star's breasts. Plus the whole process is pretty invasive.

If you've never woken up in a mortuary with a cannula inserted in your carotid artery while your face inflates like a helium balloon, then you probably wouldn't understand.

After removing the makeup with a hand towel and a bottle of 2005 Napa Valley Pahlmeyer Chardonnay, I'm wide awake and looking for something to keep me occupied. With my two options pretty much reduced to television and wine, I pick up the remote control and flip through the channels, attempting to repeat the dialogue from different programs as I work on my enunciation. But after fifteen minutes of watching *Walker*,

Texas Ranger and *The Fresh Prince of Bel-Air,* I can't take any more.

I don't want to sit inside and watch the Hallmark Channel or Nickelodeon. I want to play tennis or go for a bike ride or stagger around the streets of downtown Santa Cruz. The thought of Breathers screaming and running away at the sight of me gets me laughing and before you can say *Night of the Living Dead,* I'm out the cellar door for an early morning stroll.

Walking around past two in the morning is a good way to get yourself dismembered. But staying cooped up in my parents' wine cellar is beginning to feel more and more like a prison sentence. And after the field trip to Sigma Chi to try to retrieve Tom's arm, I'm feeling emboldened.

Still, I'm not completely brain dead. So I stick to the shadows and play homeless drunk whenever a car drives past. Sure, I'm still having to pretend I'm something other than one of the undead in order to be seen in public, but I feel exhilarated—the sense of freedom, the black sky filled with stars, the cold November air on my face. If I didn't know any better, I'd swear I can almost see my own breath.

At first I start walking with no particular destination in mind. Just your average zombie out for a dead-of-the-night stroll. But then I find myself staggering along Old San Jose Road, taking the path I've worn out countless times since the accident. Except this time, rather than continuing on to the Soquel Cemetery to visit my dead wife, my destination turns out to be the abandoned granary.

Ray is awake and tending a low, glowing fire while the twins sit to his left, leaning against each other, their eyes half open and an empty mason jar nearby. Although I'd hoped they'd managed to escape the fraternity fiasco intact, I find myself relieved and almost overjoyed to see them.

"Mornin'," says Ray, raising his right hand in a neighborly greeting that nearly gets me all choked up. Usually whenever anyone raises a hand in my direction, it's holding an expired-food projectile or a crucifix or a Taser baton.

I sit down across from the twins with a smile and a nod, happy to be out of the wine cellar and in the company of others who accept me. Even without the fire, it's warm here. Comforting. A place of refuge, free from the influence or the rules of Breathers. Even the weekly meetings at the Community Center can't offer that. After all, we're not exactly part of the community, the meetings are regulated by Breathers, and no one is going to invite us to attend the monthly Rotary Club Pot Luck.

I hadn't noticed it before, but it occurs to me that I'm hungry.

Before I can even ask, Ray gets up without a word, pulls out a jar of Resplendent Rapture and a bottle of Budweiser, opens both of them, then sets them on the ground next to me. When I reach for my pen to thank him, I realize I've left my dry erase board at home.

"Anks," I say, the word coming out in a gravelly croak. More like a cryptic death rattle than an expression of gratitude. But the message seems to get across.

Ray looks over at me with a faint smile and nods. "Anytime."

I dig in with my fingers, savoring the texture of the meat as I chew, aware of the taste that seems so rich and flavorful compared to anything else I've eaten in the past few months. Maybe it's the fire. Maybe it's the silence. Maybe it's the act of eating game meat from a jar using my fingers. But that sense of primal hunger I experienced the last time I was here feels stronger. More than that, it feels right.

For several minutes the four of us just sit there, the only sounds the occasional crackle and spit of the fire or the more frequent grunts of pleasure from me.

To my left, one of the twins lets out a belch and the other one giggles.

I finish consuming the contents of the jar, wiping my fingers on my jeans, and let out a long, satisfied sigh.

"That's a right pleasant sound," says Ray, taking a pull on his beer. "It's the sound of satisfaction."

I nod and raise my own beer in response.

"And there's nothing like a good meal and a beer to leave a man feeling satisfied," says Ray. "Isn't that so, boys?"

Zack and Luke nod in unison.

"Of course, being satisfied can have its drawbacks," says Ray. "You become too satisfied, too comfortable with your position, and you start to forget why you were unsatisfied in the first place."

The twins, who were half asleep when I staggered in, are now sitting up side by side, their eyes locked on Ray, their heads bobbing to the rhythm of his words.

"Contentment breeds laziness," says Ray. "And someone who tends toward laziness is likely to allow others to tell him what he can and can't do."

Ray's words roll out, smooth and full of conviction, with the cadence of a sermon. He's kind of like a zombie preacher. A messiah for the undead. And Luke and Zack, sitting there bobbing their heads, are his disciples.

As I listen to Ray, I notice that my head has started to bob as well.

"You don't strike me as the lazy type, Andy," says Ray.

I shake my head and say, "O."

More like a groan of pleasure than a repudiation of my slothful ways. But I make my point.

"I didn't think so," says Ray, draining the last of his beer.

Before Ray's empty bottle can touch the ground, Luke is up and handing him a full bottle, then hands one to me and returns to his brother's side, where they clink bottles and drink in unison, each a reflection of the other.

They're still kind of creepy, but in a warm and fuzzy sort of way.

"You can't afford to be lazy," says Ray. "Satisfaction is a luxury. Contentment an extravagance. Like I always say, you can't wait around for someone to solve your problems or improve your lot. Sooner or later, you have to help yourself."

As I listen to Ray, I can't help but think of Helen's words of encouragement and inspirational chalkboard expressions:

YOU ARE NOT ALONE.

I AM A SURVIVOR.

HOPE IS NOT A FOUR-LETTER WORD.

While I appreciate Helen's attempts to inspire us, to boost our morale, I think I understand what Ray's getting at. We are alone, so we need to be self-reliant. We can't be satisfied with simply surviving. And if we grow complacent, then there's nothing left to hope for.

Another one of Helen's sayings pops into my head, the one she wrote on the chalkboard near the end of the last meeting:

FIND YOUR PURPOSE.

Sitting here, listening to Ray talk, I almost believe that I can.

onight's meeting has a decidedly festive air to it, if you can use the word "festive" to describe a gathering of reanimated, partially decomposed corpses.

Our usual number has nearly doubled. Ray showed up as promised, bringing Zack and Luke with him, while Naomi, Carl, and Helen have chaperoned their own guests. The only one missing is Tom, who apparently felt too self-conscious about his mismatched arms to make an appearance.

No one else in the group knows about our attempt to get Tom's arm back. And since it hasn't been in the news, Jerry and I decided not to mention it. The three of us figured we'd make up a story about Tom going to the body salvage yard to get a new arm. It's not that uncommon for zombies to need a replacement for a lost limb and the salvage yard is zombie friendly, provided you bring a Breather and pay cash. The pickings there are pretty slim, so our story wouldn't be unbelievable. Hell, I've seen zombies with two left hands.

On the chalkboard, Helen has written WELCOME SUR-VIVORS, underlined and with exclamation points. All that's missing is a smiley face.

I hang out near the refreshment table, sampling pastries,

wishing I had the nerve to test out the few words I've learned to respeak. Actually, it's just two words: *Hi, Rita*. But the best I've managed to do is "I, Eeta," which sounds more like a proclamation of hunger than a salutation, so I remain silent and satisfy myself with just watching the object of my newfound desire, who glances my way and smiles.

Tonight Rita's wearing a white turtleneck sweater with a matching white knit cap and white jeans. She looks kind of like a zombie snowflake.

The Breather liaison from the County Department of Resurrection, obviously overwhelmed by the sheer volume of zombies in proximity, stands with his back to the wall, as close to the exit as possible. To try to make him feel more at ease, I stagger up and offer the liaison a pecan tassie. He blanches until he can almost pass for one of us.

A few minutes later, he leaves.

Except for Ray coming up to say hey, none of the newcomers approach me, so I just watch everyone mill around, eating cookies and pastries and drinking punch, making small talk.

"How did you die?"

"Were you embalmed?"

"Where were you supposed to be buried?"

"Dude, are you wearing makeup?"

Jerry is standing in front of me, his hat on crooked and the crotch of his pants hanging down to his knees. Before I can come up with some kind of lame excuse to write on my dry erase board, Rita appears on my right.

"Andy's wearing makeup," says Jerry.

"Really?" says Rita.

She turns to look at me, studying my face, her eyes dark orbs in her own pale face. I suddenly don't care about anyone else. As far as I can tell, no one else is in the room.

With her right index finger, Rita reaches up and touches

the side of my nose, pressing against my flesh and running her finger across my cheek. She holds up her finger, a thin residue of concealer and foundation on it, then puts her finger in her mouth and sucks it clean.

"Mmmmmm," she says. "Yves Saint Laurent."

Jerry looks at Rita, his mouth open, then closes it and looks at me. "Dude."

"Okay," says Helen. "If everyone would please take a seat, we can get started."

Rita, Jerry, and I sit together. Ray sits on one side of us with his backpack while Zack and Luke sit on the other, sliding their chairs closer like sibling cats seeking warmth. I half expect them to start grooming each other.

Next to the twins on one end is Carl and his guest, a fifty-ish looking woman named Leslie. She has an English accent and no visible scars, though she has a pale, bluish tint. But then, don't we all?

I don't know Leslie's story or how she and Carl met, but from the way Carl keeps fidgeting in his chair and fighting to keep a nervous smile off his lips, I swear that he's smitten with Leslie. Plus there's his lack of attitude that he usually brings to the meetings, so I know something's up.

On the other side of Ray is Naomi and a teenager named Beth, who was killed in a car accident. I'm not sure of the details, other than the fact that she took the brunt of the impact with her face.

Next to Beth sits Ian, who looks to be about my age. Ian came with Helen and that's about all I know. In the blue suit he's wearing, he looks more like a Breather than one of the undead. And he wears a lot of cologne.

"First, I'd like to welcome our newcomers," says Helen, spreading her arms toward our enlarged semicircle of plastic chairs and animated cadavers. "I know for some of you coming here tonight was difficult, perhaps even frightening, so I want to thank you for taking that first step and reaching out to us."

Carl applauds, then stops when he realizes no one else is applauding and absently picks at one of his knife wounds. The rest of us, especially the regulars, just stare at him.

"Thank you for your enthusiasm, Carl," says Helen. "Now before I get into tonight's theme, I'd like to ask everyone, newcomers and regulars alike, to share with the group your story of survival. Carl, since you seem so eager, why don't we start with you."

Carl stands up, gives another, uncharacteristic nervous smile, then clears his throat and stumbles through his story about getting stabbed to death in the face and chest. Naomi laughs at his behavior but Carl offers no rebuttal and just sits down when he's done.

"Hello, my name is Leslie," says his guest, standing up and smoothing out her cornflower blue dress, which is a shade darker than her complexion. "I'm afraid my story isn't nearly as exciting as Carl's. Just last Thursday I had a heart attack and died."

"Whoa," says Jerry. "You're like, totally new to this undead thing, aren't you?"

"Quite," says Leslie.

"How are you adjusting?" asks Helen.

"It's been a bit of a shock, naturally," says Leslie, her English accent making being undead sound so formal and proper. "But Carl's been a dear."

We all look at Carl, who offers an uncomfortable smile, then stands up. "Excuse me," he says. "I have to use the restroom."

Naomi lets out another laugh as Carl leaves.

"So what happened?" asks Rita.

"Well, when I woke up Friday morning on a table under a sheet," says Leslie, "I thought I was still alive, until I realized where I was."

"Where was that?" asks Helen, her voice soft and supportive.

"When I sat up and removed the sheet, there were two men in surgical clothes and masks cutting open the chest of a dead boy on another table."

Knowing nods and murmurs from the group.

"What did you do?" asks Rita.

"My initial reaction was one of modesty," says Leslie. "I wasn't clothed and tried to cover myself with the sheet. Then I noticed the stitches running down the length of my own chest. That's when one of the men noticed me and started to scream."

More murmuring and head-shaking.

"So how did you meet Carl?" asks Naomi.

"Well, after a bit of a scene, I was taken to the SPCA until my daughter came to pick me up," says Leslie. "Carl was in the cage next to mine."

At that moment, Carl returns from his pee break. No one says anything as he walks over to his chair. It's so quiet I can hear Jerry decomposing.

"What?" says Carl, standing there and looking down to make sure his fly is zipped up.

"Dude," says Jerry, "you were in the pound?"

Carl glances around as if he'd been caught masturbating.

"I told them that was where I met you," says Leslie.

"Yeah, well," says Carl. "It was just a misunderstanding. Can we move on?"

Zack and Luke stand up, shoulder to shoulder, and recite their story of diving headfirst off the railroad trestle into the San Lorenzo River. It's kind of eerie how they tell the story, each one saying a few words and then the other picking up the thread and continuing with it, back and forth as if they had one mind and two mouths.

Jerry follows the twins with an amusing narrative of his car accident, finishing it off by offering to let everyone touch his exposed brain. The twins take him up on his offer while everyone else declines.

I start to get up to shuffle over to the chalkboard and share my story, but Rita puts her hand on my arm and keeps me in my chair.

"Andy survived a car accident that left him severely damaged and unable to talk," she says, looking at me and smiling. "But that doesn't mean he's not a good listener."

I sit there and watch Rita tell my story, mesmerized by her lips, which are Succulent Red, as they shape the words that should be mine. I feel honored to have her speaking for me, sharing my history with everyone else. I almost think she tells it better than me.

Once she's done with my story, Rita tells her own tale of suicide. How she felt alone and desperate, an outcast among the living—no friends, no community, no sense of belonging. Then one day, while standing in the kitchen of her studio apartment eating leftover pizza and listening to The Smiths, she just grabbed a steak knife and slit her wrists and then her throat. No planning. No note. She just pressed the blade to her flesh and cut.

She's never told her story like this. Her description has always been brief and matter-of-fact, a hurried account of something she felt ashamed of. But this time there's no shame. No remorse. Instead she seems eager to share.

"I can still remember how I felt watching the blood pool on the floor around me," says Rita. "How I felt my strength ebbing, the life draining from me, knowing that I'd succeeded in ending my lonely existence, only to wake up at the mortuary two days later and realize I still wasn't dead."

Heads nod in acknowledgment, along with an empathetic "Bummer" from Jerry.

"But even though I'm still an outcast among the living," says Rita, her gaze traveling around the semicircle of zombies until it settles on me. "I don't feel so alone anymore."

If I could blush, I'd be a third-degree sunburn.

Ray introduces himself and tells how he was shot by a trigger-happy landowner with a shotgun, got kicked out of his home by his wife, and moved into the granary. Then he stands up, opens his backpack, and hands out a jar of Ray's Resplendent Rapture to everyone. Several members of the group eye the contents of the jars with skepticism, but Rita, Jerry, and I vouch for the quality, which seems to satisfy everyone.

Naomi's account of her death at the hands of her husband is short and bitter. Afterward, she lights up one of her formaldehyde-laced cigarettes and manages to smoke half of it before yielding to Helen's request to put it out, which she does in her empty eye socket.

Sometimes she's such an exhibitionist.

Naomi's guest, Beth, was killed by a drunk driver and lives with her parents and younger sister. She has stitches crisscrossing her face and scalp and the left side of her head is shaved from the doctor's attempts to stop the hemorrhaging in her brain.

"What is it like living with your family?" asks Helen.

"My mom cries a lot," says Beth, nervously playing with the hair on the right side of her head. "My dad spends most of his time at work now. And my sister invites her friends over to stare at me."

I can't help but look at Beth and think about Annie, wondering if it would be worse to have a daughter who's a zombie or to be a zombie with a daughter who's a Breather. I suppose neither one is much of an option, but at least if I were the one who was alive, I'd have the right to raise my own daughter.

Most of the time I try to avoid thinking about Annie and what she's doing and how much I miss her. It's not natural for a father to try to forget he has a daughter, but when you're not allowed to communicate with her in any way, then the only thing you accomplish by thinking about her is to create an exquisite, aching pain that never goes away.

But sometimes, when I see other children playing or walking home from school, I think I hear Annie's voice or her laugh. Other times I think I catch a whiff of her hair. She was always partial to Suave Tropical Kiwi.

When Beth finishes her story, Jerry leans over to me. "She's totally hot, dude."

"She's only sixteen, Jerry," whispers Rita.

And the side of her head is shaved. And she has stitches tic-tac-toed across her face.

"So?" says Jerry. "She's a totally hot sixteen-year-old."

Jerry takes a swig of his grape soda, then reaches into his pants pocket, pulls out a can of Altoids, and pops two into his mouth.

"Curiously strong," he says with a grin.

They'll have to be more than curious to make an impact on Jerry's breath.

Next, Helen tells her story about getting shotgunned in the chest while attempting to resolve a domestic dispute with one of her patients. When she finishes, she turns to her guest, who looks a bit out of place in his Brooks Brother's suit and Armani tie.

Maybe it's because I've had a recent crash course in foundations, concealers, and powders, but I can tell he's wearing makeup.

"I met Ian more than a year ago, when I was still a Breather," says Helen. "I didn't know he was one of us until last week. I think you'll all find his story a little unique. And perhaps inspirational as well."

Ian is a thirty-two-year-old attorney who got drunk one Saturday night and fell down in an alley, struck his head on the asphalt, knocked himself out, then choked on his own vomit.

Yes. Inspirational. Definitely.

"Six hours later," says Ian, "I woke up and didn't realize anything was wrong until I was home taking a shower. I just didn't feel right. Not sick, exactly, but as if something inside just wasn't working right. That and I could smell myself and the smell just wouldn't go away. I must have used an entire bar of soap and half a bottle of shampoo and I still stunk."

"So when did it dawn on you that you weren't alive anymore?" asks Helen.

"Well, after my shower," says Ian, "I was leaning toward the mirror, checking out my complexion, which had gone kind of gray, and I noticed I wasn't fogging up the glass. I breathed and breathed and nothing. Then I checked my pulse. That's when I passed out again."

Jerry lets out a guffaw. No one else laughs.

"When I came to," says Ian, "I thought it was just a bad dream. How could I be dead? Then I realized it was real and I smashed the bathroom mirror, as well as the toilet seat and several tiles on the bathroom floor. When I was done breaking things, I sat down and tried to cry until I felt like I would throw up. Then I fell asleep. When I woke up, I put on extra deodorant and a bunch of cologne, went down to the store, bought two more bottles of cologne, extra toothpaste, mouthwash, soap, shampoo, deodorant, and a bunch of cosmetics, then I spent the rest of the night applying makeup until I found something close to a natural look."

I have to say, Ian's natural look pretty much kicks ass on mine. I'll have to ask him what kind of foundation he uses. And if he can recommend a good concealer.

"Why did you put on makeup?" asks Rita.

"So I could keep my job," says Ian. "I make a good living as an attorney and I have a nice house. I didn't want to give any of that up."

No one says anything until Naomi finally speaks up.

"Nobody knows you're dead?"

"So far I've managed to fool everyone at the firm," says Ian. "But I've had to stop dating. And going to the gym. And playing tennis. And I had to give my dog away because he kept wanting to roll around on me."

Tell me about it.

"And how long ago did you reanimate?" says Helen.

"Three weeks ago last Sunday."

Lots of murmurs of disbelief.

"But how?" says Rita. "How do you . . . ?"

"I have a friend who runs a crematorium over in Salinas and I paid him to embalm me," says Ian. "It's more like hush money, actually. He gets five hundred a month to keep his mouth shut and provide me with enough formaldehyde to keep the decomposition to a crawl."

It hardly seems fair. I drink Alberto VO5 conditioner in bulk to get my daily recommended dose of formaldehyde and this guy gets the pure stuff.

"If no one knows you're dead," asks Carl, "then why risk coming here?"

"Helen asked me to come," says Ian. "I owed her a favor and couldn't turn her down."

"What kind of favor?" asks Naomi.

"If it wasn't for Helen," says Ian, "my sister would be dead."

Turns out the patient of Helen's in the domestic dispute was Ian's sister. Helen saved her life.

"So," says Helen. "What can we learn from Ian's story?"

Everyone looks around at one another, waiting for someone else to give an answer. Thankfully, Jerry obliges.

"It's good to know someone who works at a crematorium?" he says.

"No," says Helen. "I mean yes, that's true, but it's not the point."

"Oh," says Jerry, "if you're gonna die, make sure no one's around when it happens."

"Not exactly," says Helen, as she walks around the semicircle of chairs. "We are all survivors. We are all here, in this room together, because we've all experienced something extraordinary. We've been given a second chance. And although we face more obstacles and more heartache than perhaps we want to deal with, we can never let our spirit be broken. We can never give up."

Helen walks over to the chalkboard and underneath WEL-COME SURVIVORS, she writes tonight's message:

NEVER GIVE UP.

"Say it with me now."

The rest of the meeting is devoted to a sort of structured conversation, allowing everyone to get to know one another while helping each survivor find some action he or she can take to keep from surrendering hope.

Ray and the twins seem satisfied with their existence, but Beth and Leslie, having reanimated more recently, are more overwhelmed with the constraints and the stigma of their new status. Jerry offers to act as a sort of spiritual zombie guide for Beth, who is flattered by his proposal and they spend the rest of the evening sitting next to each other, comparing stitches and wounds. It's sweet, really. In a decaying, putrid sort of way.

As for the regulars, it seems like everyone is doing something to improve their existence.

Rita has started taking walks. Jerry is working on some kind of *Playboy* art project. Naomi has become a fan of the PGA to deal with her anger toward her ex-husband. Carl, when he's not helping other zombies he meets at the SPCA, has taken up meditation. And Helen, of course, helps the rest of us.

Which makes me wonder about my own efforts at self-improvement.

Sure, I've worked on my singing voice and learned how to blend concealer. And I've protested and been urinated on by a poodle and assaulted with food products. But other than helping to get Tom's arm back, or at least someone's arm back, I haven't really done anything to help anyone like Helen does. I haven't taken any steps to better myself like Naomi or Carl. And I haven't taken up a constructive hobby like Jerry.

So when I bring out my petition for zombie rights, thinking it's a poor excuse for making a difference but with nothing else to contribute, I expect it to be met with cursory enthusiasm. Like applause for a warm-up band from a bored audience impatient for the main act. Instead, everyone is enthusiastic. Surprised. Impressed. So I tell them about my protests and about my trips to the SPCA and about the little girl who pointed to my sign and asked me if it was true. Were zombies people, too?

"That's marvelous, Andy," says Helen, signing my petition.

"Nice work," says Carl, continuing his charming persona facade.

"You're full of secrets, aren't you?" says Rita, low enough so no one else can hear.

All of the members of the group sign my petition except Ian, who wants to keep his Breather cover intact, and Tom, of course, who isn't here. Ray doesn't think the petition will make a difference, but he signs it anyway.

Everyone shakes my hand or kisses my cheek, thanking me for writing the letter. I'm suddenly the big hero. The zombie of the hour. Regarded with respect and admiration. I'm intoxicated with pride and a sense of accomplishment. Instead of the warm-up band, I feel like the main act. Like the headliner playing to an expectant crowd. Like I have to top everything else I've done so far.

"Dude," says Jerry. "What are you going to do next?"

Before I know what I'm doing, I write:

I'm going to visit my daughter.

"That's wonderful!" says Helen.

"When are you going?" asks Rita.

"Dude," says Jerry. "I didn't know you had a daughter."

If I could talk, I'd be stuttering.

I'm going tomorrow, I lie.

"Well, congratulations," says Helen. "That's a big step. You'll have to tell us all about it at the next meeting."

If I could sweat, I'd be glistening.

Not wanting to answer any additional questions about my make-believe trip to see my daughter, I grab my backpack and excuse myself to go take a make-believe pee. When I return, I stand outside the entrance to the meeting room and watch the others.

Ray is talking to Ian, leaning in close, almost whispering in Ian's ear. Ian's head is nodding. Jerry is sitting down and leaning over while Beth pokes at his brain. Rita and Helen are laughing about something while Naomi and Leslie discuss Carl as he stands by looking awkward and annoyed. The twins don't talk to anyone but share each other's company in silence.

I can't bring myself to go back inside.

Some zombies' bodies are like walking science experiments, serving host to a plethora of bacteria, fungi, and maggots. These are the unlucky ones who didn't get embalmed and who suffer the indignities of putrefaction as they slowly dissolve—their muscles collapse, their skin slips, their internal organs turn to chicken soup.

In zombie circles, we refer to these pathetic souls as Melters.

I feel like such a Melter.

I don't know why I felt I had to make up a story about going to visit Annie. Blame it on hubris or getting caught up in the moment or a by-product of meeting the little girl in the park. Doesn't matter. I shouldn't have lied to everyone. I'm a total Melter.

Before anyone can see me standing in the doorway, I back away and head for the exit.

I know it's a bad idea to go out alone, especially at night, and that I'm probably just making things worse by leaving, but I don't want to go back inside and have to make up more lies about going to visit Annie. Especially to Rita.

At least it's not raining. And since most of the village shops close their doors by seven, I can navigate my way through the side streets without having to deal with any drive-by abuse or attempted dismemberings. Still, I know there are Breathers all around me because I can hear them waiting for a table outside of Tortilla Flats or getting into their cars after eating at the Golden Buddha or laughing and slurring their words as they stagger out the doors of Sir Froggy's Pub.

The sounds evoke a deep sense of longing. Of reverie. Of

resentment. I want to be the one making those sounds. I want to be the one enjoying a night out. I want to be the one laughing with my friends as I stumble out of a bar after having one too many cocktails. Instead, I have to shuffle along in the shadows, in silence, with only self-regret and discontent as my company.

I can't go to a bar and drown my liver in beer. I can't take a walk on the beach to reflect on my existence. And I don't want to go home and sit alone in the wine cellar and watch TV and listen to my parents argue about me.

There's really only one place for me to go.

Chapter 25

The grounds of the Soquel Cemetery aren't exactly an aesthetic comfort, even in the generous wash of light from the nearly full moon. Instead of the soft, green, manicured lawn of Evergreen Cemetery, dandelions and other weeds grow in barren patches of earth. Overgrown grass gone to seed obscures headstones and markers, many of which date back more than one hundred years. Large portions of the grass that inhabit the center of the cemetery are dead or dying.

At least they know how to set the mood.

Near the middle of the cemetery stands the tallest tree in the yard, a cypress almost perfectly straight, with a brush of foliage on the top and a single limb jutting out to one side. The other limbs have all been cut back to the trunk, leaving the cypress looking quite a bit like Tom with his missing arm.

Just past the cypress, in front of a large, white headstone that simply says Davis Peck, the ground has been dug up. I wonder if this is in preparation for his arrival or due to an unexpected departure. Either way, it's an open grave, an entrance into death's womb, and it gives me the willies. Maybe it's because I know that one of those had been prepared for me. Maybe it's because I could have literally walked across my own grave. Or maybe it's because I've seen one too many zombie movies. Whatever the reason, I give Davis Peck's plot a wide berth and distract myself by reading headstones.

Eleanor DeMont died in 1920 at the age of sixteen. Her headstone sits at the base of a leaning oak tree. Another marker has a marble cat curled up beneath the solitary name Lilith. There's a grave for Santa Claus (Albert Moyer 1917–1987) and a single headstone for a mother and her two children who all died on July 4, 1989.

Some of the headstones are unusual, some of the plots personally landscaped with lilies, Japanese maples, cactus, or flagstone paths. These are the exception. Most of the plots are neglected, the markers and headstones discolored and weather worn—some covered with moss or splattered with dried bird shit.

One of the newest markers belongs to my wife.

I still don't understand why I came back and Rachel didn't. No one does, not for sure. Not the scientists, not the government, not the *Weekly World News*. There are unproven genetic theories about why some of the dead reanimate but no one has any definitive answers, unless you believe the stock urban legends about voodoo spells and zombie viruses found on Web sites and in horror movies. What a load of crap.

I sit down at Rachel's grave and break out the jar of venison Ray gave to me at the meeting. I don't have a fork so I use my fingers, getting the juices and oils all over my hands. The meat is just as delicious as the first time I had some, but there's a sensual quality about it that's becoming addictive.

It's a bit awkward, sitting here enjoying this meal above my dead wife, conflicted with thoughts of my past and my present. If I could talk to Rachel, I'd tell her all of the obvious things—how much I miss our life together, how sorry I am for falling asleep behind the wheel, how I think I'm falling in love with another zombie.

Talk about your awkward moments.

Sometimes I try to talk to Rachel in my head and that helps, but it would be so much more cathartic if I could actually give voice to my thoughts. I know she couldn't hear me, or at least I don't think she could, but when I'm sitting at her grave in the Soquel Cemetery at night, my silence feels like an unexploded bomb.

The obvious lamentations and regrets would only take so long to unload, as I've spoken them so many times in my head that they feel like the rehearsed lines of a jaded actor. Once they had passion and substance. Now they're just words that have lost their meaning, like a mantra repeated simply because it's part of your routine, not because it makes you feel better or because it's honest. Still you continue to say the words because they're familiar and comfortable and they allow you to avoid the real issues that are at the root of your discontent.

Ask any Breather what he or she wishes for, no matter how outlandish the wish, even if it's unreasonable or improbable, it's likely not inconceivable. Riches, fame, reconstructive plastic surgery to look like Marilyn Monroe. There's even in vitro fertilization technology that would allow men to carry a fetus to term in the intestine.

Bizarre, yes. Unimaginable, no.

For the undead, who are bizarre and unimaginable to begin with, the one and only wish most of us desire is to get our lives back, which is impossible. Unreasonable. Inconceivable. Yet it's still there, floating around in our heads like a balloon that's just out of reach—a single, four-letter word that taunts us and haunts us and reminds us of just how much we've lost.

Hope.

It's human nature to want to believe that good things will happen, that no matter how many roadblocks or setbacks or disappointments we have to endure, eventually everything will work out. But since technically zombies are no longer human, where does that leave us? What is our nature? What are we supposed to hope for? To what goals should we aspire?

Personal development?

Spiritual growth?

Slower decomposition?

We don't have any civil rights, nor any constitutional rights for that matter, so why should we expect good things to happen? How can we find the impetus to set any goals when the ultimate goal, the one thing we all want, is unreachable?

I stare at the marker for Rachel's grave and trace her name with my fingers, then lie down and put my ear to the ground, listening to see if I can hear her calling to me through six feet of earth, but all I hear is the sound of an approaching vehicle.

Headlights flash along Old San Jose Road and a car drives past. I can't see any figures inside but I imagine a man behind the wheel, his wife in the passenger seat beside him, and their daughter riding in the back. That could be my family. That would be my family. If only I hadn't fallen asleep and ruined everything.

You didn't ruin everything, my mother's voice says in my head. *You just made a mistake and now you have to learn to make the best of it.*

When my mother said that to me a couple months ago, I'd wished that I had the appetite of a Hollywood zombie so I could eat her brains and make her shut up. She didn't have any clue as to what I had to deal with or what I'd lost. But now I realize she was only trying to make me feel better. And in spite of her cheery outlook regarding her son's perpetual state of decay, she was right. I need to make the best of what I have.

I stagger to my feet and think about some of the lessons Helen has tried to teach us over the past few months, about the sayings she likes to write on the chalkboard

WHY ARE WE HERE?

FIND YOUR PURPOSE.

NEVER GIVE UP.

and I realize that the protests I've made and the petition I wrote are not nearly enough. I need to push the boundaries of my existence. I need to challenge the institution that has relegated me to the status of nonhuman. After all, what do I have to lose by standing up for myself? If being a rotting corpse with no rights and no future isn't the worst thing that can happen to me, it can't be that much further to rock-bottom.

Everyone can get used to a certain level of abuse, but there comes a point when you have to take a stand. Like Ray says, if you don't have as much as you need, then take it. Or else find a way to make it yours.

Sooner or later, you've got to help yourself.

Chapter 26

The bus stop near my home is an unsheltered bench. Very pleasant on a warm sunny day. On a cold, rainy, November day, however, waiting for the bus is about as pleasant as a used diaper. But I shouldn't complain. If not for the fact that the county expects its mass transit customers to have to stand in the rain, I probably wouldn't have a chance.

None of the three Breathers waiting for the bus notice there's a zombie in a rain poncho standing six feet away. Most Breathers, in spite of their acts of bravado in large groups or from the safety of their passing cars, become nervous when confronted with a zombie. Especially in a situation when they're not expecting it.

Like waiting for the bus.

Or standing in line for the theater.

Or ordering steaks at the meat counter.

I glance around from beneath the hood of my poncho, grateful for the rain and for the ivory concealer and foundation my mother bought me. In the sunlight, with no shadows to help hide my condition, no amount of makeup would have allowed me to make it this far unnoticed. And while my left leg still drags a little, my zombie walk isn't quite as pronounced this morning.

I'm not as nervous as I thought I'd be, or as nervous as I imagined I *should* be. It's mostly memory response that reminds me I could get into a lot of trouble for this. My mind or consciousness or whatever it is understands the threat, but since my brain has stopped sending signals of alarm to my adrenal gland, which isn't functioning anyway, my body doesn't know it should be in a state of anxiety. So long as no one takes a close look at me, I should be fine.

Still, I can swear that my pores are sweating.

When the bus finally pulls up, the number 71 to Monterey via Watsonville, I wait for the Breathers to file on, then fall in behind them and manage to get up and into the bus without falling on my face. Which is always a good way to start your morning.

In spite of the fact that I don't experience sensory input the way I did before my nerve endings died and my synapses stopped firing, I'm excited. I feel a bit like a pioneer, going boldly where no zombie has ever gone before. Kind of like an undead Captain Kirk.

I wonder if Rosa Parks felt this way.

But when I drop exact change into the meter and turn and stare down the aisle at the half-full bus, I freeze up.

I'm surrounded by Breathers.

If I stagger down the aisle to seek refuge at the back of the bus, I might draw attention and get kicked off or hauled away to the SPCA before the bus ever pulls into traffic. If I claim the nearest empty set of seats, I risk having additional riders file past me, maybe even sit next to me.

"Please take your seat, sir," says the bus driver.

I'm not sure if it's the realization that everyone on the bus is staring at me or that a Breather addressed me without malice or that I'm dishonoring the memory of both Rosa Parks and William Shatner, but my paralysis breaks and I take the first available set of empty seats, two rows back on the driver's side. I sit at the window, hoping if someone sits next to me I can pretend I'm asleep, which shouldn't be too difficult to pull off considering that I just managed to pretend I'm alive.

I start to smile, sitting in my seat on a bus filled with Breathers who don't know what I am, waiting to pull away from the curb. But the bus just sits there and I see the bus driver in the rearview mirror, glancing at me, and I feel the eyes of everyone in the bus on me. They can sense something's not right, that there's something off about me, but they can't quite figure it out because the obvious answer is out of the question. A zombie would never try to get on a bus. Still, there's something out of sorts, something everyone feels but can't quite put their fingers on.

That's what I tell myself.

The memory of panic and discouragement flows through me as the bus driver glances at me one more time. Then he shifts a lever and the front door slides shut with a *whoosh*. An instant later, the bus lets out a hydraulic fart and pulls away from the curb and I'm on my way to see Annie.

It seems like more than four months since I last saw my daughter. Sometimes I have a hard time remembering what she actually looks like. But I'm excited at the thought of seeing her again, of seeing her smile and hearing her laugh. I just hope I can stand the bus ride.

I'd never been on Santa Cruz public transportation while I was alive and now I know why. The seats aren't much better than medieval torture chairs, the bus stops every two minutes to let passengers on or off, and a lot of the Breathers who take the bus don't smell much better than I do. At least I won't stand out on the olfactory front.

The bus comes to a stop in Soquel Village, near the community center where the group meets. I look out the windows, at the people walking past and the cars filled with Breathers, all of them unaware that a zombie is right here in their midst, riding a public bus, flaunting the very rules of my existence.

I'm not used to enjoying an unmolested trip through town in daylight, so this feels a bit surreal, as if I'm not really here but having an out-of-body experience. Then again, my entire existence is kind of like an out-of-body experience.

When the doors to the bus open, a mother and her young son get on board. The mother looks as if she's been awake for three days and knows she won't get to sleep anytime soon. Her son, who looks to be about eight or nine, appears to be the reason for her insomnia.

The boy stomps up the steps, jumping with both feet at once and landing with the force of a WWF wrestler. With each landing, he lets out an explosion of sound effects.

"Ronnie," says his mother, "stop it, please."

Ronnie, who has reached the top step, continues to jump up and down, releasing little explosions.

Ronnie is why contraception should be taught in schools.

While Ronnie takes off down the aisle toward the back of the bus, his mother pays the fare with a weary, apologetic look to the bus driver, then turns away and shouts at her son.

"Ronnie!"

As the bus pulls away and Ronnie's mother trudges after her son, I stare out the window and think about where I'm going and I feel a smile slip across my face. I can't wait to see Annie. I know she might not be prepared to see her father wearing makeup to hide the fact that he's slowly decaying, but that's okay. I don't want to frighten her. I don't even care if she knows I'm there. All I want is a glimpse of Annie, to see her smiling and know she's okay and healthy and happy. That's all I want.

I settle into my hard, plastic torture chair and watch the village slip away behind us, thoughts of Annie filling me with a sense of calm. Then something crawls between my legs.

"Ronnie! Come here!"

I glance down and see Ronnie on the floor, slithering between my feet on his back, facing me. I can see his little gremlin expression, his tongue hanging out, his eyes filled with mischief. Those eyes look up at me, directly into mine, and Ronnie starts to scream.

So much for my trip to Monterey.

Seconds later, Ronnie's mother is standing in the aisle next to me, yelling for Ronnie, reaching for her screaming son, who is thrashing around on the floor beneath me like a floundering fish, trying to get away. The man sitting in front of me turns around to see what all the fuss is about. When he gets a good look at me, his eyes open wide and he scrambles out of his seat, shouting, "Jesus Christ! It's a zombie!"

Pandemonium ensues. All of the passengers around me leave their seats, stumbling over one another to get away. Ronnie is still screaming on the floor of the bus, trapped by his own hysteria while his mother takes several steps toward the front of the bus, shouting out to her son and anyone who will listen.

"Ronnie! Ronnie! Somebody help my baby!"

Somebody could help her baby by pumping him full of Ritalin. Or administering some regular shock therapy.

The bus is slowing down and pulling over to the curb, the bus driver talking frantically on the radio handset to his dispatcher. Everyone on the bus is staring at me and shouting, crying, swearing, trying to get off the bus, or just scared speechless. More than two dozen Breathers and they're terrified of one, defenseless zombie.

In spite of my dismay at how my trip to see Annie has taken a dead-end detour, I start to laugh. Except it doesn't sound like laughter. It's more like the heavy, high-pitched breathing you'd hear on the other end of an obscene phone call. It's really freaking everyone out, which just makes me laugh harder.

Below me, Ronnie has stopped squirming and screaming and is now curled up in a fetal position, whimpering. The doors are open and nearly everyone else has abandoned the bus, including the driver. Only Ronnie's mother remains, standing at the front of the aisle, alternately looking from me to the door as if she can't decide what she should do. I don't want anyone to think I'm holding little precious Ronnie hostage, so I get up and move back down the aisle several rows and sit down. Eventually, Ronnie's mother gets up the nerve to collect her son and then I'm the only passenger remaining.

Approaching sirens wail from multiple directions. I suppose I could get up and exit the bus, make it easier on myself and surrender without a fuss, but that would be like admitting I've done something wrong when all I wanted was to see my daughter.

So instead, I shuffle up the aisle and take a seat in the front row to wait for Animal Control while I watch the Breathers standing outside in the rain, and I think about Annie and I wonder how pissed off this will make my father.

Chapter 27

I scribble words down on my dry erase board so Ted can't see what I'm writing as I watch him out of the corner of my eye, studying me with a mixture of aversion and interest.

"How are you feeling today, Andrew?"

I hold up my dry erase board, upon which I've already written:

How are you feeling today, Andrew?

He's so predictable.

Ted lets out an anemic laugh, followed by a strained smile. Either that or he's showing off that he just had his teeth capped.

. . . twelve . . . thirteen . . . fourteen . . .

"I understand that you've recently had something of an adventure," says Ted.

Not really, I write.

"That's not what your parents tell me," he says.

My parents.

After the bus fiasco, my parents left me at the SPCA for two days. I didn't really mind. The volunteers and staff treat me with more respect and consideration than the majority of

Breathers and it gets me out of the wine cellar. Plus they've got some really tasty dog treats.

I know my father wanted to teach me a lesson, but all he taught me was that he has no compassion. I'm an affront to his senses and an embarrassment to his sensibilities. I'm a social and economic albatross. He'd sooner see me consumed by maggots than happy.

At least my mother tries to understand me, to share in what I'm going through, even if she does spray me with air freshener and wear heavy-duty latex gloves whenever she has to come into contact with me.

My mother is sitting out in the reception area waiting for me, probably reading a *Sunset* magazine and humming to herself while my father is probably waiting for me at home with a can of gasoline and a blow torch.

"When you got on the bus," says Ted, "was there someplace you wanted to go?"

I didn't tell my parents I'd been on my way to see Annie because that would only create more problems. Maybe even encourage Annie's aunt and uncle to move her out of state. So I'm not about to tell Ted. I know there's the whole patient confidentiality thing but somehow I don't think that applies to zombies. Ted would just as likely tell my parents where I'd been going as he would get a chemical peel.

I just wanted to feel normal, I write.

"Normal," says Ted in a manner that lets me know he has no idea how to respond. "Normal . . ."

He's smiling again, caressing his teeth with his tongue. I glance up at the digital clock, at the red numbers advancing second by second, and realize I'd rather be home watching *Trick My Truck* on Country Music Television.

I erase my previous words and write:

What's going on?

"What do you mean, Andrew?" he says through a strained, artificially brightened smile.

I think he knows what I mean.

Why are you here?

"Do you mean in the emotional sense, the spiritual sense, or the existential sense?"

What does that mean?

Nothing. Just silence. I don't think he knows what he's talking about.

What are you doing?

"I'm trying to help you, Andrew."

How is this helping me?

"I don't know," says Ted. "How is it helping you?"

It's not.

No response. Just another *hiss* of lilac.

There comes a time in every zombie's existence when he realizes that the old ways of doing things aren't working anymore.

The old habits.

The old friends.

The old expectations.

Rather than providing comfort and familiarity, they create roadblocks and dependencies that prevent growth and exploration. They hold you back. They keep you from realizing your potential. Sooner or later, you have to let them all go.

. . . fifty-seven . . . fifty-eight . . . fifty-nine . . .

I think I'm done.

Chapter 28

In light of my recent displays of "spirited rebellion," as she put it, and my father's exponentially increasing resentment toward me, my mother thought we might patch up our problems and differences if we all sat down and shared a nice family Thanksgiving dinner together.

"Just like old times," she says.

The three of us are sitting around the dining room table in a stifling, uncomfortable silence. My father shovels cranberry sauce and turkey into his mouth, refusing to speak to or make eye contact with me or my mother, while Mom abandoned her attempts at making conversation after my father told her to "Shut it." Now she just sits in her chair, holding back tears and biting her lower lip as she picks at the stuffing and green beans on her plate.

My parents don't appear to be in the holiday spirit.

Meanwhile, I'm thankful just to be eating at the table. It's the first time my parents have invited me to join them for a meal since my third day back, when one of the stitches on my face popped and a piece of rotting tissue fell into my mother's homemade gazpacho.

Needless to say, Mom hasn't made it since.

Fortunately, my stitches seem to be holding fast these days, better than I would have thought after four months. So I'm thankful for that. I'm thankful for a lot of things, more than I would have imagined barely more than a month ago.

I'm thankful for my support group.

I'm thankful for Rita.

I'm thankful for meeting Ray.

And I'm thankful my speech is returning.

It's still rudimentary, but when your vocabulary has consisted of grunts and screeches that make Leatherface sound like a Rhodes scholar, anything is an improvement.

In addition to "I, Eeta," I've managed to vocalize a few other expressions:

"Ooo ook ate." (You look great.)

"Sss, eese." (Yes, please.)

"Hank ooo." (Thank you.)

And "Ow oo I ell?" (How do I smell?)

Coming from a nine-month-old in a high chair with creamed corn dripping down his chin, the brief explosions of half-English would probably sound adorable. But coming from a thirty-four-year-old decomposing half-corpse with mashed potatoes and gravy dripping down his chin . . . well, let's just say it's probably not going to make anyone reach for the video camera.

So I keep quiet and eat my dinner and look around the table, at my disappointed mother and my brooding father, at all of the food and splendor of this silent, oppressive Thanksgiving feast, until my gaze falls on the turkey with its blistered skin and its vanishing flesh. The more I stare at it, the more I realize that I can relate to it, empathize with it, and it strikes me how much we have in common. True, it's dead and cooked and partially devoured, but is that so different from me?

As it's slowly consumed, the bones appear bit by bit, the cartilage and ribs revealing themselves as meat is stripped from the skeleton. Eventually, it will be nothing but a carcass. And I wonder: Am I being destroyed by Breathers?

Is the process of decomposition gradually consuming me?

Or am I being consumed by the degradation of having to exist in a world ruled by the living?

The longer I stare at the turkey, the more I begin to feel a sort of kinship with it. The more I see it as a metaphor of my current existence. The more I begin to understand why Tom would want to become a vegetarian.

Before my father can cut off another slice of breast or tear off a wing, I reach over and grab the turkey by its leg and drag it off the serving platter, across the table toward me.

"Hey," says my father, his mouth filled with stuffing, pieces of it spraying across the table. "What the hell do you think you're doing?"

Intervention.

Deliverance.

Redemption.

Take your pick. All I know is it feels right.

The turkey overturns the gravy boat on its way toward me, dumping its contents onto the tablecloth and into the cran-berry sauce.

"Goddamn it!" yells my father, dropping his knife and fork and reaching for the turkey.

"Honestly, honey," says my mother, happy just to have some sort of interaction taking place. "If you wanted some more, all you had to do was ask."

Before my father can grab the other leg, I pull the sixteen-pound Butterball into my lap, knocking my plate aside and off the edge of the table, where it lands on the hardwood and cracks in two, spilling my dinner across the floor.

"Andy!" says my mother. "Those are my best dinner plates."

"Give me that turkey," says my father, who gets to his feet and comes around the table with his head thrust out in front of him the way he does whenever he means business. It used to scare the crap out of me when I was a kid. But I'm not a kid anymore. And I'm not giving up my turkey.

I push back in the chair and stand up, more sure of myself than I've been in months, and cradle the holiday personification of my essence against my stomach with my right arm as I back away toward the cellar door. Just before my father reaches me, he steps in my spilled mashed potatoes and goes down hard, smacking his elbow on the table.

"Are you all right, dear?" asks Mom, who is still sitting in her chair as if all of this is completely normal.

My father doesn't answer, just gets to his feet and comes after me. I've almost reached the wine cellar door when he catches up and grabs hold of an exposed leg. I don't think he even cares about eating the turkey anymore. He just doesn't want me to have it.

Part of me wonders just what the hell I expected to accomplish. How I thought this would improve my situation. Another part of me finds this more fun than any recent Thanksgiving I can remember, so I start to laugh.

"This isn't funny," says my father, trying to pull the turkey away from me, but I've got a firm grip on the other leg with my right hand and I'm not letting go. Over my father's shoulder, I see my mother cleaning up my broken plate as she complains about how we both ruined a perfectly lovely meal.

My father and I continue to fight over the turkey, each of us pulling on a leg, skin and meat sliding off in our hands. And I'm reminded of sloughage.

During the initial stages of human decay, liquid leaking from enzyme-ravaged cells gets between the layers of skin and loosens them. Sometimes the skin of an entire hand or foot will come off. As the process continues, giant sheets of skin peel away from the body.

Like the piece of skin that just slipped off the leg my father is holding.

If I hadn't already ruined my appetite for turkey, that definitely did it.

An instant later, the leg in my father's hand rips away and he stumbles back and falls into the antique black buffet hutch containing my mother's tea cup collection. The hutch topples over and lands with a thunderous crash of wood and broken china cups as I fall to the floor laughing with the turkey in my lap and my mother starts to cry.

Just like old times.

Chapter 29

Mom and Dad have escaped the disaster of our Thanksgiving dinner to play tennis at the Seascape Resort with the Putnams and they won't be back until after lunch, which leaves me with at least three hours to practice my newfound abilities without feeling self-conscious or irritating my father.

My parents keep the door to the wine cellar locked when they leave the house in order to prevent me from smelling up the place, so my repeated trips up and down the stairs have a futile, Sisyphean flair. However, instead of feeling condemned, I feel empowered. It's as if I'm relearning how to walk.

That and I've discovered that it's getting easier for me to negotiate the stairs.

As I reach the top of the stairs and turn around to make my way back down again, I keep talking—repeating the same phrase over and over: "There's no place like home."

I've been saying this now for nearly an hour. At first, most of it came out sounding like the chorus of "Old MacDonald": "Ee no aa eye oh."

But after a while, the words start to take shape, as if by repeating the syllables hundreds of times, I'm managing to sculpt them into intelligible sounds. Now when I speak the words, they come out just a few letters shy of perfect: "Air's no play like ome."

I haven't felt this excited since, well, since Rita and I walked into Soquel Village hand in hand. I want to share this with someone, this moment of triumph, of self-actualization. But my only companions are a 2001 Dominus Cabernet and a half-finished jar of Ray's Resplendent Rapture.

I sit down on my mattress and shovel another forkful of venison into my mouth, then wash it down with the last of the Dominus, both of which taste exquisite. While I've always been able to appreciate the savory and musky flavor of Ray's delectable treat, it seems to have taken on a stronger taste. More flavorful. I'd attribute it to something as simple as a different batch of venison, except all the food I've eaten over the past few weeks seems to have developed an improvement in flavor. At first I thought Mom was just adding more seasoning, but that wouldn't account for the wine. And the Dominus isn't the first bottle of wine I've actually enjoyed of late, though if I didn't know better, I'd swear I was beginning to feel a bit tipsy.

Probably just the excitement of all the walking and talking I've been doing.

As my feelings of exultation begin to ebb and the empty jar of venison joins the empty bottle of Dominus on the bedside table, the silence of the house and the solitude of the wine cellar start to close in around me like a burial vault.

I need to find someone who understands what this means to me, someone who will appreciate what I've accomplished, someone who can relate to the excitement of discovering that I'm not the rotting, croaking, shuffling zombie I used to be. And there's only one someone who comes to mind.

I get dressed as fast as I can, then check my reflection like a teenager checking for zits. I consider putting on some of my mother's makeup, then remember the cellar door is locked from the inside.

"Uck it," I say.

Before I head out the back door, I grab a bottle of 1982 Borgogno Barolo Reserve and wrap it in a towel, then stuff it into my backpack. From under my pillow I grab an envelope and slide it into my back pocket. With a final glance in the television screen to check my stitches and gray pallor, I'm out the back door and headed for the gully.

It's a perfect late-November morning—blue sky, cirrus clouds, and all around me the trees still burn with the colors of autumn while dead, fallen leaves scatter in the breath of the wind.

I'd forgotten what it felt like to experience the nuances of the changing seasons, to appreciate the light filtering through the trees or the grace of a leaf drifting to the ground. In spite of the sun, there's enough of a chill in the air to warrant a sweater. Not that the weather has much of an impact on my wardrobe decisions. Since zombies don't exactly get hot or cold, we can pretty much wear whatever we want, whenever we want. Still, that doesn't mean we don't realize what we're supposed to wear.

It's confusing being a zombie, for reasons other than the obvious. You don't experience sensory input the way you did when you were alive, yet you have the memories of how that input made you feel. So you rely on those memories to help you adjust, to help you try to fit in. Except you don't fit in, you never will, and you know it. But that doesn't stop you from trying.

I'm wearing a hunter green cable-knit sweater from Macy's, a pair of Levi's, Columbia hiking shoes, and a black knit beanie from The Gap. To some extent, I'm dressed based on my expectations of what I should be wearing. And strangely enough, it even feels a little cold, though I attribute that more to learned perception than an actual sensory experience. But to a larger extent, the clothes I'm wearing I chose because I wanted to make a good impression.

As I traverse the gully, aware that I'm not dragging my left foot as much as yesterday, I keep reciting the haiku I've written for Rita under my breath—just loud enough so that I'm able to hear what I'm saying. Not every word is intelligible, but I manage to enunciate about every third or fourth word. Granted, in a haiku, that doesn't come to more than four words. Five, tops. But other than my linguistic exercise this morning, that's more than I've managed to spit out in the past four months.

Maybe there's something in my genetic structure that is somehow helping to heal me. Or maybe I'm just getting used to my physical limitations instead of fighting them. Whatever the reason, I'm not complaining.

I check my back right pocket to make sure the haiku I wrote for Rita is still there, the folded envelope with a single piece of paper containing three lines that came to me without effort, as if they'd been in my head all along and were just waiting to be written:

lips colored crimson
dead flesh like alabaster
my lifeless heart pounds

I just hope her mother's not home.

Chapter 30

People who've lost an arm or a leg to combat, infections, or chainsaw accidents frequently report experiencing phantom limb syndrome, where they can still feel their missing arms or legs.

Standing in front of Rita's, raising my fist to knock on her door, I swear I can feel my heart thumping and the sweat flowing from my pores, pasting my shirt to my skin. It's been more than a dozen years since I had romantic intentions toward a woman other than Rachel and I'm more than a little rusty. I feel like I'm in high school, going to get my prom date. But instead of feeling self-conscious about a zit that just erupted in the middle of my forehead, I'm concerned about the stitches that run from my chin to my left eye socket.

An instant before my knuckles hit wood, the male self-destruct system for confidence kicks in and I wonder if I'm making a mistake. I wonder if she'll laugh at me. I wonder if I should have applied more cologne to mask the stench of decay.

I knock three times and wait, hoping Rita answers and not her mother. Even if a Breather has a zombie living at home, answering the door to find a card-carrying member of the living dead standing on your doorstep has to be somewhat un-nerving. And I'm not in the mood to have someone scream at the sight of me. It's not exactly a confidence builder.

After a few moments of silence, I hear the sound of ap-proaching footsteps that stop at the door. There's a peephole mounted in the door at eye level and I sense someone study-ing me. It can't be more than a second or two but it seems as though I've been standing on the doorstep for hours. I almost turn to leave but then the door swings open and Rita is step-ping across the threshold with a smile on her lips and her arms open and all of my anxiety drains away.

Rita's wearing a short-sleeved, white T-shirt and faded blue jeans. She's not wearing socks, makeup, or a bra. Even with my diminished vision, I can see the outline of her nipples pressing against white cotton.

"Hi, Andy," she says, wrapping her arms around my shoul-ders, enfolding me in her embrace. My right arm encircles her waist. Although she shouldn't have any body heat, I feel a warmth radiating from her skin.

We stand holding each other for I don't know how long but it's not long enough. When she pulls away and takes my hand, I'm aware that I've got what Jerry would call a stiffy. Apparently, Rita is aware as well.

"Come inside," says Rita. The look on her face and the sensation in my pants makes me wonder if her words were meant as a double entendre. It doesn't matter. I'm following her wherever she wants me to go.

She leads me down the hallway, past the kitchen and the living room, past the bathroom and a bedroom, to the last room at the end of the hallway. The bed is unmade, clothes lie strewn across the floor, and a half-empty Mason jar of Ray's Resplendent Rapture sits on the bedside table. Cylinders of lipstick in dozens of colors and shades cover the dresser.

Rita closes the door behind us, leads me to the foot of the bed, sits me down, then grabs the Mason jar and joins me. With a fork, she removes a chunk of venison and offers it to me without a word. I open my mouth and accept. It's amazing how much better food tastes when it's fed to you by a beautiful zombie.

Rita takes a bite and lets out a little moan of pleasure. I watch the fork withdraw from her lips and let out a little moan of my own.

She feeds me again and then herself, back and forth in silence until the jar is empty, then she runs her index finger inside the jar, takes her finger, glistening with the juice from the meat, and offers it to me.

I've completely forgotten about my haiku.

I suck on Rita's finger and watch her smile, keeping my eyes open so I don't miss anything. When I'm finished, Rita puts her finger in her mouth, watching me while she does things to her finger that would make me blush if I were still alive, then she gets up and steps over to her dresser, where she picks up a cylinder of lipstick, an Optic Fuchsia, and coats her lips so they look like she's just eaten a candy apple. After pursing, she licks her lips and smiles, then extends the lipstick out to its full length and bites it in half.

This is more than I can stand.

Before I can get to my feet and stagger over to her, Rita is on top of me, pushing me back onto her bed, her lips against mine, her tongue searching for the back of my throat. I taste lipstick, I feel the chunk of Optic Fuchsia pressing against my teeth, and it's exquisite.

Rita pulls away and slips out of her T-shirt and blue jeans like a magic trick. The next thing I know she's naked and straddling me, unzipping my pants and disappearing from view.

This time, I close my eyes.

Chapter 31

Is it necrophilia if we're both dead?

Rita is curled up next to me, my right hand caressing her bare shoulder as she traces the stitches on my face. The rest of my clothes have joined hers in a pile on the floor.

Some zombies, like Jerry, due to a physiological reaction immediately after death, continue their existence with permanent erections. I am not one of those zombies. I haven't experienced an aroused physical state since the accident and because reanimated corpses can't produce erections or sperm, I never expected to have sex again. But I've already had two orgasms in thirty minutes and, apparently, I'm interested in pursuing a third.

How is this possible?

Rita raises herself on one elbow and looks at me as if she just realized I was Elvis Presley. "What did you say?"

I don't know what she's talking about, until I realize that I must have spoken out loud.

"Ow is iss ossibul?"

"How is what possible?" asks Rita.

The fact that she understands me nearly brings me to tears.

I point to my throat. "Iss," I say, then point down at the erection below my waist. "An at."

A wicked smile crosses Rita's face. "I'll tell you what I think about this," she says, brushing my throat with her fingers before pulling the covers back. "But first, let me take care of that."

I don't know if it's because I haven't had sex in nearly five months or if the undead have less self-control, but Rita takes care of me in less than five minutes.

"Yummy," she says, returning to the crook of my arm.

Yummy indeed.

And to think that, a month ago, my biggest thrill was Dinner and a Movie on TBS.

We lay on the bed in silence, Rita playing with my chest hair and me rethinking my position on God, because if my existence before today was hell, then this is most definitely heaven.

I look at Rita, with her dark hair and her pale skin, with her soft, young lips and the way her fingers brush against my rotting flesh, and I'm overwhelmed with her sexuality. I hope my dead wife understands that just because I've had sex with a living corpse, that doesn't mean I don't cherish her memory. But there comes a point where you have to let go of the past in order to embrace the future.

I'm not sure what surprises me more—my lack of guilt regarding my newfound romance or that I'm starting to sound like Helen.

"I think I know why your voice is returning," says Rita into my chest.

"Ow?" I say, hoping it sounds like a question and not an exclamation of pain.

"Do you remember the first time you felt different?" asks Rita.

I don't understand.

She raises up again on one elbow and looks at me. I can see the stitches on her throat. They're sublime.

"That Sunday after Halloween," she says. "Why did you go for a walk down to the village?"

I don't know, I say in Andy-speak. I just had to get out.

"You felt restless?"

I nod.

"And emboldened?"

I nod again.

"You felt different."

I think back to that Sunday, to what ultimately drove me to leave the wine cellar, and nod a third time.

Rita sits up, her nipples pink and hard, and reaches across me to the bedside table, her breasts brushing against my chest. I feel a now familiar stirring beneath my waist and wonder if I can last more than five minutes this time.

Rita returns to her position next to me and holds the empty Mason jar in her hand.

"We each consumed a jar the night we met Ray," she says. "Jerry didn't eat any that night. Just you and me."

I nod absently, thinking about how good the venison tasted, how juicy it was, how much I wanted another one when I'd finished.

"How many jars have you had?" she asks.

I think for a minute, adding up my trips to see Ray and the jars of Rapture he's sent home with me, and hold up four fingers, then add a thumb.

"I've had three," says Rita. "And ever since that first jar, I've felt something growing inside of me. An understanding. An awareness . . ."

"An awakening," I say, though it comes out "A a-akeknee."

"Exactly. Now look at this," she says, holding out her wrist.

I notice, for the first time, that the stitches on her right wrist are gone. A raw, healing scar remains.

"The last few days it's been itching," she says. "This morning, the stitches just fell out."

I stare at her wrist, brush my finger against the pink flesh of the scar, and immediately Mr. Stiffy returns. This realization isn't lost on Rita, who swings one leg across and straddles me, her knees pressing against my waist, her thighs hovering inches above me.

"You know what I think?" she whispers, her lips brushing against my ear.

I shake my head. I can barely focus on my own thoughts, let alone figure out what she's thinking.

"I don't think it's venison in those jars."

"Ut is it?" I ask, though I think I already know the answer. I've probably known it intuitively from the beginning and just allowed myself to think otherwise. But instead of feeling disgusted or sick to my stomach, I find myself craving more.

"Breathers," she says, whispering the word into my ear as her thighs slide down to meet my hips and I'm once again enveloped in a warmth that shouldn't exist yet exceeds any carnal pleasure I've ever experienced.

My senses are overwhelmed.

I forget about the empty Mason jar and the human flesh it once contained and I focus on Rita, on the sensation of her body pressing against mine. I turn my head and find her wrist, the one that's newly healed, and suck on the scar. Rita moans and asks me to do it again. She says "Suck on me" and I have to think of something to keep from losing control right then.

I was never much of a sports fan, so thinking about baseball won't do the trick. And dead dogs in a ditch is just a little too close to home. So instead, I find myself running through the titles of as many zombie movies as I can think of. I barely make it through the first three George Romero films before I explode.

Chapter 32

Who wants to start tonight?" asks Helen.

Rita and I look at each other and smirk. Jerry sits next to us, his road rash clearer and less inflamed than it was several days ago, like poison oak that's finally turned the corner, though he doesn't seem to notice. Tom sits across from Jerry wearing a pissy expression, his right arm two inches shorter than his left and the knuckles covered with black hair. Naomi and Carl are next to Tom looking pretty much the same as always—Naomi with her sagging eye socket and Carl picking at his open knife wounds—while Leslie, the only consistent return newbie, is knitting a blanket.

On the chalkboard is the phrase:

BELIEVE IN YOURSELF.

For the first time since the accident, I think I actually do.

Once the realization of what we were eating sunk in, I had a few moments where I felt a little weird about the idea of consuming human flesh. It's more a question of morality than guilt. After all, I'm only a little over four months removed from Breather status. But considering the transformation I've gone through since I tasted my first jar of Ray's Resplendent

Rapture, I'm willing to look the other way on the whole morality issue.

Over the past few days, Rita and I have discovered that the rehabilitative effects of eating Breather extend beyond our physical injuries. We each feel changes taking place inside of us, inside our bodies and our heads, as if the wiring has been shorted out for the past few months and circuits are beginning to fire again. Slowly but surely, the power is starting to come back on.

We've also discovered that zombie sex is phenomenally superior to Breather sex.

Think MP3 compared to 8-track.

Think first class compared to coach.

Think filet mignon compared to ground beef.

At first I just figured it was the excitement of experiencing physical pleasure again. Except Rita noticed it, too. I'm not sure if it was before or after she had an orgasm that lasted for ten minutes, but I think that was pretty much the clincher for her. For me it was when we had sex five times in one hour.

I really need to work on my stamina.

Still, it's like I'm seventeen again, sneaking over to my girlfriend's house to have sex while her mom is at work. Or sneaking my girlfriend into the wine cellar of my parents' house while they sit upstairs oblivious to Rita's muffled cries of passion. Honestly, I doubt my parents would care if they knew. Just so long as I'm not out protesting for my civil rights or trying to ride public transportation.

"Would anyone like to share something personal with the group?" asks Helen.

Rita glances at me, the way she looks at me when she wants to try a new sexual position, and I let out a single burst of laughter.

"Is it just me," says Naomi, "or is something going on?"

"What do you mean?" asks Helen.

Naomi looks around the room, her one eye settling on Rita and me a moment. "I don't know exactly," she says. "Something just feels different. I feel different."

"Yeah, you know what? I feel it, too," says Jerry. "Only I thought I was stoned or something."

"Me, too," says Tom, nodding. The fingers of his shorter right hand twitch. "Well, I mean, not the stoned part."

Rita and I have had three and five jars of Breather, respectively, while by my count Tom and Jerry have each had two. No one else in the group has had more than one. But they don't know what Rita and I know.

"I don't think I feel any different," says Leslie. "But then, I'm new at this. What should I be feeling?"

No one gives her an answer.

"Carl," says Helen. "Do you feel anything out of the ordinary?"

"I don't *feel* anything," says Carl.

"That's nothing new," says Naomi.

Carl ignores her. "But I notice that Jerry's face is clearer and Andy doesn't seem to be walking with as much of a limp. And Rita's not wearing any makeup."

She's not. Her face is pale and unadorned. She's wearing blue jeans and a red turtleneck sweater that covers her neck and wrists. But instead of concealing her stitches, she's hiding the fact that she's healing.

Everyone stares at Rita, who giggles, then they stare at Jerry, who says, "What?"

"Is this true, Jerry?" asks Helen. "Is your skin improving?"

"I don't know," says Jerry, picking at his face. A scab comes off and falls to the floor, leaving a pink patch of flesh from where it fell. "Maybe."

Helen walks over to Jerry and studies his face, raising his chin with her fingers and then turning his head from side to side.

"What have you been up to?" asks Helen.

"Nothin'," says Jerry. "I swear."

Helen glances at us. Rita smiles and I say, "On't ook at ee."

Everyone's mouths drop open but no one says a word. Finally, Helen says, "Oh dear," and staggers to her chair, where Leslie and Naomi help her sit down.

"Dude," says Jerry. "Have you been able to talk this whole time?"

I shake my head.

"When did you regain your ability to speak?" asks Leslie.

"Ast upple eeks," I say.

"But how?" asks Naomi. "How is that possible? You're dead. We're all dead."

"Undead," says Carl.

"Whatever," says Naomi. "Andy shouldn't be able to regain his voice, your road rash shouldn't be able to improve, and Rita . . ."

Rita pulls her sleeve up and holds her healed wrist up for everyone to see.

"Holy shit," says Jerry.

"That's impossible," says Tom.

"Apparently not," says Leslie, who seems to be much more accepting of these revelations than anyone else.

"What the hell is going on?" asks Naomi, standing up, hands on her hips. "What have you three been doing?"

"They've been eating Breather," says Helen, her voice flat.

Rita and I exchange surprised looks.

An awkward silence follows. If this were a scene in a movie, somewhere in the distance you'd hear a dog bark.

"What do Breathers taste like?" asks Leslie.

"How should I know?" says Jerry. "I haven't eaten any."

"Yes, you have," says Rita.

"No, I haven't," says Jerry. "I think I'd know if I'd eaten Breather."

I reach into my backpack and remove an empty Mason jar of Ray's Resplendent Rapture.

Jerry looks at the jar in my hand and says, "You're kidding."

I shake my head.

"He gave each of us a jar," says Naomi. "Are you telling us we all ate Breather?"

Tom is suddenly out of his chair and running for the bathroom, his left hand covering his mouth as he makes little gagging sounds.

"Actually," says Leslie, "I thought it was quite good."

"Why didn't you tell us what was in those jars?" asks Naomi.

"We didn't know," says Rita. "We didn't figure it out until a few days ago."

"But how do you know for sure that it's Breather and not deer meat?" says Jerry. "Did you talk to Ray?"

Ray wasn't home when we stopped by for a visit. But in the ashes of his fire, we did find a human femur, which I'm guessing he didn't use to toast marshmallows.

"They don't have to talk to Ray," says Helen, her voice regaining some of her trademark energy. "The undead don't just miraculously heal by eating venison."

"You knew about this?" asks Carl. "That this was possible?"

Turns out, one of the zombies Helen counseled when she was still among the living claimed he'd found a way to not only reverse decomposition, but to heal wounds and injuries.

"Though I'd only seen him three times, I noticed that he

appeared healthier than your average zombie," says Helen. "When I asked him how it was possible, he just smiled and told me I'd rather not know. Of course, I suspected he was eating Breathers, but I didn't report it to anyone."

"What happened to him?" asks Rita.

"He said that as soon as he could pass for a Breather, he was going to move someplace where nobody knew what he was so he could start a new life," says Helen. "I never saw him again after that. According to the records, he just disappeared."

"Did you ever tell anyone else about what he'd said?" asks Leslie.

Helen shakes her head. "Not until now."

"Do Breathers know about this?" asks Naomi.

"I don't know," says Helen. "I presume someone at some level knows. Or at least suspects. But if they do, it's not something they've revealed to the general public."

I can understand now why we're not allowed to have access to the Internet. Sharing information like this on a global level would create a lot of problems for the living.

"But I guarantee that if the Department of Resurrection comes in here and realizes our physical conditions have improved," says Helen, "we'll all get reported."

In addition to being used for crash tests, plastic surgery, chop shops, and an assortment of unspeakable scientific experiments, abandoned or fallen zombies can end up in what is commonly known in the undead community as "reanimated purgatory"—discarded in landfills, sold to zombie zoos, or enslaved on one of a handful of television reality shows. *Zombie Nanny* is probably the worst of the bunch, though I hear *Survivor Zombie* runs a close second.

"So, where do we go from here?" asks Leslie.

"We don't go anywhere." Helen stands up, walks over

to the chalkboard, and starts writing. "We don't accept any more jars of Ray's venison, we don't share this information with anyone outside of the group, we use makeup and props to conceal any visible improvements, and we practice restraint."

Helen steps aside and reveals what she has written:

I WILL NOT CONSUME THE LIVING.

"Say it with me now."

Chapter **33**

Jerry, Rita, and I are walking along the side of the road on our way to see if Ray has any more jars of Breather.

Initially, Jerry was concerned that we were in direct conflict with Helen's instructions, but Rita convinced him that since the Breather who donated the meat is already dead, technically we're not consuming the living.

"What if Ray's not home?" asks Jerry.

I shrug. It's the first time I've been able to shrug with both shoulders since the accident. Not exactly headline news, but when your left shoulder has been a useless mass of bone and tissue for nearly five months, a shrug is like winning the lottery.

Jerry takes off his baseball hat and scratches at his scalp. In the wash of light from a street lamp, I can see there's less of his brain exposed than before.

"Do you think he'd mind if I borrowed some more *Playboys*?"

At some point along the way, Rita slips her right hand into my left. I shiver as much from her touch as I do from the fact that I can actually feel her hand in mine. I'm also aware that I'm growing more aroused by the second. Fortunately, Jerry has scampered ahead to chase after a possum, so he doesn't see Rita's hand slide out of mine and down the front of my pants.

By the time we reach the back door of the granary, it's nearly ten o'clock. A couple of weeks ago, the prospect of breaking curfew, even with an hour or so to spare, would have given me the phantom sweats. But once you've eaten Breather, all the other rules and taboos just don't seem like such a big deal anymore.

"Doesn't look like anyone's home," says Rita.

"Well, since we're already here . . . ," says Jerry.

Just as Jerry reaches for the door, we hear muffled voices inside, male and female, followed by the sound of glass breaking.

"Shit," says a female voice.

This is followed by another voice, this one male. "I think I'm going to throw up again."

Footsteps are suddenly coming toward us from behind the door. Before we can move away, the back door swings open and a figure lurches out and throws up all over Jerry's shoes.

"Oh man," says Jerry, walking away and trying to kick the vomit off of his shoes. "These are my favorite pair of Converse."

"Sorry," says Tom.

"Are you all right, dear?" asks Leslie as she arrives in the doorway behind him.

"Yeah, kind of," says Tom, standing up and wiping his mouth with his hand.

Naomi appears next to Leslie and sees us. "What are you three doing here?"

"Apparently, the same thing you are," says Rita. "Any luck?"

"No," says Naomi. "Just a bunch of warm beer and *Playboy* magazines."

"Don't touch those!" says Jerry, wiping his shoes on some weeds. "I need to borrow them."

"Ss Ray ear?" I ask.

"No," says Leslie. "No one's here but us."

Out on Old San Jose Road, headlights flash past and tires hum on asphalt.

"I think we should get out of sight," says Rita.

The six of us go inside, which is lit up by Ray's propane lantern. Carl is crouched near one of the grain storage areas trying to clean up a couple of broken bottles of beer with a magazine. Which explains the glass we heard breaking.

"Dude!" yells Jerry as he runs over to Carl and takes the magazine from him. He wipes the magazine on his shirt, then holds it up. "This is the Fiftieth Anniversary Playmate issue."

I wonder where Ray is. When I check the coals in the fire pit, they're cold. But in addition to the femur, there's a pair of shoulder blades.

I suddenly feel like it's wrong for all of us to be in here searching for Ray's jars of human flesh.

"I hink we sood eeve," I say.

"Andy's right," says Rita. "Let's get this place cleaned up and go home."

While Rita, Leslie, Naomi, and Carl pick up the pieces of broken glass, Tom waits by the back door, just in case he has to throw up again.

"Erry," I say. "Et's go."

"Hold on," he says, rummaging through the grain storage area. "I just want to grab a few more *Playboy*s."

Before I can say another word, we hear the sound of a car approaching alongside the granary.

"Shit," whispers Naomi.

We all freeze and listen as the car pulls up and then stops near the back door.

"What do we do?" says Tom, joining the rest of us as the car engine shuts off.

Rita turns off the propane lantern. "Hide."

Other than the two grain storage bins, there's not any-place to hide, and all seven of us won't fit, so Rita and Leslie crawl into one while Tom joins Jerry in the other. Naomi hunkers down behind one of the bins and I do the same behind its twin. Carl, with no place left, climbs halfway up one of the ladders.

Outside, a car door opens and closes. Footsteps approach the back door. Unable to help myself, I peek up over the top of the storage bin as the back door swings open and a figure appears in the doorway. A flashlight beam stabs into the granary.

I realize that I'm actually perspiring.

Before I can fully appreciate the significance of the sensation I'm experiencing, the figure's voice intrudes upon the moment.

"Hello? Is anybody home?"

Carl and Naomi start laughing. I can't help myself and I start to laugh, too. Seconds later, Rita and Leslie's muffled giggles drift out from the storage bin.

The flashlight beam sweeps back and forth, searching for the source of the laughter, finally settling on Carl fifteen feet up on the ladder.

"So," he says, laughing so hard he nearly loses his grip, "is this what you meant by practicing restraint?"

"Oh, son of a bitch," says Helen.

Chapter 34

In addition to an improvement in physical appearance and an increase in self-confidence, another side-effect of eating Breather is that once you get a taste for them, you tend to want more.

Unless, of course, you're a vegetarian.

"I can't believe I ate two jars," says Tom. He hasn't thrown up since we left the granary, but he has the look of a man who might change his mind at any second.

"Believe it," says Jerry, sitting beside Tom in the backseat of Helen's sister's minivan. "I mean, come on. You had to know that stuff wasn't tuna."

"Can we not talk about this, please?" says Tom.

"You brought it up," says Jerry.

"Will you two be quiet," says Naomi from the front seat. "You're making Helen nervous."

Helen has already dropped off Carl and Leslie, but she's had to take the long way to avoid the main streets. A car full of zombies cruising around late at night isn't exactly something the police would consider business as usual.

Rita and I sit in the center seat section, holding hands. We haven't told anyone about us yet, but I think they kind of get the idea. Leslie even told me she thought we made a cute couple.

"Did you think it tasted like tuna?" asks Jerry.

"Can someone please roll down a window?" says Tom.

I can't help but laugh.

"Tom," says Rita, turning around in her seat. "Have you looked in the mirror lately?"

"Not really," says Tom. "I kind of avoid mirrors altogether. Why?"

She pulls a compact out of her purse and opens it up for him. "Why don't you take a look."

Tom reluctantly takes the compact and holds it up in front of his face. At first his expression doesn't change. Then he adjusts the compact and holds it up closer, trying to get a better look. In the dome light of the minivan it's hard to see, and the improvement isn't obvious at first glance, but the flap of skin that is Tom's right cheek has begun to heal.

As if unconvinced, Tom reaches up and touches his face. In spite of the fact that he's still holding the compact with his good left hand, he doesn't seem to realize that his alien right hand is the one exploring his cheek. Apparently, his face isn't the only wound that's healing.

"Holy cow," he says.

"Kind of makes you rethink being a vegetarian, doesn't it?" says Jerry.

This time, Tom doesn't offer up a retort.

After dropping off Tom and Naomi, Helen asks Jerry, Rita, and me if we'd mind walking home so she can get the minivan back before her sister realizes it's gone. When Helen pulls up along the side of an uninhabited stretch of road to let us off, I get out and approach the driver's side, where Helen rolls down her window.

"What is it, Andy?"

I lean through the window and kiss her on the cheek. "Hank yoo, Lllen," I say. "Hank yoo or eh-ee-hing."

She looks up at me and offers a smile filled with compassion and understanding. "You're welcome, Andy."

The three of us watch her drive away, then head off in contemplative silence. I don't know about Rita, but I can't stop thinking about how long all of us can manage to keep our little revelation a secret. As for Jerry, chances are he's just thinking about busting out a clean towel and a brand new bottle of hand lotion.

After a few blocks, Jerry breaks away and heads off to his parents' with his backpack full of *Playboys*, while I insist on walking Rita home before getting back to the wine cellar. She declines my offer initially, until I convince her that I'd just follow her home one way or another.

"Like a puppy dog?" she says.

"Oof," I say, then start panting.

She stops me from panting by pressing her lips against mine, her tongue probing the inside of my mouth. Sensations and feelings that I'd assumed were lost forever overwhelm me—warmth, desire, passion. Standing there in Rita's embrace, it's as though I'm intoxicated with heat.

For the second time tonight, I'm aware that my pores are releasing fluid.

"I'm edding," I say.

Rita pulls away and gives me a questioning look. "You want to get married?"

"Oh," I say, shaking my head. Although I can't see myself, I swear I'm blushing.

I lift up my right arm and show her my armpit, which is a little damp. I heard once that humans don't technically sweat. Cows sweat and we perspire, but it's hard enough for me to say "cow." Besides, I'm not technically human.

"I'm *etting*."

An odd smile steals its way across Rita's lips. "Tell me if this makes you sweat."

She takes my right hand and places it against her chest. I feel her nipples growing hard beneath my fingers, feel the soft flesh of her breast giving in to the weight of my palm. The longer she holds my hand there, the harder it is for me to keep from sliding my hand under her shirt.

Then I feel something else, a faint vibration that occurs every five to ten seconds. I press my hand firmly against her chest, holding it there, forgetting about her breasts and her nipples, waiting for the next vibration. When it comes again, I look up at Rita and see that her eyes are filled with tears.

Her heart has begun to beat again.

Chapter 35

It's not often you reconsider your stance on something as fundamental as your belief in a higher intelligence. An omnipotent deity. A supreme being.

But only a higher intelligence could have made Breathers taste so good. Only an omnipotent deity could have given human flesh its healing power. Only a supreme being could have been ironic enough to allow the walking dead to impersonate the living by eating them.

That's what I'm here to determine, anyway.

Not that I'm trying to impersonate anyone. I still have a patchwork of stitches across my face and a stilted walk that makes Frankenstein's monster look like a dancer in the Joffrey Ballet. But at least I'm able to sit in one of the pews at the back of the Congregational Church of Soquel without anyone gasping or screaming or scrunching their face up in disgust.

Not the type of confirmation that generally evokes a case of the warm fuzzies, but I'll take what I can get.

There aren't any services taking place on a Wednesday evening, so it's not like I have to contend with a church full of worshipers. Only a handful of Breathers are present and people don't tend to bother you if your head appears to be angled in prayer. But praying isn't what I came here to do.

After feeling the miracle of Rita's heart beating, I wondered if perhaps there wasn't something inexplicably religious going on here. The only miracles I've ever heard about have all been attributed to either God or Jesus, so I figured I'd check it out, see if I believed in the possibility that a supernatural presence was responsible for the healing taking place within us. Not that I'm looking for validation or excuses. It's more out of curiosity. Just in case I've been wrong all this time.

I don't expect to have any revelations or get struck by lightning or hear the voice of God. I'm just here to see if there's something I missed. After all, when you've started eating human flesh, even if you've never believed in God or heaven, you still tend to wonder about eternal damnation.

In spite of how good Breather tastes, it's not something you just accept without question, being a cannibal. I'm sure when it's the lifestyle for a society and you're born into it, you take to it like a piranha to a drowning cow. But when you've spent more than thirty years as an omnivore, having dinner parties and barbecues with your friends and neighbors, and suddenly you begin to wonder how your friends and neighbors would taste between two buns with a little mustard and ketchup and maybe a slice of tomato, the idea takes a little getting used to.

Which is probably why Ray introduced us to eating Breather the way he did.

Had I known definitively what I was eating, what was being offered to me, I doubt I would have dug into it with such enthusiasm. But to be honest, even that first jar of Breather, I think I knew what it was. I just didn't want to consider the possibility. I wanted to consume it in blissful ignorance. Except it's kind of hard to ignore what you're eating when your undead girlfriend's heart starts beating again.

Which brings me back to why I'm here.

I'm hoping that our gradual transformation can be attributed to a divine miracle, to the hand of God—not to the salubrious nutritional benefits of my friends and neighbors. If it's the former, then I'm hoping I can find the willpower to forgo these cravings I have for human flesh. If it's the latter, then I'm hoping I can find a good meat tenderizer.

Of the half dozen Breathers in the church, one is a woman praying several pews ahead of me, two are a couple discussing their upcoming wedding in the vestibule behind me, while a fourth, a man, sits on the left near the front pews. Another woman who appears to be upset about something is talking with the minister at the altar—the minister being the sixth.

For the past thirty minutes I've been trying to ignore them. To pretend they're not here. So I just close my eyes and bow my head and continue with my pretense of praying, waiting for the sign I've come here hoping to find. But every now and then I get a whiff of one of them and I find myself wondering how they would taste.

I probably should have eaten something before I left the house.

I think that's been the hardest part to get used to. My appetite. Before I started eating human flesh, I tended to eat more out of habit than hunger and I would crave anything that had any flavor, anything that didn't taste like steamed rice or white bread or plain pasta. Now, more and more, I find myself craving steamed rice with stir-fried Breather, a Breather and cheese sandwich, and spaghetti with Breather sauce.

This isn't how I imagined I would end up. I didn't ask for

this. I didn't ask to reanimate. I didn't ask to eat human flesh from a Mason jar. But now that I have, I'm finding it's hard to turn back. Something inside me has changed. Something more than physiological. Something instinctual. I can feel it growing, wanting to take over. And I can feel myself succumbing, seduced by this new feeling.

But there's still a part of me that wants to fight against it. That wants a reason to believe that there's another way. That I can exist among Breathers without thinking about how succulent they would taste. But that part is steadily growing smaller and more silent.

So I sit here in this church with my eyes closed and my head bowed and I realize that in spite of my spiritual skepticism, in spite of my pious artifice, I'm praying. Hoping for some kind of sign, some indication that divine intervention is at work within me, healing my injuries, bringing me back to life. At least that way, I can treat my Breather cravings as an addiction, a lifestyle choice, something to overcome. Otherwise, I'm going to have to accept the fact that eating Breathers is necessary for my survival.

Behind me, the voices of the couple discussing their wedding have suddenly grown silent. When I open my eyes and glance up, I notice that the woman and the minister who were standing at the altar are no longer in the church. Neither is the man who was sitting near the front pews on the left. The only Breather remaining is the woman a couple of pews ahead of me, her head still bowed in prayer. I have to admire her devotion. She's been at it since I showed up. But in the silence of the church, with only the two of us in attendance, I finally hear the snores and I realize she's been faking it, much like me.

I'm still waiting for my sign when I hear a commotion outside the church. I can't tell what's going on and I don't recall hearing any sirens, so I figure it doesn't have anything to do with me. Then the back door of the church opens and the minister walks in, flanked by two men from Animal Control.

"There he is," the minister says, pointing at me. "There's the blasphemous abomination."

So much for divine intervention.

ndy, can you come upstairs for a minute, dear?"

When I woke up this morning, two inches of stitches running down my cheek had come loose, so I cut them off with a pair of scissors. Now I'm putting on makeup to make it look like I'm trying to cover up my stitches when I'm actually trying to hide the fact that I'm healing.

"Andy?" my mother calls again.

Without the makeup, I still wouldn't pass for a Breather, but I would definitely look like a new and improved Andy to anyone who's seen me before. Like my parents.

"Andy?"

"Okay, okay," I mutter, then smile when I realize it's the first completely clear response I've spoken.

I remind myself to keep from talking because that would most likely freak out my parents and give my father another excuse to ship me off to Cadavers R Us. Still, I'd love to see the expressions on their faces. It would almost be worth it, except I'd never get to see Rita again. And that would definitely be a deal breaker.

I hang my dry erase board around my neck, then try to drag myself up the stairs as if my left arm and leg still don't work. But when you've suddenly found your body healing and your basic motor skills returning, faking mangled limbs and decomposing flesh is harder than it looks. It's like pretending you're a woman and walking into the men's bathroom to use the urinal.

Sometimes you just forget.

From upstairs, I smell homemade Christmas cookies baking while Frank Sinatra croons his version of "Mistletoe and Holly." Mom always loved the Rat Pack.

Christmas is just around the corner, which seems appropriate since each day I wake up with the anticipation of discovering the new gifts awaiting me. But instead of finding them beneath the Christmas tree or in my stocking, I find them within myself or in my reflection in the mirror.

When your ability to walk and talk begins to return, when you experience pleasure and excitement and other physical sensations that you thought were no longer possible, when you can once again taste and smell and feel, the moral questions surrounding these changes lose their power. Grow moot. Become just another distraction on the way to self-discovery.

As for God, I'm not concerned about him anymore. God had his chance. And he sent me to the SPCA.

The entire way up the stairs, I keep checking to see if I can feel my heartbeat.

I'm beginning to wonder, if my heart starts beating again, am I still a zombie? Am I technically one of the undead if I have blood pumping through my veins? And what if I start to breathe again? Does that make me human? Will I regain the rights and opportunities that once defined my existence?

I suppose it doesn't really matter, since I don't have any control over what Breathers think of me, of my kind. They're going to believe what they want to believe, even if they're family.

When I reach the top of the stairs and stagger into the kitchen for effect, my father is sitting at the kitchen table watching me while absently thumbing through a stack of papers. My mother stands at the sink doing dishes, apparently oblivious to my entrance.

"Take a seat," says my father.

Other than the Thanksgiving turkey debacle, my father has seldom addressed me directly since I reanimated and my mother is oddly aloof, yet this feels vaguely familiar—a scene I've participated in before. The unease I feel is also familiar, not a zombie-living-in-a-Breather-world unease, but something less recent. A memory from my youth.

Then it hits me.

Whenever my parents felt the need to discipline me as a child or an adolescent, my mother would call me into the room and then retreat to some mundane task while my father handed out the punishment. This time, however, I get the sense that getting grounded is the least of my worries.

"Take a seat, Andrew," my father says again.

Now I know it's serious. My father only calls me Andrew when I'm in big trouble.

I shuffle over to the table and do my best to sit down awkwardly in the chair across from my father. I glance at my mother, who has been washing the same glass since I came upstairs.

I remove the dry erase board from around my neck, then set the board down on the table and write: *What's up?*

My father stares at the words I've written, then finally looks up into my face and makes eye contact with me.

"We have a problem," he says, continuing to thumb through the stack of papers. "Do you know what these are?"

I shake my head.

"These," he says, holding the papers up for effect, "are individual invoices for every bottle of wine I've purchased over the past ten years."

Uh oh.

"Every time your mother and I consume a bottle, I file the invoices away," he says. "These invoices here, which number one hundred and seventy-two, represent the wine that should still be in the cellar, minus the bottles you've broken in fits of anger."

Oops.

"The other night," he says, "while you were at one of your meetings, I took inventory and discovered that of the one hundred and seventy-two bottles of wine that should be in the cellar, forty-seven are missing."

Somehow, I don't think telling my father that I share the bottles with the undead would improve my situation.

"According to my figures," he says, removing the top page from the stack, "the total replacement value of the missing bottles of wine, as well as the eleven other bottles you've broken, comes to just under seven thousand dollars."

Yet another reason to drink beer. The price of wine is almost as bad as the price of real estate.

"Add to that the cost of your therapist, the numerous times we've had to pay to get you out of the SPCA, and the damage you did to your mother's tea cup collection," says my father, "and that brings the total to just under ten thousand dollars."

I sit and stare at my father, listening to Frank Sinatra and the *squeak squeak squeak* of sponge against glass as my mother continues to wash the same glass over and over.

I'm beginning to perspire.

Hospitals pay good money for cadaver-derived human tissue. Skin can fetch up to $1,000 per square foot. Corneas go for $2,000 apiece, femurs $3,800 each, and patella tendons $1,800 to $3,000. Heart valves run from $5,000 to $7,000.

Granted, hospitals are paying not just for the tissue but for the removal of the tissues in a ready-to-use form that has undergone significant quality testing. Prices for research items are usually lower because the tissue undergoes less testing and processing, but even so, my father could recoup the entire $10,000 by selling me off to a research facility.

And I thought being sent off to summer camp was bad.

I wipe my previous question off the dry erase board and write another one: *What do you plan to do?*

"You know what I'd like to do," says my father, studying me with an expression of disgust and resentment. "But your mother can't stand the thought of you getting cut up into pieces and sold off."

I look over at my mother, who refuses to offer me even a glance of recognition.

"You've worn out your welcome here, Andrew," my father says, and I can tell from the hint of a smile on his face that he's been waiting to say that since I came back. "The dead don't belong with the living. They belong in the ground."

I'm not dead, I almost say. *I'm undead.*

"Your mother and I are driving down to Palm Springs tomorrow morning for a few days," he says, collecting the stack of papers and standing up. "When we get back, we'll contact the zoo up in San Francisco and make arrangements for you to join their family and earn back the money you owe us."

A zombie zoo. That's worse than a research facility. At least in a research facility, you're being destroyed for some sort of noble purpose. But a zombie zoo strips you of any remaining dignity. You're on display for everyone to abuse and you spend the remainder of your existence slowly rotting away until you're nothing but tissue and bone. I hear that at some zoos, Breathers are even allowed to take home a piece of preserved zombie as a souvenir.

I stand up, leaving my dry erase board on the table, then shuffle over to the cellar door, where my father stands holding the door open, waiting for me to pass. I look him in the eye, almost catch myself, then blurt out the words I've been wanting to say for the past several months.

"Fuck you, Dad."

Behind me in the kitchen, a glass shatters on the floor.

My father stares at me, his jaw slack, the confident expression in his eyes replaced by doubt. Maybe it was a mistake to let him know I could talk. I don't know. But I do know that it's worth seeing that smug look of his clouded by a trace of fear.

I glance back once more at my mother, who stands with the sponge in her hands and pieces of broken glass at her feet, then begin my descent. As soon as I hit the second step, the door slams and locks behind me. From the other side, I hear my mother start to sob.

Back in the wine cellar, I sit down on my mattress and wonder what's going to happen to me. I've just started to feel alive again, to feel a sense of belonging, a sense of self-worth, and it's all going to be taken away—my new friends, my new existence, Rita. Everything.

Before I realize what's happening, I start to do something I never thought I'd do again.

Tears build up in my ducts and spill out of my eyes, coursing down my cheeks, across my makeup and healing stitches. At first I laugh, elated at the fact that I'm crying, then I remember why I'm unhappy and I cry harder.

I am a survivor. I am a survivor. I am a survivor.

I know I shouldn't just sit here getting angry or feeling sorry for myself. I should try to figure out a way to avoid being shipped off to the zoo. Instead, I open a 2002 Kistler Pinot Noir from the Sonoma Coast and start drinking.

Chapter 37

I'm standing in the kitchen in a puddle of defrosted frozen food items just after midnight on an early December morning, listening to Christmas music—my stomach empty and the refrigerator filled with my parents.

Not exactly a Hallmark moment.

On the CD player, Frank Sinatra is singing "White Christmas."

I think this is where we came in.

I still can't piece together how this all happened. Or how I got into the house. The door to the wine cellar is standing open, but for the undeath of me I can't recall a single moment that transpired after the third bottle of wine, which I think was a 1995 Barbaresco from Italy.

I also have no idea how I managed to do all of this considering my left arm still isn't much better than fifty percent. I must have surprised them somehow, caught them off guard. Maybe I coaxed my mother into opening the cellar door. Maybe I went outside and climbed in through an unlocked window. I guess it doesn't matter. All that matters is that I've suddenly got bigger problems than getting grounded or sold off to a zombie zoo.

Coming to terms with the fact that I've killed my parents

is enough of a shock without having to think about how I'm going to get rid of the evidence. Not that my only regrets have to do with how I'm going to explain this to the police or how I plan to dispose of my parents' bodies. It's just that I've got a lot of processing to do. After all, it's not every day you wake up drunk on the kitchen floor and realize you've dismembered your parents and stuffed them into the refrigerator.

I'm not sure what's more disconcerting—the sight of my parents' disembodied heads staring out at me from the freezer through gallon-sized Ziploc bags, or their dismembered and headless torsos squeezed into the refrigerator where the eggs and cream cheese should be.

It's at times like this I'm grateful I don't believe in eternal damnation.

Of course, you could argue that I've already reached that particular destination and have been renting a penthouse suite there ever since I climbed out of my coffin. Though *eternal* tends to have an expiration date when your body is gradually decomposing. And *damnation* is only a punishment if you have something to lose.

It's not that I don't feel bad about what I've done to my mother and father. But up until recently, I expected to just eventually rot away. And anything I had to lose had already been stolen from me. Then I meet Ray and fall in love with Rita and I feel like I have something to exist for again. I have something that matters. And my parents were going to take that away from me because of ten thousand dollars and a few acts of civil disobedience.

I know I wasn't the easiest zombie to raise, but my father could have shown some compassion and my mother could have let me hug her without screaming and gagging. Maybe it wouldn't have mattered. Maybe this would have happened sooner or later. Maybe my father was right.

The dead don't belong with the living.

As I study the remains of my parents, the initial cold shock of disbelief at what I've done gives way to a flash of hot guilt that makes me wonder if there was any way to avoid this. If maybe I might have overreacted. Still, I have to admit that I'm impressed by my efficient use of shelf space. I never would have thought you could fit two adult bodies into an Amana bottom freezer and still have room for leftovers from Thanksgiving dinner. But that doesn't mean I don't feel like I've made a mistake.

The longer I stare at my parents, the more I wonder if I should have put their extremities in the vegetable crisper.

In the wash of light from inside the refrigerator, I see flour tortillas and a package of wheat bread mixed in with the contents of the freezer on the floor. I open up the tortillas and start chewing on one as I stare into the refrigerator, at the headless torsos of my parents, trying to figure out what I'm going to do, and before I realize what's happening, I'm thinking about having a midnight snack.

Maybe it's because I'm hungry. Maybe it's because I've tasted Breather. Maybe it's because their heads are in the freezer and that makes it easier to disassociate their bodies from their identities. But the thought of barbecued ribs almost starts me salivating.

Still, it's a bit of a dilemma. In spite of their failings and the fact that they were willing to sell off their son to settle a ten-thousand-dollar debt, they were my parents. And I feel like I've kind of failed them by killing them and stuffing them into the refrigerator. But now that it's done, I can't help but think about how they would taste with a little Bull's Eye barbecue sauce.

The UA handbook doesn't exactly cover this type of scenario. And there aren't any role models for the undead to follow. Hollywood zombies don't tend to exhibit any senti-mentality when eating friends or loved ones. And I've never seen a hungry, reanimated corpse in a movie stop to consider the consequences of its actions.

If I were a religious creature, the decision might be more difficult to make. And even though I don't believe in a heaven, hell would be spending the rest of my existence in a zombie zoo. So as far as I'm concerned, I've escaped hell. And since I've already dismembered my parents and put their body parts in Ziploc bags, I don't see how eating them can make things any worse.

After all, I am a zombie.

The first thing I need to figure out is how to cook Breather. Is it like beef? Like chicken? Or is it more like pork? Or kanga-roo? Or ostrich? And what parts are the best to eat?

In my mother's cookbook, under the section titled Meat, it says you can learn the difference between the tender and less tender cuts by remembering that exercise and age are what toughen meat. The most frequently exercised parts—the legs, neck, shoulder, rump, and flank—will be far tougher than the seldom exercised rib and loin.

I'm guessing that Breathers are more like cows than pigs or other farm or game animals. Cows are a lot bigger, obviously, but at least all of the parts sound the same.

The chuck primal cut runs from the neck to the fifth rib and includes the shoulder blade and upper arm. The shoul-der blade portion includes blade roasts and steaks, cross cuts, mock tender cuts, and of course, neck. The upper arm half in-cludes the arm roast, cross-rib roast, boneless shoulder roast, and the short ribs.

I decide to go with the ribs. Number one, it's what I'm craving. Number two, the loin portions of both of my par-ents would need to be defrosted. And number three, if I don't eat my mother and father's torsos soon, I'll end up having spoilage. And rotting human flesh doesn't smell like normal leftovers.

If you've never spent several hours in a closed room with half a dozen living corpses in various states of decay, then you probably wouldn't understand.

Putting my mother's torso into the refrigerator was apparently easier than getting it out. In retrospect, it would have been a good idea to leave at least one of her arms to use as a handle, but since I didn't have the foresight, I have to settle for using a two-pronged barbecue fork and a pair of tongs.

According to the cookbook, meat cut from the ribs is ideally cooked with high heat methods such as broiling, roasting, and grilling. Broiling seems like the easiest choice to me, so I turn on the oven and pull out the broiling pan, and then spray it down with some Pam to make sure my mother doesn't stick to it.

I look at my mother, sitting on the large wood cutting block on the kitchen counter, then grab the butcher knife and stand over her dismembered torso, trying to figure out where to start and if I should at least honor her with some kind of ceremony or ritual. Before I can make the first cut, I hear the sound of footsteps coming up the stairs from the wine cellar and turn around in time to see Rita appear in the open doorway.

"What's for dinner?" she asks.

Chapter 38

R ita and I are sitting at the kitchen table, eating by candle-light. More than half of the candles are gone, as is most of the 1978 Mondavi Cabernet Imperial Reserve. According to my father's ledger, this one is valued at $300.

When I didn't show up for the December World Death Tour at Holy Cross Cemetery, Rita and the others were concerned, so after she returned home, Rita snuck out and came over to see if I was okay. I would have enjoyed eating my parents alone, but having someone to share it with makes the experience that much more special.

In addition to the ribs—which Rita dressed up with a homemade sauce using lemon juice, Worcestershire sauce, and Dijon mustard that really brought out the natural flavor of my mother—we steamed an artichoke and some rice, then turned down the lights and lit the candles. I put on some Billie Holiday to make the meal complete.

When we finally sat down to eat, I thought I might hesitate at the thought of eating my mother. Oedipal complexes aside, it's just not something you ever think about when you start to plan out your future. But my mother's ribs were delicious. Except that doesn't do them justice. While the preserved

Breather that Ray gave us was salubrious and tasty, freshly cooked Breather is ambrosial. It's the difference between alba-core tuna salad and a freshly caught, seared ahi steak.

"Do you want any more ribs?" asks Rita.

I shake my head. Although there wasn't much meat on them, I can't eat another bite. I know that in the movies, zombies devour limbs and buckets of internal organs and can't seem to get enough. But that's just more Hollywood propaganda. Breathers are as rich and filling as a double chocolate soufflé. Granted, they're more savory than sweet, but it doesn't take much Breather meat to fill you up. Instead of craving more, you just want to loosen your belt and sit on the couch and watch Letterman.

I bet Hollywood zombies all end up with stomachaches.

Once we've finished our meal, I clear the dishes while Rita puts the leftovers into the refrigerator. As I stand at the sink and watch Rita pack my mother's barbecued ribs into a plastic Rubbermaid container, I'm overwhelmed with images of my parents, with memories of them that rush through my mind. Birthdays and holidays and graduations. My wedding and the birth of my daughter. Random snapshot moments shared with my parents who are now dead and stored in the Amana bottom freezer.

The last memory is of my mother, helping me apply foundation across my stitches.

Before I realize what's happening, I'm doubled over on the floor sobbing. Rita is behind me an instant later, her arms around me, her cheek next to mine. She doesn't say anything but just holds me, offering the comfort of her embrace. The slow, infrequent beating of her heart against my back soothes me, reminds me that my own heart stopped beating nearly five months ago and that those memories of my parents were from a life that has not only passed me by but has forsaken me. And I realize that the grief flowing out of me is not so much for the lives of my parents but for the life that I once shared with them, for the memories they gave me, and for the future memories that died when my Passat slammed into that redwood tree.

On top of the grief and regret, I realize that eventually someone's going to notice my parents are missing. Which means I'm up the proverbial stream without a paddle. Or a boat, for that matter. I can't take back what I've done and I can't expect to get away with it.

This is not a Disney movie.

I have no fairy godmother.

My life is not a do-over.

Except, in a way, it is. I died and was reborn. Not in a Jesus Christ sort of way, but then it's kind of hard to follow up the son of God, if you believe in that sort of thing. But like JC and all the born-again Christians, I've been given a second chance at life. True, Christ never officially rejoined the ranks of the living and I'm technically undead, so even if my heart starts beating and the blood starts pumping through my veins again, I don't think I'll reach Breather status. But I have another opportunity here and I can't capitalize on it by sitting on the kitchen floor and crying.

Gradually, the sobs taper off and I sit up. I burp once, tasting my mother in the back of my throat, but it doesn't set off another emotional release or make me want to vomit. I killed and ate my mother. Part of her, anyway. And that's something I just have to accept. It's part of who I am now and I can't do anything to change it. It is what it is.

I think that should be the new proclamation Helen puts up on the chalkboard at the next meeting:

IT IS WHAT IT IS.

While most of Helen's quotes are well-intentioned inspirations

I AM A SURVIVOR.

YOU ARE NOT ALONE.

FIND YOUR PURPOSE.

they don't offer the freedom of imperfection and the immunity from stigmatization of IT IS WHAT IT IS. After all, I can't change who or what I am any more than I can develop mammary glands and start breast-feeding.

And just like that, the catharsis from the release of grief is replaced by the liberation of accepting my situation, of accepting what I've become.

I am a zombie. One of the undead.

I am most definitely not alone.

And I believe I've found my purpose.

As if in response to my revelation, a flash of light fills the morning sky, followed by a boom of thunder. Moments later, it starts to rain.

Rita apparently senses the change in my mood and shifts around until she's in front of me. "Feeling better?"

I nod. I also believe I've come up with a way to buy some time regarding my parents. But the first thing I need to do is find out how much of a mess I made when I killed them.

Chapter 39

There's not as much blood as I expected. And most of that is in the bathtub. Apparently, an artery or two got a little out of control and sprayed across the tiled shower walls, but for the most part, the evidence of my parents' demise is an easy cleanup. Rita uses bleach and Lysol to cleanse and disinfect, then she takes a shower to give it that lived-in feeling.

My parents' bedroom is where I presume I ambushed them before dismembering them in the bathtub. The bed is in disarray, with the pillows on the floor and the bedding pulled halfway off. I find a few drops of blood on one of the pillowcases, so I remove it and its twin and stuff them into a plastic garbage bag, then strip the sheets and throw them into the washer while Rita puts a fresh set of linens on the bed.

Fortunately, my father is a preparation freak, so his and my mother's suitcases are packed and ready to go. Even the clothes they planned to wear for the drive to Palm Springs are hanging on the back of the bedroom door.

I'm a forty-four long while my father is a forty-two regular and Rita's at least a size smaller than my mother, but appearance is all that matters. And so long as the rain sticks around, no one's going to get a good look at us anyway.

Of course, if we can't get Jerry out of bed then we'll have to wait another twelve hours and I'd just as soon get this over with while I'm on a Breather high.

In addition to its restorative properties, fresh Breather provides an increased confidence, like a rush of adrenaline, only longer lasting. Kind of like Viagra. Of course, if I start to come down, I can always help myself to another serving of Mom or Dad. I have to get rid of the evidence eventually. But I'd prefer to take care of this part of saving my ass with the cover of rain and in the less-traveled hours of early morning.

By the time Rita and I get dressed and pack my parents' BMW 740 with the suitcases, the garbage bag, and the ice chest, it's pushing five in the morning. My left leg and arm still aren't better than sixty percent, so Rita has to drive.

Dressed in an Ann Taylor lavender pantsuit and ivory London Fog raincoat with matching gloves, Rita looks eerily like my mother, so I have to remain focused on the task at hand to keep from grossing myself out.

It's one thing to broil and eat your mother with homemade minute sauce. It's another to imagine taking her clothes off with your teeth.

We back out of the garage and into the rain. None of the neighbors are out before five on a Saturday morning, but I'm not worried about anyone witnessing our departure. My father always did like to get an early start. I just don't want anyone who knows my parents to flag us down for a chat.

Before we head to Jerry's, we swing by 7-Eleven. I wait in the car and watch through the store windows while Rita goes inside. The woman behind the counter doesn't give Rita a second glance. So far so good. And I doubt the clerk would suspect that the woman who just drove up in a BMW and walked into the store at five in the morning on a rainy December Saturday is one of the undead.

While I'm waiting, ready to join Rita if anything goes wrong, I notice a vibration, faint at first, but growing stronger. The vibrations are spaced out about every ten to twelve seconds, but there's no doubt where they're originating.

They're coming from inside me.

Less than two minutes after entering 7-Eleven, Rita walks out the door with her purchase and I pop the trunk. Once she puts the block of ice into the ice chest, she's back in the driver's seat.

"Piece of cake," she says.

I lean over and kiss her, taking her hand and holding it against my chest. When she tries to pull away to start the engine, I hold her there and she gives me a look of surprise.

"Isn't this a little . . ."

I put my fingers to her lips. A moment later, she realizes what I'm doing and when she feels my heart beat, her face breaks open in a beautiful smile and we embrace, our two hearts beating irregularly, but together.

Both of us would like to have more time to enjoy the moment, but time isn't a luxury we have. Number one, the sun will be coming up in less than two hours. And number two, we need to get to where we're going before the block of ice melts.

It's only a few minutes' drive to Jerry's, but every time headlights appear on the road ahead of us or in the sideview mirror, my heart starts racing. True, it beats once every nine seconds instead of ten, but when your heart hasn't worked for more than four months, "racing" becomes a relative term.

Fortunately, Jerry's awake. I don't know what he's doing up at five in the morning, but when I tap on his window, his face appears from behind the curtains within seconds. At first he has his scary face on, the one zombies use to chase away lookie-loos, until he realizes it's me.

"Dude," he says, opening the window.

I hold my finger to my lips and then motion for him to come outside. He disappears behind the curtains again, then reappears in a hooded sweatshirt, jeans, and black Converse All-Stars and climbs out the window.

"What's going on?" he whispers.

"I need your help," I say.

The fact that he doesn't ask me what the help is for lets me know that he's going to give it no matter what. And I realize that Jerry is one of the best friends I've ever had.

"Hey, Rita," says Jerry, once we're in the BMW. "Nice ride. Is this yours?"

"Andy's parents'," she says, putting the car in drive and pulling away.

"Dude," he says. "Won't they be totally pissed?"

Rita and I look at each other and smirk.

"What?" says Jerry.

As we drive, I fill Jerry in on what happened and what we plan to do. When I'm finished, Jerry sits in the backseat, picking at the healing scabs on his face, staring at me.

"Dude, you ate your mother?"

I nod.

He's silent again for a few seconds.

"What part?"

I tell him.

"How did she taste?" he asks.

"Better than what Ray gave us," I say.

Jerry doesn't say anything for nearly a full minute and I'm beginning to think that maybe this was too much for him to absorb. Sure, we're zombies. And yes, it turns out we tend to have an affinity for human flesh. But they were still my parents. They were still family. Maybe that's taboo even among the undead.

Then Jerry leans forward between the two front seats and says, "Can I come over for lunch?"

We pull up behind the granary at a quarter after five. No one is around when we arrive and I hope we can get out of here before any Breathers drive past. Ray's Lumina is still parked behind the bushes. So long as the keys are in the glove box, we shouldn't have a problem.

"We have a problem," says Jerry.

I glance back at the granary. A few days ago, I wouldn't have been able to see anything but rain and darkness surrounding the dilapidated building. But with my improved vision, I can make out smoke rising through the broken roof.

When we enter the back door of the granary, I expect to see Ray sitting on the other side of the fire, drinking a beer and eating some Breather meat out of a jar like a scene out of an old western. Instead, Ray is joined by Zack and Luke. A fourth figure is lying on the ground between them. He's not moving.

"Howdy," says Ray, his mouth half full. "Pull up a seat and join the party."

The three of them are roasting limbs over the open fire. A makeshift curing rack sits above the fire with thin strips of meat hanging from hooks. Several jars of freshly packed meat sit off to the side next to a bloody saw and several curved hunting knives. While the limbs are roasting, Luke reaches into the body cavity of the dead man on the ground, pulls out what looks like the liver, and bites it in two, giving the other half to his twin brother.

Rita and I had a snack before we left, so we're not hungry. Jerry, on the other hand, is salivating.

"Dude, is this what you did with your parents?"

Not exactly, I tell him.

Ray finishes cooking the dead guy's right arm and starts

tearing into it with his teeth. Zack and Luke follow suit with the lower right and left legs, ripping off pieces of blackened flesh and washing them down with beer.

Not to mince words, but watching the three of them roast and devour human limbs over an open fire seems less civilized than broiling my mother's ribs and eating them by candlelight with a steamed artichoke while listening to Billie Holiday.

Or maybe it's just me.

Jerry approaches the fire and helps himself to a piece of partially cured meat.

"Guess you kinda figured out it wasn't venison in those jars after all," says Ray, talking around a piece of forearm.

"Kinda," I say.

"Hey," he says. "That's pretty good. Your limp seems mighty improved, too. I think it took less than a week for my gunshot wound to heal up once I started eatin' Breather regular."

It occurs to me that Ray's wife probably never kicked him out due to the fact that she couldn't stand the smell. Or if she did, Ray went back and packed her into Mason jars.

"Ray," says Rita. "We need to borrow your car."

"Sure thing," says Ray, picking at his teeth with an exposed finger bone. "Keys are in the storage bin. You folks got some cleanin' up to do?"

"Something like that," says Rita.

While Rita grabs the keys, Jerry grabs a piece of Breather jerky and stuffs the whole thing in his mouth, then grabs another piece for the road. Never once does he ask to see any of Ray's *Playboys*.

As we leave the granary, I glance back inside and Ray waves a hand at me—not his own, but the dead guy's left hand, which he then skewers and holds over the fire. Next to him, Zack and Luke gnaw on a fibula.

So much for your kinder, gentler zombies.

Chapter 40

Highway 1 south of Santa Cruz winds through Monterey and past Carmel before becoming a truly coastal highway. Trees and cliffs line one side of the two-lane road, while on the ocean side, waves crash against the rocks more than a hundred feet below.

About fifteen miles past Big Sur, all signs of community vanish and there's nothing but uninhabited highway, almost deserted just before sunrise. It's still raining, which makes the road a little treacherous, perfect conditions for an accident.

At a turn in the road where the guardrail gives way to a natural overlook, the only barrier between the road and the fifteen-story drop to the ocean below are some shin-high rocks. After checking to make sure there aren't any cars coming from either direction, we double back to a spot in the highway just before the overlook, pull over, and keep the cars running. We transferred the ice chest, my backpack, and the garbage bag with my parents' contaminated bedding into the Lumina before we left the granary, so all we need to do is grab the block of ice and hope no one shows up.

Rita gets in behind the wheel of the Lumina while Jerry

carries the block of ice over to my parents' BMW. After I make sure the car is pointed straight at the turnout, I disengage the emergency brake, put the car in neutral, then roll down the driver's side window and get out of the car. I realize leaving the window open might look suspicious considering the weather, but I'm just trying to buy some time, not commit the perfect crime. Besides, I can't figure out any other way to get the car into drive while I'm standing outside of it.

Jerry places the block of ice on the gas pedal and the tachometer needle pushes up to over 4,000 rpms. As soon as he's out of the way, I slip a piece of cord around the automatic gearshift in the center console, then take both ends and slide them out through the window after closing the door.

Part of me thinks I should say something to mark the occasion, or at least ask someone to forgive me for what I've done. So I tell my parents I'm sorry and that I hope they can understand. Then I pull on both ends of the cord until the shifter slips into drive and I let go of one end of the cord as the BMW's rear wheels spin on the wet asphalt for a few seconds before the car takes off, racing toward the overlook.

I have a moment to consider what I'm going to do if the car veers off course or if the block of ice falls off the accelerator, but then the BMW zooms onto the overlook, hits the rocks, and flies out over the cliff before it starts to nosedive and disappears from sight.

Jerry runs over to the edge and looks down. I know we should probably get out of here before someone comes by, but I have to look. I get there just in time to see the BMW hit the water roof first with a distant crunch. For a few seconds it floats there, tires spinning, undercarriage pointing toward the sky, then it vanishes beneath the waves.

Jerry turns to me and says, "Dude, that was awesome."

Except for a couple of large rocks that are knocked out of place, you'd never know a car had driven over the edge of the cliff.

Rita pulls up in the Lumina. "Come on, you two. Show's over. Let's get out of here."

Jerry climbs into the backseat while I join Rita up front. After checking once more to verify the highway is clear in both directions, Rita turns around and drives back the way we came.

"Any problems?" asks Rita.

I shake my head.

My parents' bags are packed and in the BMW's trunk. Rita and I both wore gloves so we wouldn't leave any fingerprints. The block of ice will melt away. And by the time someone ever finds the car, hopefully the fact that there aren't any bodies in it will be chalked up to tides and undercurrents and scavengers.

At least that's what I'm hoping. Eventually, someone's going to realize my parents aren't home and even if I've managed to get rid of the physical evidence, I'm going to be suspected in their disappearance. But once you eat part of your mother during a candlelight dinner with your undead girlfriend, you pretty much know that you've chosen a path most people just aren't going to understand.

We only see one other car on the highway between Big Sur and Carmel, and only light traffic through Monterey as the dawn comes and goes. We exit the highway and find a Dumpster behind a closed grocery store where we dispose of my parents' bloodstained linens and the clothes Rita and I wore. We brought a change of clothes in my backpack and Jerry gawks as Rita strips down to her underwear before slipping into her own clothes. For some reason, he's not as interested in watching me get undressed.

As Jerry drives us out of Monterey, it occurs to me that Annie is less than five minutes away. I think about how easy it would be for us to drive over to where she lives so I can tell her that I'm still here and that I still love her. I can almost imagine myself walking up to the front door and seeing the look on her face when she opens it. But that would create all kinds of problems, not only for Annie but for me and my current predicament. The last thing I want to do is let my former sister-in-law and her husband know that I was in the neighborhood. That would pretty much kill my cover.

But in addition to personal prudence, going to see Annie just doesn't seem like a good idea.

First of all, I'm not really her father anymore. I understand that now. Killing and eating your parents has a kind of illuminating effect on one's true nature. Better for Annie to remember me the way I used to be. As a human. As a loving father and a good son. Second, I just don't think it's a good idea to expose her to what I've become, for me or for her. I don't know what I would say or how I should act or what kind of role I could play in her life.

Plus I'd hate to think that I'd look at my daughter and wonder how she'd taste in an asparagus and cheese casserole.

Chapter 41

One good way to use leftover Breather is to mix together ½ pound cooked macaroni, 1½ pints canned tomato sauce, 2-3 cups diced cooked Breather, ¼ pound sautéed sliced mushrooms, some minced garlic, salt and pepper. Spoon mixture into a greased 2½-quart casserole dish, top with grated cheese, and bake, uncovered, about 30 minutes at 375 degrees F until bubbly. Makes about six servings.

In addition to my initial late-night snack with Rita last Saturday, I've had three square meals of fresh Breather for the past three days. Breather bacon, Breather burritos, Breather and cheese sandwiches, roast Breather, Breather burgers, Breather hash, Breather stroganoff, teriyaki Breather, spaghetti with Breather balls, and old-fashioned Breather stew.

And it shows.

My left ankle is a little unstable and there's still a hitch in my step, but other than that, I don't notice any structural difference between my left and right ankles. The tibia, fibula, and talus seem to have reconnected completely, while all of the ligaments have reattached.

In addition to my ankle, my left arm is functional and regenerating muscle and bone on a daily basis and my stitches have completely fallen out. The makeup my mother bought for me sits unused and forgotten at the bottom of a wastebasket.

Although my pallor is still pasty, all shades of gray have vanished. My heart beats twelve times a minute now, which is a 100 percent increase since it first started beating. At that rate, it'll be beating over sixty times per minute by Christmas.

I'm sweating. I'm talking. I'm respirating and pumping fluid through my veins and engaging half a dozen other physiological functions that I never thought I'd be capable of again. But I've moved beyond wonder at the changes taking place within me. Now, it's a matter of acceptance, of understanding what I'm becoming. What we're all becoming.

We're healing. Evolving into a subspecies of humans. Neo-Breathers. The self-healing, walking undead. And if Rita and I are any indication of what can happen when we eat fresh Breather on a regular basis, then I can't wait to share Mom and Dad with the rest of the gang.

But even though we're redeveloping definite human physiological functions, I wonder—are we still able to reanimate if fatally injured? Will the genetic abnormality that turned us into zombies in the first place prevent us from being killed? Will the healing effects of Breather prevent us from having to worry about Band-Aids and Neosporin and health insurance?

Last night, while preparing a Momloaf with mashed potatoes and fresh spinach, I sliced open the index finger on my left hand. A Breather would have been gushing blood, applying gauze, probably getting a ride to the hospital for stitches. But since my body hasn't replenished my full ten pints of red cells, white cells, platelets, and plasma, the blood barely trickled out. This morning when I woke up, the wound had nearly closed up.

Somehow I doubt the USDA is going to rush out and add Breather to the food pyramid, but a diet that includes fresh or recently prepared Breather has nutritional qualities that make the recommended daily servings of fruits and vegetables seem like five to eight bowls of Cocoa Puffs.

After having leftover Momloaf, I decide to take a leisurely stroll through town to clear my head and to take care of some unfinished business. The weekend rain has moved on but the clouds are still thick, blocking out the moon. Save for the occasional illumination from a street lamp, the road is completely dark before six o'clock. But even if it wasn't, I wouldn't need to disguise what I am. No one can tell. Not at first glance. Or even second glance. Not unless you get right up in my face would you be able to see that there's something not quite human about me.

With my parents out of the picture, I don't have to keep up the daily pretense of being the consummate zombie, which makes taking walks much less arduous. And with my improved physical appearance, no one throws tomatoes or Big Gulps at me out of car windows.

It's the simple things that make undeath pleasant.

Rita thinks excessive public exposure is risky. If anyone suspects I'm a zombie and calls Animal Control, then I'll end up at the SPCA without any next of kin to bail me out. She has a point. But other than a handful of unchaperoned excursions and the weekly UA meetings, I've been more or less imprisoned in the wine cellar for nearly five months. With Mom and Dad gone in almost every sense of the word, I feel like I've been paroled. And honestly, when your wounds heal overnight and you start to feel a bit like an immortal, playing it safe just seems so Clark Kent.

I pass by the granary and consider stopping by to see if Ray and the twins are dining on another homeless person, but I'll have to pay a social call another time. Besides the fact that it would be bad form to drop in unannounced for dinner, I have something I need to take care of. And I already ate.

As usual after sundown, the Soquel Cemetery is deserted. Other than teenagers on a dare or out for some thrills, Breathers pretty much stay away from cemeteries at night. I don't blame them. Even in my new and improved condition, I wouldn't want to run into me walking out from the shadow of my wife's tombstone.

I didn't bring any flowers this time, but then I'm not here to pay my respects or to seek solace. I'm here to say good-bye.

I still miss my wife. I still miss the life we shared. But she's dead and I'm a zombie. I have to let go. I have to move on.

"Hi, Rachel," I say out loud. It's the first time I've spoken her name since the summer heat of late July. In the cold bite of December, her name explodes from my mouth in an ephemeral cloud that vanishes before it reaches her headstone.

I tell Rachel how much I love her. How I'm sorry she died. How I wish things wouldn't have ended like this. I tell her about Rita and Ray and the venison that wasn't really venison. Then I tell her about my parents. Well, not everything. I leave out the part about the chocolate fondue.

They say confession is good for the soul. But then, I don't know if I have a soul. If I had one, it probably departed my body when I died. Or maybe it never left. Maybe it's just trapped in a dead vessel, a purgatory of decomposing flesh, waiting for a second chance. But whatever sins I may have committed as a Breather to deserve being sentenced to zombie prison, I don't think I'm exactly making a good impression on the parole board. My guess is, I won't be getting an early release for good behavior.

I finish with my confession and realize this is it. This is the last time I'll ever come out to visit Rachel's grave, to touch the memory of the life we once shared. And even though it's necessary, even though I know I have to move on, it's harder than I imagined it would be. Harder than saying good-bye to my parents. Harder than saying good-bye to Annie.

For the first and last time, I cry for my lost wife.

Just as I'm wrapping up my good-byes to Rachel, something comes crashing through the brush at the south end of the cemetery. I don't know who or what it is, but more than one set of feet are running my way.

I duck behind Rachel's tombstone, which isn't big enough for me to hide behind. My ex-in-laws never lavished much attention on their daughter in life, so it's no surprise they stayed true to form in death. I make a mental note to eat them if at all possible, then hunker down and hope whoever I heard doesn't see me.

Two figures run behind the main building, then reappear on the other side and race past me among the headstones and trees. Even in the darkness I recognize Zack and Luke. They never look my way but keep running until they arrive at the far north corner, near the back of the cemetery, where an old, shingle-covered wooden storage shed sits bordered on two sides by ivy-covered oaks. Moments later, they crawl through an opening and vanish from sight.

I get the impression they're not playing hide-and-seek.

I stay where I am, not wanting to move and give myself away to anyone who might be following the twins. But after several minutes, I decide that whatever Zack and Luck were running from didn't pursue them this far. Maybe they weren't pursued at all. Maybe they were just trying to get away from a bad scene.

I suddenly wonder where Ray is.

I'd ask the twins but they've never done more than grunt, purr, or giggle, so I figure I have to find out for myself.

Staying back from the road as far as possible, I work my way through the brush and along the edge of Soquel Creek until I reach the granary. Even before I arrive I hear voices and see the flashing lights. And Breathers. Lots of them. When I finally get a glimpse, I understand what sent Zack and Luke running.

Several police cars and an Animal Control van are parked around the rear entrance to the granary with two spotlights illuminating the scene. From my vantage point behind a thicket of manzanita, I can see into the granary through the open doorway, out of which stumbles a police officer who staggers over to one of the cars and throws up.

Nearly everyone is wearing some kind of particle mask or covering their mouths and noses. Although I can't make out everything being said, I hear words and phrases like "carnage" and "mutilated bodies" and "spit-roasted." Even from where I'm hiding more than a hundred feet away, I can smell the aroma of barbecued Breather.

I'm beginning to think that maybe Ray managed to get away before the raid like Zack and Luke, but then I see him brought out, strapped down to a gurney. Ray's struggling to get loose, without success, and I can hear him trying to shout through the restraint strapped across his mouth.

In spite of the fact that Ray's gagged and bound, everyone gives the gurney a wide berth, moving away from it as if it's transporting nuclear waste. Not until Ray is loaded into the back of one of the Animal Control vans and the rear doors close do the Breathers relax.

I want to help Ray but I know if I tried I'd just end up in the back of the van with him. This is a trip Ray's going to have to make on his own. He won't get to make a phone call, he won't get a trial by his peers, he won't be protected by any of the First Amendment rights of the Constitution, and no one will come to his defense.

I stay hidden and watch as the van drives off, knowing that I'll never see Ray again.

Chapter 42

"Poor Ray," says Rita.

She's wearing a pink V-neck cashmere sweater with skin-tight white polyester/Lycra blend pants, and black boots. Her lips are Euphoric Pink.

"Poor Ray?" says Carl. "What about the rest of us?"

"Jesus, Carl," says Naomi, lighting another cigarette and exhaling. "Don't you ever think about anyone but yourself?"

The irony of her accusation drifts through the group in a cloud of secondhand smoke.

"I think about you every time I see a commercial for golf clubs," says Carl.

Naomi responds with the requisite hostility, prompting another exchange from Carl, while Tom and Leslie try to play peacemaker. Jerry finds the entire scene amusing and just laughs. Beth laughs along with him in a show of solidarity.

"Carl's right," says Helen, her voice rising above the din.

Everyone stops talking, laughing, or arguing and looks at Helen. On the chalkboard behind her is written:

I WILL NOT BE A VICTIM.

A little more proactive than her usual inspirational

quotes, but considering what happened to Ray, it seems like bad timing.

"The local authorities aren't likely to treat what they found at Ray's as an anomaly."

Jerry looks around with a blank expression. My guess is he's never heard the word "anomaly" before. "Is that, like, some kind of Indian food?" he asks.

"It means they won't think he's the only one eating Breathers," says Rita.

"Oh," says Jerry. "Bummer."

Bummer is right. I've got two big bummers in the freezer at home.

"Chances are they're going to monitor our activities much more closely," says Helen. "Scrutinize our behavior, maybe even remove some of us from circulation to keep the rest of us in line."

"That totally sucks," says Jerry.

"Totally," agrees Beth.

The two of them knuckle five each other softly, then each take a swig from their cans of Orange Crush. All Beth needs now is an Oakland A's baseball cap on sideways and pants hanging off her ass.

"So what should we do?" asks Tom.

"First thing," says Helen, "is we all need to try to be discreet and not draw attention to ourselves."

I feel the temperature in the room rise about ten degrees.

"And it would probably be a good idea if we all refrained from eating Breather."

I'm driving through Death Valley in a car without air conditioning.

"What about Andy's parents?" says Jerry.

I hear the Kalahari Desert is nice this time of year.

Discussing how you've killed and eaten your parents is personal—it's something you'd prefer to share with others when the timing seems appropriate. But the UA handbook doesn't address zombie etiquette when dealing with something like this, so I have to cut Jerry some slack.

"What about your parents?" asks Helen.

With Rita's help, I explain what happened. Then I bring out the Ziploc bags with cooked pieces of my parents to share with everyone. No one refuses the offering. Not even Helen.

"Well," says Carl, licking his lips as he devours part of my father's shoulder. "So much for refraining."

For the next few minutes, the only sounds are those of teeth tearing into flesh and moans of carnal pleasure that are impossible to describe.

If you've never been in a roomful of zombies eating freshly cooked pieces of human flesh, then you probably wouldn't understand.

"Mmmmm mmmmm," says Naomi, savoring the last of one of my mother's breasts. "This is better than sex."

"Speak for yourself," says Rita.

Everyone looks at Rita and me with varying degrees of surprise or mirth, followed by laughter and whistles and good-natured teasing.

"I hate to break the good mood," says Helen, "but if Andy gets caught with a refrigerator full of Breather, every one of us will probably get donated to science."

"So how do we get rid of his parents?" asks Tom.

No one says anything. They just look at each other, then at the floor, then at the chalkboard. Anywhere but at me.

"If I might make a suggestion," says Leslie, stripping the last slivers of flesh from the bones of my father's left hand. "I think it would be best if we ate them."

"You mean like a barbecue?" says Jerry.

For good barbecued Breather, add 1 tablespoon each ketchup,

Worcestershire sauce, red wine vinegar, and chili powder, ¼ teaspoon salt, and ⅛ teaspoon cayenne pepper. Mix with ground Breather, shape and cook over an open fire.

"What part of 'being discreet and not drawing attention to ourselves' did you not understand?" says Carl.

"We're zombies," says Rita. "We draw attention to ourselves simply by existing."

"Existing and standing around with a beer and a Breather burger aren't exactly the same thing," says Carl.

"Actually," says Leslie, "I was thinking more along the lines of a dinner party."

"Didn't you listen to Helen?" says Carl. "The zombie patrol is going to monitor our behavior more closely after what happened out at Ray's."

"I heard what Helen said," says Rita. "But I think the longer we wait, the greater our chances of being caught."

Carl offers up a counterpoint but his argument is met by a chorus of support for the barbecue. Even Helen seems to acknowledge that we need to get rid of the evidence before Sunday, though Tom sides with Carl because he's afraid of what will happen if we get caught.

In the middle of everything, I get up from my chair and walk over to the chalkboard and erase the quote that Helen had written earlier:

I WILL NOT BE A VICTIM.

No one tries to stop me or asks me what I'm doing. I didn't even know I was going to do it. But then I'm picking up the chalk and writing down my own quote. I feel the same way I did when I made my signs before I went out to protest for zombie rights. But this time, my message is reaching the right audience.

When I finish, no one is arguing. No one is talking. They're all just staring at the chalkboard, at the six words I've written, and nodding their heads:

WE HAVE THE RIGHT TO EXIST.

"Okay," says Carl. "Where should we have this barbecue?"

"How about Andy's?" asks Tom.

Rita explains that we don't want to draw attention to the fact that my parents are dead, so throwing a party at my house with them as the main course probably isn't a good idea.

"We could have it at my place," says Jerry. "My parents are out of town all weekend."

Rita suggests Saturday after sunset to cut down on any excessive lookie-loos. Helen offers up transportation to get the rest of my parents over to Jerry's. Leslie and Naomi offer to make hors d'oeuvres. And Carl offers to cook. I, of course, will bring the wine.

"All right," says Helen. "We're all agreed. Now let's just try to keep this as discreet as possible."

Chapter 43

Oingo Boingo's "Dead Man's Party" is blasting from the stereo speakers when Rita and I arrive at Jerry's.

Waiting for an invitation to arrive
Going to a party where no one's still alive

Rita is wearing a sheer red blouse with a red bra and a matching miniskirt. She's also wearing red thong underwear that says *Thursday* even though this is Saturday. Red knee-high platforms complete the outfit.

Out back, Carl is tending the barbecue.

He's prepared the lower portions of my parents' anatomy into multiple edible forms, including top loin strips, bottom round steaks, flank steaks, and ground Mom and Dad shaped into burgers. Since I'm in the mood for steak and since I don't trust what part of my parents Carl ground up to make the burgers, I choose a top loin strip, while Rita opts for the bottom round.

"How do you want it cooked?" asks Carl.

"Medium well," I say.

I still have problems with the concept of eating uncooked

human flesh, though I don't need mine cooked well-done like Tom, who still insists on throwing a couple of tofu dogs on the grill so he feels like he's maintaining a vegetarian diet.

Rita asks for hers rare.

While Carl throws our Breather steaks over the coals, Rita and I wander inside in search of the host.

Naomi and Leslie are in the kitchen splitting a bottle of 2000 Beringer Merlot and preparing appetizers. There's liver pâté with homemade crostini, kidney-stuffed mushrooms, beer-battered fingers, and fresh Breather cocktail.

Apparently, my parents aren't the only ones on the menu this evening.

"You two hungry?" asks Naomi, offering us a plate of deep fried fingers with ranch sauce.

Rita takes one but I decline. I'm not much for finger food.

I set down two bottles of wine from my father's collection—a 1992 Au Bon Climat Pinot Noir and a 1990 Chateau Latour Bordeaux. The Pinot runs $1,500 a bottle, so I pour Rita and myself a glass each, then ask if anyone's seen Jerry.

"He's giving tours of his bedroom," says Leslie, pouring the last of the Merlot into her glass.

"His bedroom?" says Rita. "What's so special about his bedroom that he's giving tours?"

"Oh, you have *got* to check it out," says Naomi, opening the Bordeaux. "You will not believe it."

As we walk through the house and down the hallway to Jerry's room, I try to imagine what it is that Jerry has done with his room that is so outlandish as not to be believed, but nothing I can come up with compares with the reality.

When Rita and I walk into the bedroom, Jerry is sitting on the foot of his bed with Beth. No one else is in the room. At least, no one three-dimensional.

Dozens of naked women from the pages of *Playboy* stare

out at us from the walls. Not a single square inch of plaster is visible. But it's obvious from the positions of the women, from their poses and expressions and the way they're arranged on the walls, that Jerry didn't just tack them up at random, without any thought or purpose. There's a definite design here, a creation of art that strikes me as familiar but escapes me until I look up at the ceiling.

"Oh my god," says Rita.

It's the Sistine Chapel.

Directly above us, Miss February 1998 is accepting the forbidden fruit while two other Playmates are expelled from the Garden of Eden. Next to that panel, in the center of the ceiling, the Creation of Eve is an homage to the 1997 Playmate of the Year.

The Deluge is an erotic creation of various Playmates dripping wet in showers, bathtubs, and waterfalls, while the Separation of Light from Darkness features a fair-skinned Miss September 2000 surrounded by four nude black Playmates.

Each panel, from the Separation of Light from Darkness to the Drunkenness of Noah, is re-created with naked, beautiful women in erotic poses. There's Miss January 1994 and Miss May 2000 among the Ancestors of Christ, while the Prophets are depicted by an apparent chronological representation of the Playmates of the Year. Granted, it's not perfect. After all, you can't expect to find an exact match for every image created by Michelangelo in the pages of *Playboy*. But when you look up and see Miss June 2003 in a swirl of lingerie reaching out to an awaiting Miss January 1994, there is no doubt that you are beholding the Creation of Adam.

It's very artistic, almost spiritual. In a tits and ass kind of way.

"What do you think?" asks Jerry.

"Unbelievable," says Rita, moving about the room to get a closer look. The two walls on either side of Jerry's bed depict the life of Moses and the life of Christ, while the Last Judgment forms the centerpiece of Jerry's work on the wall above his bed. "And I just thought you spent a lot of time masturbating."

"Yeah, well, there's that, too," says Jerry.

Beth giggles and squeezes Jerry's hand.

Maybe it's just the overwhelming sexuality of being surrounded by dozens of naked women, but I get the feeling Jerry won't be servicing himself tonight. True, Beth is only sixteen, but somehow I doubt anyone is going to charge Jerry with statutory rape.

Once Carl has finished cooking up Mom and Dad, everyone gathers in the dining room for dinner. All counted, there are twelve of us—including Zack and Luke, who I suggested we invite, and Ian, whom Helen invited. He's still legally a Breather. And a defense attorney. Which will both be helpful if any neighbors call the zombie patrol.

I'm sitting at one end of the room, flanked by Rita and Carl, surveying the spread of food laid out across the table. Brussels sprouts and butternut squash, mashed potatoes and Breather gravy, baked tofu in spinach with peanut sauce for Tom. And, of course, my parents, prepared and cooked in various ways for all to enjoy.

"Andy," says Helen, "would you like to say a few words?"

I keep it brief, thanking my parents for making this meal possible. I say it perfectly. Except for an occasional problem with pronouncing soft consonants, my speech has returned to normal.

I walk without a limp.

My heart is now beating once every two seconds.

As far as I know, other than Rita and me, none of the others have had a revival of their internal organs. But they're all healing.

Tom's alien right arm has reconnected to his socket and the flaps of skin on his face have begun to reattach.

Jerry's skull has almost completely reformed.

Naomi can't put her cigarettes out in her eye socket anymore because the nerves have started firing again.

And Helen's exit wound has started to close up.

Helen adds her own words about being grateful that she's able to share this meal with all of us. "You are my family," she says. "You are what comforts me."

Everyone raises a glass to toast. I notice Leslie and Naomi are wiping away tears. Even Carl's eyes are moist. Helen is right. We are a family. Gathered around this Thanksgiving-like feast, we could almost pass for Breathers.

Then we all dig in.

In zombie movies, whenever the undead dine, there's no conversation, just the primal rending and devouring of flesh. True, we have vegetables and tofu and we're using plates and utensils instead of our laps and hands, but nobody says a word. All you can hear is the sound of consumption. So for once, Hollywood got it right.

After dinner is finished and the dishes are all cleaned up, the lights are dimmed and everyone gathers around the television with popcorn and Breather jerky to watch George Romero's original *Night of the Living Dead*. I snuggle up with Rita on the couch next to Carl and Leslie, while Beth sits on Jerry's lap and Zack and Luke curl up in a single chair.

When the movie starts, everyone is in a festive mood—laughing and making lewd comments, throwing popcorn at each other. It's an interactive experience. We all cheer whenever a Breather gets killed and boo whenever a zombie gets destroyed. But when the zombies start to feed, the audience falls silent.

I'd seen *Night of the Living Dead* a few times while I was alive, but not since college. And I'd never really taken the movie seriously. This time I find it fascinating. Not from a filmmaking standpoint—plot, story, direction, all that artsy crap. I'm talking about something more spiritual.

A moment of clarity.

An epiphany about my own existence.

And I don't think I'm the only one who feels it.

While it's doubtful I or anyone else legally classified as one of the undead will ever regain our status among the living, that doesn't mean we don't have aspirations that go beyond keeping our bodies maggot-free.

The undead aspire to be Breathers. It's what we once were and what we wish we could be again. But in a world that considers us inhuman, there is no hope of reclaiming our humanity. There is no one to redeem us. We've been forsaken—by society, by friends, by family. So we have to find a way to redeem ourselves.

There are defining moments in everyone's existence, some more monumental than others:

Neil Armstrong's first step for mankind.

Bobby Thompson's shot heard round the world.

Rosa Parks refusing to give up her seat on the bus.

Each of them found their moment and seized it, turned it into an act that embodied a quest. A triumph. A dream.

Sooner or later, everyone reaches their moment. For some it passes by unnoticed or unrealized. For others, it hits them while watching a black-and-white B horror film from 1968.

This is our moment. This is our time.

Chapter 44

When you die, your Social Security number gets retired, which isn't a problem if you stay dead. But if you come back, become a zombie due to some latent genetic abnormality or because you consumed too many Twinkies while you were alive, well then, you're pretty much screwed. Since the undead aren't considered human beings, even by Breathers who don't belong to organized religions, the chances of reclaiming your Social Security number are about as good as a town in Wyoming electing a gay sheriff.

Without a Social Security number, you can't get a job, apply for federal or state assistance, or get financial aid to go to school. Which makes earning a living tough to do, even if you haven't reanimated from the dead and started eating human flesh. Except in Tennessee. I hear they have more relaxed guidelines there.

After some searching of my parents' house, I find my birth certificate and driver's license in a box in the master bedroom closet. I also find a book on Kama Sutra, a bottle of massage oil, a set of leather wrist cuffs with restraints, a dildo, and three Polaroids of my naked mother.

I think I need to make another appointment to see my therapist.

In order to reclaim a Social Security number from an erroneous death, you need to prove U.S. citizenship, age, and identity. If you're over the age of twelve, you have to appear at a Social Security office in person.

Back when most people still didn't own a television, you could obtain a birth certificate, photo ID, and a Social Security number entirely through the mail. But in the post 9/11, post–Patriot Act United States, that's no longer possible.

Even if it was, I have no intention of getting my Social Security number fraudulently. I don't want to make up a fake name and a fake identity to subvert the system in order to get my life back. I want to level the playing field. I want Breathers to *know* I'm a zombie. I want them to fear my existence in a way they never considered.

As equals.

Like all government agencies, the local Social Security Administration office has about as much warmth and charm as a Turkish prison, just without the beatings, torture, executions, extortion, and occasional hostage-taking.

There are four service windows in the back, with a security door adjacent to the first window and a waiting area that consists of four rows of chairs. The rent-a-cop podium inside the front door to the left is unoccupied when I enter. Opposite the podium is a computer check-in system:

Select 0 if you have an appointment.

Select 1 if you have other business.

I didn't bother to call ahead for an appointment, which doesn't look like a problem since there's a solitary Breather sitting in the waiting area and another one standing at the only open service window, talking to the clerk. So I press 1 and the thermal printer spits out a ticket with A75 on it.

I take a seat in the third row, two chairs over and one row back from a middle-aged woman who's reading a magazine.

Less than ten seconds after I sit down, the woman shivers once and pulls her sweater close around her. Before her number is called, she gets up and leaves the building.

I have that effect on people.

The elderly man at the counter finishes up his business and walks toward the exit, turning a shade of gray as he passes me. Then the service representative calls out my number.

The first thing I do now when I see Breathers is size them up. Would they be good in a stew or are they better suited for charbroiling? Do they look more like filet mignon or more like sloppy joes? It's a matter of preference, really. Or how much effort you want to put into preparing your meal. If you can't make up your mind, you can always just club them, gloss with olive oil, add some anchovy fillets and capers, and call it carpaccio.

The Social Security service rep looks like sloppy joes.

"How can I help you?" he says with a smile that's more of a grimace.

He reminds me of Ted that way, minus the gold hoop earring and the collagen injections.

I tell him I'd like to get my Social Security number reinstated.

"Reinstated?" he asks. "Why was the number originally flagged?"

"An erroneous death," I say.

He stares at me for several moments, that false smile still stretched across his face. "That's a little complicated."

I show him my birth certificate and driver's license, as well as my passport, and give him my Social Security number.

He takes my documents, then types my number into his computer. Perspiration is forming on his forehead, beading up in little drops. Whatever shows up on his computer monitor drains the color from his face.

"It . . . it says here you're deceased," he says, his voice cracking.

An erroneous death, I remind him.

He looks at me, then at the monitor, then turns and looks behind him. He's all alone.

"Gary!" he calls out.

"Is there a problem?" I ask.

"Gary!"

"Excuse me," I say.

He turns back to me, his face ashen, then he glances at the monitor. "Our records show that you . . . that Andrew Warner . . . that he died on July fourteenth and reanimated three days later."

"Just like Christ," I say. "And now I'd like to have my Social Security number reinstated, if you don't mind."

"That's . . . ," he says, stepping back from the counter. "That's not possible."

"Why not?" I ask.

"Because . . . ," he says, backing up and reaching for the telephone. "Because . . ."

"Step away from the window."

I turn to look and Gary, the rent-a-cop, is standing to my left near the security door. His right hand hovers near his gun. Like that's going to help him. He could pump every round of his clip into me and I'd still manage to have him spit roasted before *Oprah*.

Behind the counter, the service rep is calling the police.

"I just want my Social Security number," I say.

Gary removes his gun from its holster and levels it at me. "I said, step away from the window."

I don't particularly want to get shot, so I step back.

"Put your hands on top of your head."

I do it with a sigh. This is just so inconvenient.

"Be careful," says the service rep, who is off the phone. "He's a zombie."

Gary's eyes, previously filled with resolve, widen with fear and uncertainty. His hands begin to shake.

The police station is just two blocks away, so I hear the sirens in seconds.

"Don't move," says Gary, his voice trembling.

My nose itches and I need to scratch it. Out of the corner of my eye, I see the service rep escaping through a door in the back, leaving Gary and me alone.

Gary realizes this as well, which doesn't seem to help his confidence.

"You don't need the gun," I say.

Gary doesn't respond, though his hands start to shake more. Yeah, this is who I want protecting me.

"I'm not going to hurt anyone."

The itch in my nose is maddening. I wonder if I'm coming down with a cold.

"I just need to scratch my nose."

Outside, the sirens grow louder, followed by the sound of tires squealing to a stop on asphalt. Car doors open, voices shout out. Gary steals a glance at the front door.

I sneeze.

His gun explodes. The first bullet tears into my chest, hot and searing. The second bullet slams into my forehead above my left eye before exiting through the back of my skull.

I would have preferred a *Gesundheit*.

I don't know if Gary keeps firing, but if he does, I don't feel any more bullets. I'm just staggering back, reminded of that first morning when I awoke walking along Old San Jose Road. Then I'm falling, my limbs useless, the sound of voices shouting and sirens blaring filling my ears.

Then nothing.

Chapter 45

I wake to the sound of sirens wailing.

At first I think I'm in the Animal Control van, but we're not moving. And I hear multiple alarms going off one after another, blending like a symphony of sirens. Either that or I'm in hell, which isn't completely out of the question considering the smell.

When I open my eyes and sit up, I'm on the floor in a cage. All around me, dogs are howling. The German shepherd across from me is snarling, flecks of foam flying from his mouth as he barks and growls and tries to chew his way out of his cage. Someone must have forgotten to give him his meds.

Most of the other inmates aren't candidates for Ritalin, though they might need a good therapist.

On my right, a generic-looking shaggy terrier is trying to scratch his way through the concrete floor. The dog in the cage to my left, a black lab male, is pressed into the far corner of his cage, whimpering. When I look directly at him, he pisses on the floor.

Apparently, the zombie kennel was all filled up.

"Hello?"

No one answers.

One of the bonuses of being a card-carrying member of the undead is that no matter what kind of physical abuse or injuries you're subjected to or sustain, you don't feel any pain or discomfort. But for the first time in months, I have a headache.

I reach up and finger the hole above my left eye, which is sticky with congealed blood. I don't know how long I've been out, but it's good to know I'm still healing. How long that'll keep up without any fresh Breather, I don't know. But considering that it's more than likely I'll be here at least a couple of days, I guess I'll get a chance to find out.

The German shepherd across from me has stopped snarling and is now unleashing a relentless barrage of barking. The golden retriever in the adjacent cage decides this looks like fun and joins in, as does the rottweiler next to him.

I could really use some Tylenol.

"Hello?"

The exit wound in the back of my skull is at least three times as big as where the bullet entered and I can feel pieces of skull and brain matter tangled up in my hair. I try using the contents of my water dish to wash it out but I really need some good shampoo to do the job.

There's no exit wound from the bullet that took me in the chest, but there's a ragged opening just beneath my right nipple and a good deal of blood that soaked into the fabric around the dime-sized hole in my black DaVinci Gambino shirt.

That's just great. My favorite shirt, ruined.

The bullet wounds will heal and my skull and brain tissue will regenerate, but it's just so hard to replace good-quality apparel.

I stand up to stretch my legs and to make sure my motor functions are still working, then I walk to the front of my cage.

"Is anyone here?"

From the amount and the angle of sunlight coming in through the windows above, I'm guessing it's late afternoon, which means I've been unconscious at least five hours.

There's a bowl of dog kibble for me to eat, along with a rawhide bone, neither of which is likely to satisfy my hunger. I could go for a Breather burrito with some rice and black beans. Or a roast Breather sandwich with Dijon mustard and potato chips.

I'm sure I could get Rita or Jerry to smuggle something in for me, even if it's just some jerky. But somehow, I don't think I'm going to get my one phone call.

"Hello?"

Nobody answers.

I think about dumping out the rest of my water dish and clanging it against the bars of my cage. Instead, I join the rest of my inmates and howl along with them.

Chapter 46

"I can't believe they shot you, dude."

It's day three of my captivity and Jerry is sitting on the floor, rubbing his eyes and occasionally letting out a trio of sneezes. At first I thought he'd caught a cold, but it turns out he's allergic to cats.

The staff couldn't handle the constant howling and urinating, even though my voice had grown hoarse and I'd pretty much emptied my bladder, so since the zombie kennel was at capacity, they moved me into the feline kennel. The accommodations aren't as spacious and with all of the hissing I keep dreaming about snakes and vampires and Vaudeville melodramas, but I always was more of a cat person.

Jerry sneezes, then wipes a hand across his nose. His eyes are red and swollen and he keeps having to clear his throat. I'm touched that he asked for a cage near mine rather than with the others in the dog kennel, but I hope his parents come to get him before he develops a rash.

The day after my aborted trip to the Social Security office, Jerry walked into Fast Eddie's to have a drink and shoot some pool. Said he "just wanted to see what would happen."

What happened was that Jerry had one drink and then

another and then another and after less than two hours, he'd torn up the *Breathers Only* sign posted at the front door and then removed his baseball hat to display what remained of his exposed brain, giving everyone the chance to touch it.

Needless to say, the place emptied out faster than a bulimic's stomach. When Animal Control showed up, Jerry was sitting at the bar, drinking a Jack and Coke and lighting the pieces of the *Breathers Only* sign on fire.

The day before, about the same time I was walking into the Social Security office, Carl showed up to play a round of golf at the Seascape resort, where he'd been a member in good standing prior to his death and reanimation. But Seascape has a strict and long-standing No Zombie policy, so Carl was denied access the moment someone recognized him. In other words, they locked the doors and started screaming for help.

Carl didn't run away or put up a fight, but waited outside for the police and went peacefully, unlike Naomi, who had to be subdued with restraints and a Taser baton before they could get her out of the movie theater.

Buying her ticket and getting through the door proved to be uneventful in spite of her empty eye socket, but while she was waiting in line to get some popcorn, a little boy standing with his mother in front of Naomi kept turning around and staring at her, so she finally said, "What? You never seen a zombie before?"

At least she didn't get shot in the face.

I reach up and touch the ragged hole above my left eye. While I managed to clean it up and rub some Neosporin on it, without any fresh Breather I'm not healing like I used to. And I can't expect Rita to show up with any contraband since she got locked up with Leslie, Beth, and Tom for picketing outside of the SPCA, protesting our incarcerations.

Of course, everyone else can get released as soon as their

appointed caretakers show up to bail them out. I, on the other hand, am in a somewhat more precarious predicament. Not only are my parents not around to pay my fines but the police have realized they're missing. Naturally, I'm the prime suspect even though no evidence has been found, but even if they never dig up anything to prove I killed my parents, I've got four more days before I'll be transferred to County for redistribution. Unless someone steps forward to foster me.

ZOMBIE SEEKING BREATHER
House trained
Likes cats and walks on the beach
Good in the kitchen

The only problem is, even if someone agreed to foster me, the county wouldn't allow it to happen because of the questions regarding my parents' disappearance. I'm considered a high-risk zombie, which means when the seven days are up, so is my luck.

This was bound to happen eventually. You can't expect to eat your parents and not have someone notice they're missing. But you just don't think about the consequences of your actions when you're turning your leftover parents into croquettes.

Jerry lets out another series of sneezes, followed by several violent, hacking coughs. Any moment I half expect him to spit up a hairball.

The only one of our original group who didn't get busted is Helen, though when she stopped by for a visit she did confide to me that she keeps thinking about eating her sister.

"She just looks so succulent."

Yes. Succulent. My mouth salivates at the word.

Instead of eating her sister, Helen took down a homeless

person with help from Zack and Luke, then they cut him up and stored him in a freezer in Ian's garage.

If green is the color of envy, then I'm split pea soup.

For a great green pea Breather soup, melt 2 tablespoons of butter in a large saucepan, blend in 2 tablespoons flour, add 1 pint each milk and Breather broth and bring to a boil. Smooth in chopped Breather and green pea puree, salt and pepper, then cover and simmer 5–10 minutes. Makes six servings.

Helen told me not to worry, that she and Ian were working on a way to get me out of this. I hope they figure it out soon so I can get some fresh Breather because I keep picking pieces of my brain out of the exit wound in the back of my head.

Chapter 47

D ay five of my captivity.

Jerry was released two days ago. I can't say I miss his constant wheezing and coughing, but at least it broke up the monotony of hissing.

The red Persian in the cage next to mine is the worst. He doesn't hiss at me as much as the others, but since his face is mashed in, his respiratory system is apparently dysfunctional, causing him to have sneezing fits twice a day that spray me with globs of orange mucous.

When Jerry's parents showed up to claim him, I expected them to react in typical Breather fashion. But whereas my mother would have refused to touch me and my father would have berated me with the expense and inconvenience of my condition, Jerry's parents smothered him with affection and apologized for not being able to pick him up sooner.

And I thought everyone wanted to eat their mother and father.

So I'm all alone now, unless you count the ninety-three cats and twenty-four kittens currently sharing the kennel with me.

After Jerry's departure in the morning, Carl and Naomi

left later that afternoon. Rita, Leslie, Beth, and Tom went home yesterday. Rita stopped by on her way out and slipped me a kiss along with some dried Breather, but it didn't help much. I'm beginning to deteriorate. My fresh wounds are suppurating, turning black, and my heart has slowed to less than five beats per minute. It's hard to tell if my flesh is starting to rot because of the overwhelming litter box odor. That and a couple of the new arrivals in adjacent cages have sprayed me.

And I'm developing cramps.

If you've never been confined to a five-foot-long, three-foot-wide, three-foot-high cage for five days, then you probably wouldn't understand.

> wire cage confines
> muscles cramp and wounds fester
> smells like cat urine

Right about now, my parents' wine cellar looks like the penthouse suite at the Ritz-Carlton. What I wouldn't give for a bottle of 1999 Arietta Merlot and back-to-back episodes of *Spin City*.

On the bright side, according to Helen, several personal effects belonging to my parents washed ashore just south of Big Sur, prompting the police to switch their investigation to the stretch of ocean from Carmel to San Simeon. With any luck they'll find my parents' BMW and rule their deaths accidental and let me go, which I realize is about as likely as a good Hollywood movie based on a bad television series. But at least it gives me something to think about other than whether I'll be dissected, chopped up, or flambéed.

Ian petitioned the county for an injunction on my behalf in an attempt to keep me from being destroyed until the police investigation regarding my parents' disappearance has been resolved. He thinks he has a good chance of making it happen. He even contacted the *Santa Cruz County Sentinel* hoping to get some local media coverage. I don't exactly know what he hopes to accomplish by pissing off a bunch of Breathers who will complain about their tax dollars being wasted on a sub-human, but Ian seems to think it could help my cause.

All I know is that unless my parents show up in the next two days, which isn't likely considering that they've been completely digested and passed through my system, then I get a full scholarship to Cadaver College.

I hear the entrance exams are brutal.

Chapter 48

"A ndy! Andy! How are they treating you?"

"What's it like being a zombie?"

"How are you dealing with the disappearance of your parents?"

It's day nine of my captivity and I'm fielding questions from more than half a dozen reporters standing outside my cage, which is actually more of a deluxe private kennel than a cage.

Measuring ten-feet long, ten-feet wide, and eight-feet tall, my new accommodations come with a sofa that pulls out into a queen-sized bed, a mini-refrigerator, a microwave, a portable toilet with privacy veils, a DVD player with a nineteen-inch flat-screen monitor, and my own personal attendant. Circuit City donated the DVD player and flat-screen, but all of the other accessories came from local organizations who wanted some good PR. The personal attendant is a kid named Scott who volunteers for the SPCA but who wants to be an actor and thought this might be a chance for him to get discovered.

When you're suddenly famous, everyone wants a piece of you.

Two days ago, I awoke to the sound of sirens pulling up out

in front of the SPCA. I figured that was the end of me, that I'd wind up rooming with Ray in a dormitory for the harvested undead, which was beginning to look like a pretty attractive option considering that I'd spent the last couple of days with cat litter stuck to my ass.

Turns out one of the regional media outlets picked up on a local story about an outbreak of civil disobedience among Santa Cruz County's undead and sent someone to investigate. When they discovered that one of the undead was an orphaned zombie who had sent a petition to a member of the House of Representatives asking for the government to restore his constitutional rights and that a local lawyer was fighting to save said orphaned zombie from destruction, the story went national.

Turns out my petition was completely disregarded by my would-be representative and instead was posted outside his office as a running joke on Capitol Hill. But when my name showed up on the news and someone figured out I was the author of the petition, the joke became a public relations nightmare.

So far my story's been reported on *World News Tonight,* the *CBS Evening News,* and *Headline News,* debated on *Crossfire, Real Time with Bill Maher,* and NPR, and even made it into a press conference given by the president's press secretary. I think the official stance taken by the president was "No comment."

On the morning I was scheduled to be discharged to the county, the media descended upon the SPCA with a convoy of television vans, video cameras, satellite feeds, and dozens of reporters. Protesters lined up on both sides of the issue, yelling at each other. And hundreds of local citizens showed up to either voice their opinions or to see if they might catch a glimpse of Andy the Zombie. Apparently, it was quite a circus.

The police showed up to try to keep it from turning into a zoo.

"Andy, what do you think is going to happen to you?"

"When do you think you'll get out of here?"

"What are your favorite foods?"

Next question.

When the media arrived, the SPCA locked down the building for the first twenty-four hours, preventing reporters from having access to me—in part because they didn't want to disturb the other animals but also because they realized they would have their own public relations nightmare on their hands if any images were broadcast of me cramped up inside my coffin of a cage, with nothing but a water dish, a bowl of kibble, and a bag of catnip. Which, by the way, tastes like dead grass but really packs a punch.

So in the middle of the night I was moved into one of the large cages the SPCA keeps available for livestock and game animals. Some of the volunteers even pitched in to supply me with some pillows and blankets.

In spite of the fact that they're Breathers, most of the volunteers genuinely care about the fate of their undead charges. I think it's that sentiment that has helped to fuel the growing support for me and for zombies across the nation over the last couple of days.

All of the donated accoutrements started showing up within hours of my first television broadcast on network news. My current accommodations showed up this morning, courtesy of a local entrepreneur who builds custom cages and figured he could boost his sales with my constant media exposure.

"Andy, how did you die?"

"What was your life like before you became a zombie?"

"Do you feel like you've been abandoned?"

The police investigation into my parents' disappearance is

still ongoing, but that hasn't prevented stories from circulating in tabloid magazines, on Internet Web sites, and on shows like *Entertainment Tonight* that my parents either committed suicide because they could no longer deal with having a zombie for a son or else they faked their deaths in order to avoid the responsibility of caring for me.

Some of the other claims being reported about me:

I spent the last three months enslaved in my parents' basement, where I was sexually abused by corpse fetishists.

I had my internal organs sold off one by one to pay for Mom and Dad's heroin habit.

My parents cut off my genitals and kept them in a jar because they thought it would help them to win the lottery.

I guess you can lead the media to a story but you can't make them report it accurately.

In spite of their speculative reporting, the tabloid news stories have more credence with the public than the truth, so I've been turned into this tragic, sympathetic zombie figure.

A human interest story about a nonhuman.

A cult hero for a society that abhors me.

I think about how I sat on my parents' lawn and picketed in front of the mortuary and sat on a bench in the park trying to give Breathers something to think about, trying to give a dissenting point of view. I think about how I got urinated on and spit on and bombarded with food and insults, how I got carted off by Animal Control time after time for my efforts and how nothing I did seemed to make a difference.

And now, all of a sudden, here I am.

I used to think that saviors and saints were for the religious and for those who had no faith in their own abilities, who had to believe in someone or something bigger than themselves in order to find their place in the world. But now I realize that not every savior is holy. Not every saint is a paragon of virtue.

You can have your Jesus Christ.

You can have your Mohammed.

You can have your Krishna, your Confucius, your Buddha.

Take your Martin Luther and your Gandhi.

"Andy, what are your thoughts on world hunger?"

"Andy, do you believe in life after death?"

"Andy, how does it feel to be a celebrity?"

My savior is the American media.

Chapter **49**

It's amazing how cramped a ten-by-ten cage can get when you try to fit an entire television production crew and their equipment inside.

"I need more lighting in this corner," shouts the production assistant. Or maybe he's a gaffer. Or a best boy. I have no idea. All I know is that I'm feeling a little insecure about going on national television with a bullet hole above my left eyebrow.

I asked the makeup artist to cover it up with concealer, but the director wants to accentuate my zombieness so the audience can feel for me, so they can understand my anguish. My anguish is that I have a hole in my forehead that looks like the world's largest blackhead.

As if that isn't bad enough, the makeup artist keeps applying too much foundation. And the concealer she used is the wrong color for my skin type. And the blush makes me look like Bozo the clown. I try to explain this to her but she just ignores me, so I don't bother to tell her that she needs to use a softer sponge.

Around my cage mills an audience of SPCA volunteers,

police officers, local news media, invited guests, and several VIPs, including the mayor of Santa Cruz. I keep looking to see if Rita or Jerry or someone from the group is in the crowd, but apparently they couldn't make it tonight.

Outside the SPCA, protesters shout their opposition to my existence:

"Zombies aren't human!"

"Death to the undead!"

And my running favorite:

"Go back to your coffin!"

Like I'm a vampire. Please. Keep your undead creatures straight.

My personal attendant, Scott, walks up to me and lets me know that Beringer just donated several cases of their 2001 Private Reserve Cabernet Sauvignon and where would I like them? He also tells me that Katie Couric is on the cell phone again and can I take her call?

"I can't," I say. "I'm doing a live remote for *Larry King Live.*"

Over the last three days, I've appeared live via satellite on CNN, *Good Morning America, Live with Regis and Kelly,* CNBC, the *Best Damn Sports Show,* and Howard Stern. Howard even asked me to come back with Rita once I'm cleared of killing my parents because he's always wanted to have a live zombie sex act on the show. I told him I'd think about it.

"Okay, people," says the director. Or is it the production assistant? All I know is that I'm wearing more makeup than Elizabeth Taylor in *Cleopatra.* "We've got three minutes until we're rolling, so we need everyone ready and in position in two."

I feel concealer and powder caked on my skin, but the makeup artist keeps applying more. And she's brushing it on in the wrong direction. And the eyeliner she used makes me look like a Las Vegas whore. I have half a mind to bite her, but that would probably kill the Larry King interview.

Initially the news programs and talk shows wanted to book me for interviews because of the hype and the sheer novelty I brought to the table. Even though the undead are considered health hazards and a public nuisance by the masses, an interview with a zombie equals big ratings. So no one wanted to get left behind.

But after the ACLU filed a class action lawsuit on behalf of the undead claiming our civil rights have been trampled for decades, I started getting calls from *Newsweek* and *Rolling Stone,* Matt Lauer and FOX News. Like I'd ever do an interview with FOX. They're about as fair and balanced as a Ku Klux Klan barbecue.

Apparently, the KKK, the AMA, the AFL-CIO, the Republican Party, and dozens of religious right groups have lined up to fight against the ACLU's claim that we, as former Breathers, are being deprived of our right to life, liberty, and property without due process.

My petition, thank you very much.

Granted, the right to life and liberty doesn't include the consumption of the living, but you can't expect Breathers and zombies to see eye to eye on everything.

"Two minutes, people!"

While most of the heavy hitters have lined up on the other side of the ACLU, there are historical precedents to back up their case. After all, at one time African Americans were considered property, not human beings. True, we haven't been enslaved but the parallels are hard to discount.

We're disparaged by a class that considers us inferior.

We're used for entertainment purposes and medical research.

We're frequently strung up and tortured for fun.

And the comparisons to the plight of African Americans is just the beginning.

Hell, less than a century ago, women weren't even allowed the right to vote. In the 1940s, Japanese Americans were rounded up and interred in camps. Then came the civil rights battle for gays and lesbians. And at the turn of the century, after 9/11, Muslims were persecuted and racially profiled.

Zombies are just the latest in a long line of those who've been oppressed by the ruling elite. Of course, that's never stopped other minorities from discriminating against us, too, which makes about as much sense as a David Lynch film.

"One minute!"

My makeup bib is removed and the lights given one final adjustment, then everyone takes their places as the director shouts out for everyone to be quiet.

I'm wearing a hunter green short-sleeved silk shirt with brown cotton slacks and black Italian leather shoes. With all of the lights on in my cage it's getting warm and I'm starting to perspire, so I hope the pancake batter of makeup I'm wearing doesn't slide off my face and into my lap. Not unless someone wants to donate a washer and dryer.

The first few times I sat down for an interview, I was nervous, like a kid going to a new school or an adolescent about to get a glimpse of his first, honest-to-god breast. Now it's routine.

Been there, done that.

Next!

Hell, I've had to turn down interview requests from ESPN and *60 Minutes* simply because I just don't have enough time. Everyone wants a piece of me. I've become the poster child for zombie civil rights.

"Okay, we're on in ten, nine, eight . . ."

From what I've been told, the shows I appear on get higher ratings than God on Sunday. Of course, I'm not making any money for any of these interviews because I still don't have a Social Security number. But the exposure is good.

On three, two, one . . .

Chapter 50

Sleigh bells ring, are you listening?
In the lane, snow is glistening . . .

The deliberate, gravelly bass voice of Louis Armstrong drifts through the cage, emanating from the speakers on the Sony CD Micro System donated by the local Best Buy. Personally, I would have preferred a collection of Elvis Christmas songs, but Rita is a sucker for old-time jazz.

Rita is curled up next to me under the goose down comforter on my queen-sized sofa bed. She's not wearing anything, which is how I like her best.

All of the cameras and reporters and production crews are gone, as is most of the SPCA staff. The county hired extra security to keep the protesters, autograph seekers, and fraternity pledges away, so I gave my personal attendant the night off. It is, after all, Christmas Eve.

Somehow, this isn't how I envisioned I would be spending the night before Christmas. Not six months ago. Not even two weeks ago, which is how long I've been locked up. And with all of the media attention I've had over the past week, I haven't been able to get my Breather fix, so Rita made me a special Christmas meal of Breather and potato pancakes with a nice dill sauce. True, she had to make the pancakes at Ian's and smuggle them in and they weren't as fresh after we heated them up in my microwave, but it's not as if I can really complain.

I reach over to the side of the bed and grab a piece of the candied Breather that Leslie made for me, then wash it down with a Churchill 1985 Vintage Port. I offer some of each to Rita, who declines without saying a word, maintaining the pensive silence she's had for most of the evening. I've asked her twice if there's anything wrong but she claims she's fine.

I stroke her hair as she lies with her head on my chest while Satchmo gives way to Judy Garland's version of "Have Yourself a Merry Little Christmas."

"Wanna fool around?" I ask.

Nothing. She doesn't even finger my bullet hole, which has finally started to heal.

"Andy," she says, finally. "Do you miss your daughter?"

Not exactly the type of playful bed banter I was fishing for, and definitely a deal breaker as far as having sex anytime in the next hour, but I guess it's worth considering.

Do I miss Annie?

I should. After all, it is Christmas. And watching Annie experience the magic of believing in Santa Claus was almost enough to make me believe again. But honestly, over the past three weeks, I haven't thought about her once. It's for the best, really. For her and for me. Though when Larry King asked me the same question, I lied. For all I knew, Annie might have been watching. I didn't want her to think her father was a monster.

"No. I don't miss Annie. Why?"

No response. Not even a shrug of the shoulders.

In the canine kennel, one of the dogs lets out a single, mournful howl and then falls silent.

"Do you miss your family?" asks Rita.

I wonder where she's going with this.

Family? Which family? Do I miss Rachel and Annie? I used to, but I've done my grieving and moved on. Sure, if I think about them long and hard enough, I can conjure up feelings of loss, maybe even some tears, but what's the point? Not even Oprah's going to get me to go there.

Do I miss my father and mother? I guess that depends on what she means by *miss*.

Do I miss my father's naked contempt? Do I miss my mother's cold affection? Or do I miss how they tasted covered in a chilled aioli sauce?

No. No. And yes.

"Is that what you wanted to know?" I ask.

On the CD player, Judy gives way to Frank Loesser's playful "Baby It's Cold Outside."

Yeah. And it's cold inside, too.

"What is this all about?" I ask.

Is she threatened by my previous relationship? Does she want to get married? Is she thinking about killing and eating her mother?

When she doesn't respond, I place my fingers under Rita's chin and turn her face toward me. There are tears in her eyes, but I can't tell if she's happy or sad. She looks somewhere in between. As if whatever is on her mind both troubles and pleases her.

After a few moments, she raises herself off my chest and props herself up on one elbow, her eyes level with mine. I was mistaken. There is no sadness in them. Only joy.

"I'm pregnant."

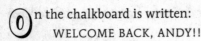

Chapter 51

On the chalkboard is written:

WELCOME BACK, ANDY!!

And beneath that:

NEW YEAR'S EVE PARTY AT JERRY'S—BYOB.

Which, in zombie speak, means Bring Your Own Breather.

A couple of weeks ago, Jerry might have been able to get away with actually writing out the words on the chalkboard, but with the paparazzi following me around since I got out of the SPCA, we have to use a little common sense.

Helen and Leslie come up to hug me, followed by Naomi, who plants a kiss on my cheek. Jerry gives me a high five and an enthusiastic "Dude!" while Carl just smiles and nods from across the room. Tom comes up to me and shakes my hand with his short, hairy alien appendage, then gives me a hug and starts to cry.

"I missed you, too," I say.

The day after Christmas, the police located my parents' BMW in the ocean just off the shore south of Big Sur. Although they didn't find their bodies, they did find enough evidence to corroborate my claim that my parents had been driving down the coast to stay at their timeshare in Palm Springs. So I was allowed to go home.

I have to admit, it's good to be out and to see everyone again, but I kind of miss the SPCA—the food, the wine, the women willing to have sex with me. It's not often you get an opportunity to live that kind of lifestyle without any personal responsibility. It was kind of like being in college again, only with national media exposure.

And a private servant.

Although the case surrounding my parents' disappearance hasn't been officially closed, the police have initially declared their deaths accidental, clearing the way for me to go home. Technically, I'm not supposed to be released without a guardian, so Ian signed the consent forms. Not that I needed any help in that area—more than a dozen Breathers, all of them single or divorced women over forty, stepped forward to volunteer as my foster guardian.

Regardless of their motives—compassion, desperation, kinky fantasies—I'm flattered. It's nice to be wanted, even if it's by the same people who despised me yesterday. But I've got more important responsibilities than feeding my own ego.

As Rita settles into her chair for the meeting, I make sure she's comfortable and ask if there's anything she needs. Sure she's only five weeks pregnant, but I enjoy doting on her. And in spite of the recent positive publicity for the undead, finding an ob-gyn who would treat Rita and keep her pregnancy a secret isn't likely. So we have to be careful.

The push for zombie civil rights has created the social equivalent of a tornado, spinning across the country, tearing holes in the cultural fabric. Zombies procreating would produce a category-five hurricane.

Still, we can't wait for society to catch up to us. Rita and I have to think about our future—retirement accounts, college savings, whether to use a diaper service or disposables. But the first thing we need is the ability to earn a living.

My second visit to the Social Security office didn't go much better than the first, except this time I didn't get shot. At least Gary the rent-a-cop apologized to me before he asked me to autograph his holster. When he asked about what happened to my bullet wounds, I told him I have a good makeup artist.

It's becoming more difficult to hide the fact that I'm healing, so I've had to cut back on my Breather intake. Needless to say, it's made me a little cranky.

That and I still can't get my Social Security number reinstated.

I don't know what I expected. Social change doesn't happen overnight. But considering how much progress we've made in just the last week, my inability to earn a living to support my new family is a disappointment. And with interviews lined up with Letterman, Leno, and Oprah, all I can think about is the potential income I'm losing.

Rita tells me not to worry, that everything will work out, that the exposure I'm getting is more important than any financial loss, but I can't help feeling like I'm being taken advantage of.

"Okay, everyone, please take a seat," says Helen. "We have a lot of important things to talk about tonight, so let's get started."

Helen erases the messages on the chalkboard, then writes down the topic for tonight's meeting:

HOW TO DEAL WITH CORPORATE MEDIA.

Naomi and Carl are booked on Conan O'Brien, Jerry is promoting his Playboy Playmate Sistine Chapel on *The Daily Show,* and Tom is scheduled to be the first contestant on *Extreme Makeover: Zombie Edition.* Zack and Luke, meanwhile, have been asked to participate in an upcoming "Ghouls vs. Fools" episode of *Fear Factor*.

I'd put my money on the ghouls.

All across the country, zombies are appearing on talk shows and television programs, in news magazines and advertisements, pitching everything from funeral homes to deodorant. Several companies have even started merchandising the undead—creating action figures, trading cards, and even T-shirts that say "Got Zombie?" I hear McDonald's is offering a new Zombie Happy Meal.

At some point we all expect the novelty of zombies as media darlings to die down, but you never can tell. I thought reality TV shows would eventually lose their appeal, but now they number more than sixty, from *Amazing Race* to the upcoming *Zombie Life*. Who knows? Five years from now, I could have my own talk show.

But would I get paid for it?

"Andy," says Helen. "Would you like to lead the group?"

I stand and walk up to the chalkboard, then turn and face the group. Jerry, Beth, Tom, and Naomi applaud while Carl and Leslie laugh and Rita gives me an affectionate wink. It's enough to bring me to the verge of tears. This is the first time I've addressed the group at a meeting without having to rely on visual aids.

Looking at everyone, I'm reminded of the first time I attended a UA meeting, back in August when I was just getting over the shock of what had happened to me. Then there were just the five of us—Helen, Naomi, Carl, Tom, and me. The future looked bleak. No one believed in anything.

Now it's hard to fathom everything that has transpired since then. In spite of the potential roadblocks we still face, the dead-end, unpaved road we'd been headed down has taken a detour and we find ourselves traveling on a new highway, a ribbon of asphalt stretching away from our past toward the horizon and a new existence which lies beyond it.

It's a classic story of suffering and redemption, like *The Color Purple* or The New Testament.

Only with cannibalism.

Chapter 52

I'm beginning to think I need a bodyguard.

Increasingly, someone calls and threatens me, usually with promises of ripping my arms off or sending me back to hell where I belong. Standard stuff. But sometimes women will call and threaten to perform certain sexual acts on me until specific body parts fall off. Actually, I think it's the same woman.

Most of the real trouble comes from enthusiastic autograph seekers who want me to sign photographs and breasts and copies of *Shaun of the Dead.* More than once I've had to call the police to keep them away. Talk about irony.

Even though Ian is my legal guardian, the county allowed me to return to my parents' house until a final ruling is made on their deaths. According to their will, which they never got around to changing once I died, I'm the lone beneficiary, so it's not like I'm squatting. Still, I do have to check in with Ian once a week and he's supposed to come by to make unannounced visits just to keep up the pretense of a foster-guardian relationship. Mostly it's just to keep the courts happy, but so far nobody really seems to care. I'm a national celebrity.

I'm sitting in my father's office going through a stack of

interview requests, endorsement offers, and a movie script based on my as-of-yet unwritten memoir, when Zack walks in to tell me that Steven Spielberg is on line one and wants to know if I'd be interested in his latest project and can I meet with him.

This is the third time Spielberg has called and I've already told him that I couldn't possibly meet with him until after the holidays. Still, I have to admire his persistence. So I tell Zack to take a number, then I tell him to have Luke check my schedule to see what next month looks like. I also remind him to pick up my dry cleaning.

Zack and Luke moved in with me the day after I got out. At first I just wanted to give them a place to live, but it turns out they both have exceptional secretarial skills.

Legally I have no right to have other zombies living with me, but with the ACLU and several prominent civil rights leaders applying pressure, the powers that be seem content to look the other way, so I don't see any reason to fill out the appropriate paperwork. And it's not like my neighbors are complaining.

During the first five months after I reanimated and came to live with my parents, the property values on our street dropped more than twenty percent. No one wanted to live next to a zombie. But ever since my first interview, the property values in the neighborhood have reversed course and are now up more than 15 percent from six months ago. In the short time I've been home, at least two of my neighbors have fielded offers from buyers willing to pay nearly twice the county median.

Two weeks ago, I was getting shot by a rent-a-cop and tossed into a cage at the SPCA. Now, I'm a celebrity. We all are. Elevated to stardom through the power of the Internet and cable television. Packaged and sold to the public in a new, shiny box with a bright, colorful bow.

It's amazing what a little positive media attention can do for your social status.

So in spite of all the negative publicity that has been built up around the undead over the decades, we're suddenly a boon to the real estate market, the entertainment industry, and the local economy. Tourists flock from over the hill and from up and down the coast to see the famous Santa Cruz zombies, pumping money into local restaurants, hotels, and boutiques selling the latest in zombie-wear.

Sure, there are always drawbacks to the influx of out-of-towners, from the headaches of traffic congestion to an increase in public intoxication and violent crimes. But at least we help to keep the homeless population down.

Which reminds me, I need to go grocery shopping. But first I have to take a call from Jesse Jackson on line two.

Chapter 53

What is it you're looking for, Andy? What is it that you want?"

I'm watching myself on television, the Oprah Winfrey interview, and thinking I should have worn something that made me look less pasty.

"Equality," the television version of me says. "We want the same rights as Breathers."

The reaction from the audience is more Jerry Springer than Oprah, with men and women yelling out their opinions and slinging expletives. I half expect someone to pick up a chair and throw it at me.

I don't have to watch the rest to know what happens. While several audience members voice their support for me and for my cause, most of the studio guests disagree with my answer. Several of them become rather vehement in their objections and are escorted out. One of them hurls a raw egg that misses me and explodes on Oprah's forehead.

Not surprisingly, that part got edited out.

I switch the channel to CNN, where a panel of political, scientific, and social "experts" debates the adverse health effects of allowing the undead to associate with the living.

"We still don't have any definitive data proving that, as a species, the undead are a health threat to the living," says the moderator.

"Hello?" says one political analyst. "They're zombies. They eat human flesh. Didn't anyone else see *Dawn of the Dead?*"

The debate disintegrates into a discussion of Hollywood versus the real world, so I flip over to MTV, where *Real World: Zombie in the House* portrays a house full of Breathers living with a zombie.

"He stinks," says one of the housemates. "Worse than garbage. I can't even describe it."

"Kind of like hot, stale vomit," says another housemate.

"Yeah. Except only worse. And he keeps drinking my shampoo. Do you know how much a ten-ounce bottle of Paul Mitchell costs?"

I switch over to the *BBC World News* on KQED and watch a report about zombies in Rome rioting outside the Vatican after being refused entrance. On CNBC, I get to watch a rash of zombie beheadings in the Middle East, while in Germany, Breathers are shown celebrating around the burning body of an unidentified zombie.

Channel to channel and program to program, the living dead are being debated, debased, and destroyed. While I expected an inevitable backlash against all of our recent media exposure and push for civil rights, I didn't anticipate that it would come this soon. Or with this much fervor.

Our right to exist, to pursue life, liberty, and happiness, is being disputed, challenged, and condemned—politically, socially, philosophically. Even athletically.

On ESPN's *Outside the Lines,* a Miami college football player who collapsed and died during practice has been banned from rejoining the team.

"I don't want to eat anyone," he says. "I just want to play football."

I don't have to hear the prognosis of his chances of ever playing football again to know the answer.

I continue to flip through the channels, searching for a news program or a talk show or a deodorant commercial that puts a positive spin on zombies, but all I find is the same message, repeated over and over: We're not any closer to being accepted as members of society.

If anything, it seems like we're moving further away from that possibility. Before we developed a social cause, we were at least tolerated. Sure, there were the occasional dismemberments or rides through town attached to the bumpers of SUVs, but for the most part Breathers tried to pretend we didn't exist. Kind of like the homeless.

Or sexually transmitted diseases.

Now, we've alerted everyone to our presence, made them aware that we have a voice, and they're not happy about it. It's not that they don't want to hear us. It's more like they're angry we had the audacity to speak up.

"They're nothing more than animals."

"Pit bulls with opposable thumbs."

"Inhuman."

On the *Fox News Report,* the talking head is venting his fair and balanced opinion about zombies and, the next thing I know, a photo of my face appears on the screen over his shoulder. Seconds later, there's a split screen and my therapist is staring out at me from my television.

It's strange seeing Ted's face this way. I'm used to seeing him in artificial light, catching glimpses of him over my shoulder. But on my parents' fifty-two-inch, high-definition flat-screen television, tinted and colored and sharpened, Ted looks more plastic, more fake, more wrinkle free. Maybe it's the stage makeup and the lighting. Either that or he's had another glycolic acid peel.

At first Ted starts talking about what it's like to treat a zombie psychologically, which is something he must have read in a book because he never actually treated me. He drones on and on for a couple of minutes and I'm about to change the channel, when he starts talking about me, about all of the sessions we had together—the way I smelled, the way I walked, the way I had to write everything on a dry erase board.

And I realize I might be in big trouble.

He keeps talking, sharing all of the details of our sessions—all of my anguish, all of my guilt, all of my hopelessness. Then he relates how that all changed, how I suddenly became more self-assured, more combative, more independent.

What ever happened to doctor-patient confidentiality?

I wonder how bad this is going to be. If I need to call Ian. If I need to schedule a news conference. If I can diffuse the situation before it explodes in my face.

I wonder if I can play this off as though I'd been pretending all those months. Playing the part of the consummate zombie. Kind of like a sociological experiment.

I watch Ted, with his smug little smile and his stupid gold hoop earring and his artificially colored hair, spilling his guts about me, and I wonder . . .

Maybe there's another option.

Chapter 54

Ted is smiling at me with that strained, fake plastic smile of his. It's been more than a month since I've seen him in person, but I think he's had his teeth whitened.

"Hello, Andy," he says. "This is a pleasant surprise."

A surprise? Yes.

Pleasant? Only in the way that passing kidney stones is pleasant.

No one else is in Ted's office. The receptionist has gone home. His last client left ten minutes ago.

"How have you been?" he says.

"I've been busy," I say.

He stares at me from behind his desk, still smiling, his gaze eventually shifting from me to the phone on his desk, then to the red, digital clock on the wall.

. . . thirty-nine . . . forty . . . forty-one . . .

"Yes," he says, finally. "I've seen you on television. You seem to have made quite a remarkable recovery."

"Just eating right."

Ted's smile falters, exposing several wrinkles at the corners of his mouth. Must be time for his monthly Botox fix.

"Well," he says, swallowing. "What can I do for you, Andy?"

"I was hoping we could talk," I say.

He makes a noise that sounds like a cross between a cough and nervous laughter.

"Sure," he says, reaching across his desk and grabbing a business card. "Just give Irene a call tomorrow to set up an—"

"I was hoping we could talk now."

Ted sits there with his hand extended, the business card held out, shaking in his fingers. He's smiling so hard I can almost hear his caps crack.

"That's . . . my office is closed," he says. "Perhaps you can come back—"

"All I need is a few minutes."

Ted looks at the clock, perhaps hoping that if he stares long enough, my few minutes will be up and I'll just leave.

. . . twenty-two . . . twenty-three . . . twenty-four . . .

He swallows with an audible *click*.

"Is there a problem?" I ask.

Ted turns to look at me, then shifts his gaze past me to the open door leading to the outer office. I'm not a mind reader, but my guess is Ted's wondering if he can get out from behind his desk and make it to the door before I can reach him.

"No," he says, standing up. "No problem."

"Good," I say, then walk over and close the office door.

Ted freezes halfway out of his chair. "What are you do-ing?"

"Just ensuring our doctor-patient confidentiality," I say. "You do believe in doctor-patient confidentiality, don't you?"

Ted doesn't say anything. Just stays there, halfway out of his chair, his lips twitching.

I made sure to lose the paparazzi on my way to Ted's. And, as far as I know, no one saw me enter the building.

Sure, I'm taking a risk hunting white-collar Breather rather than trolling for a nice, juicy homeless person, but you never really know what you're getting on the street—cirrhosis of the liver, drug abuse, skin ulcers, respiratory infections. At least with Ted, I know I'm getting someone who took care of himself, even if he is a little artificially preserved.

Besides, there's this desire in me, this animal hunger and need for revenge that I just can't seem to ignore.

Ted watches me approach, his eyes filled with a wild look that only a predator can appreciate. His eyes dart from me to the phone to the door to the window with the knowledge that escape is unlikely. But he still has to try.

Just before I reach the other side of his desk, he makes his move.

All the zombie folklore and the films that portray the living dead as slow and plodding hunters?

Please.

We move fast. And we're tenacious.

Before Ted can take more than two steps from his chair, I'm across the desk and all over him, driving him to the floor—my knees pinning his arms, my hands finding his throat. He opens his mouth to scream but I've already crushed his windpipe.

Eating a diet of fresh Breather has given me an almost supernatural strength. Although I can't tear the living limb from limb, I feel like it's possible.

I imagine it's like taking steroids with a PCP chaser.

When I killed my parents, it was in a wine-induced haze that left me with virtually no memory of what transpired. I think, for that, I'm somewhat grateful. I'd hate to think that I enjoyed killing them as much as I'm enjoying this. Well, maybe I wouldn't mind so much about my father.

Ted's arms and legs thrash to no avail. I want to bite into him, to feel his flesh in my mouth—a confection, sweet and decadent, the food of the gods. The temptation is so strong I can almost feel the invincibility seeping into my blood vessels and flowing down my throat, but I don't want to make a mess. A pool of blood and stray bits of human flesh on the floor tends to shout "zombie attack." Besides, I just got my shirt back from the dry cleaners.

Ted's eyes find mine for a moment and I smile.

"How are you feeling today, Ted?"

Somehow, I don't think he appreciates the irony.

He looks away, his mouth opening and closing in silent gasps. His struggles taper off and his head twitches once as his final glance falls on the clock, on his life ticking away.

. . . fifty-seven . . . fifty-eight . . . fifty-nine . . .

For a moment I feel sorry for him, for the fear he felt and the life he lost and the way he died. But then the moment passes. After all, I've got a family to feed.

Chapter 55

Rita is walking around the family room, offering plates of Breather-stuffed mushrooms and other appetizers to everyone while Jerry plays DJ, spinning tunes like "Monster Mash," "Werewolves of London," "Thriller," John Lee Hooker's "Graveyard Blues," and a selection of songs by The Zombies.

"If he plays 'Monster Mash' one more time," says Carl, "I swear I'm going to set him on fire."

All the gang's here except Beth, whose parents wouldn't let her come to the party. It didn't matter that Ian would be in attendance as a token Breather chaperone. Beth's parents weren't trying to protect her from exposure to any potential illegal zombie activity, but from the pornographic influence of Jerry's Sistine Chapel bedroom.

It's too bad, because she missed a real spread. Nothing quite as simple as the barbecue we had nearly a month ago. Of course, it's pretty common for zombie potlucks to end up with a buffet table filled with savory dishes and no green vegetables or sweets. Tonight is no exception, as we have a selection ranging from deep-fried finger rolls and canapés to Breather à la béarnaise and Breather fried rice. Though Zack and Luke did bring some creamed brains, so at least we won't have to run out and get any ice cream.

With all of us bringing Breather, it's apparent that I'm not the only one who recently went shopping. And according to the news, I'm not the only one who's noticed.

Over the past few days, half a dozen Breathers in Santa Cruz County have been reported missing, including Ted. Other than me, everyone at the party claims to have obtained their Breather off the street, which means that if the other five missing residents are all the victims of zombie attacks, then some of the local zombie population has grown bolder.

The problem with being a zombie in a world of Breathers is one of supply and demand. When Breathers go to the supermarket or the local corner grocery store and an item in the store is running low or out of stock, the inventory manager just places another order. But when the number of Breathers starts to run low, it becomes a bit more problematic than just restocking the inventory.

Apparently, the local zombie population has started to go grocery shopping.

Who can blame them? For decades we've lived in the shadows and been beaten down, forced to accept our place in society. Now, in less time than it took for my heart to start beating again, we've been thrust into the limelight and elevated to celebrity status, tempted with the expectation of improving our social stature.

What can prove more tempting, however, is the power that comes with the knowledge of understanding what you're fully capable of doing, of realizing your true potential. Noble causes and social evolution don't stand much of a chance when they're up against virtual immortality. And virtual immortality doesn't stand much of a chance when it's up against the glare of the media spotlight.

Which is one of the reasons why Rita and I have decided to leave.

There's no foreseeable manner in which the child Rita is carrying can be delivered into a world where Breathers know that we are the undead. Which is a bit problematic, considering my recent celebrity. And the television interview Ted gave is bound to cast some serious doubt on my physical condition. In spite of the recent cutbacks I've made in Breather consumption to deflect suspicion, it's only a matter of time before someone who saw that interview does some investigating and discovers that I've been eating the hand that feeds me. When that happens, I'll be destroyed along with my dreams of a new family.

Ian has arranged to get Rita and me fake passports and airplane tickets to Scotland, where he has family who will help us get a fresh start and a place to stay in the remote West Highlands—"remote" being the operative word. The last place we want is somewhere with lots of media outlets or tourists or people with cameras. We considered Montana and Wyoming, but decided it was a good idea to get away from the influence of the great big American media. Of course, we had to promise Ian we wouldn't eat any of his family, which wasn't much of a problem since I've never been a big fan of Scottish food.

Naturally, we'll have to take some precautions before we leave—like changing our physical appearance, which means I have to eat enough Breather to heal my wounds and stay out of the limelight as much as possible. But other than that, a little makeup, colored contacts, fake glasses, and some hair coloring and we should be good to go.

While neither one of us is thrilled about having to leave, we realize our options are pretty limited. Sooner or later things will catch up with us here and I have a feeling it's going to be sooner. According to Ian, the passports should be ready within a week. After that, it's just a matter of packing our suitcases, liquidating as much of my parents' wealth as possible, and getting on an airplane.

We've told the others about Rita's pregnancy and our plans to leave. They were all supportive and sad and excited for us and everyone cried. Even Carl. So while tonight is New Year's Eve, it's also something of a good-bye party for all of us. An end to not only the existence we once knew, but to the friendships we've developed and the experiences we've shared. It's tough enough to maintain friendships across continents and oceans. But when you've changed your identity and are pretending to be human, having zombies back home as pen pals tends to run up a red flag.

So as the final minutes of this year wind down, we all grab our glasses and cups to toast one another. And it's not just in celebration, but in appreciation for how much we've meant to one another and how much we've overcome.

We are not alone.

We have found our purpose.

We are all survivors.

After the toasts are all done and we wash down our final bites of Breather with champagne, we all head out for the year's inaugural World Death Tour. Leslie stays behind with Ian to help clean up, while Zack and Luke opt to head back to my place to get some sleep so they can get an early start tomorrow preparing my schedule.

I need to give them a raise.

The Santa Cruz Memorial Park and Funeral Home is located just off Ocean Street near the intersection of Highway 1 and Highway 17. None of us have any family or friends buried here so we've never made this one of our stops, but it seemed like a good way to kick things off. Or end them, depending on your point of view.

The sky is clear and the moon is waxing, two days away from a full moon, bathing the cemetery in moonlight. Occasionally, I can see my shadow. When I glance over at Rita beside me, she looks ethereal, her face floating along inside the black hood of her sweatshirt. Every now and then I see her exhale of breath in the cold January air.

"Hey, dude," says Jerry, noticing the same thing about himself and blowing out puffs of white breath. "Look . . . it's like I'm totally blowing out a bunch of bong hits but I'm not even stoned."

"Really?" says Carl. "You could have fooled me."

Tom and Naomi laugh. They're holding hands. I don't know when this happened, but good for Tom. He needs to get laid. But it must be kind of weird for Naomi when he fumbles for her breast with that one short, hairy arm.

The seven of us gather around an oak tree located near the east end of the cemetery and hold hands, then Helen asks us to mark a moment of silence for all of the lost souls entombed before they reanimated. I can't imagine what that would be like, to wake up inside your coffin, encased in mahogany and velvet, screaming and pounding, wondering how anyone could have mistakenly buried you alive. I wonder how long it takes for them to figure out what happened or if they think the gradual decaying of their bodies is just normal.

In a coffin, with no insects or animals to destroy the body, the hair, nails, and teeth generally become detached within a few weeks. After a month or two the tissues liquefy. Shortly thereafter, the main body cavities burst open.

My guess is, if you're still thinking and talking to yourself at this point, you've probably realized that something's not quite normal.

Granted, bodies in a coffin aren't exposed to beetles or maggots or other insects, unless your family really scrimped and buried you in quarter-inch plywood held together with glue, but I can't help imagining what it would be like to get eaten alive by maggots:

> *maggots feast on fat*
> *subcutaneous buffet*
> *sounds like Rice Krispies*

I think I'll title that one "Snap, Crackle, Pop."

Once we're done at the oak tree, everyone wanders off for personal reflection, though after the incident with Tom's arm at Oakwood a couple months back, we buddy up instead of going solo. Helen and Carl head off one way while Naomi and Tom wander off another. Jerry tags along with Rita and me.

For the first few minutes Jerry actually manages to be quiet. I don't know if he's spending time on personal reflection or thinking about his next porno masterpiece, but it doesn't take long for him to get chatty.

First he starts in with a comment about Tom and Naomi. A minute later, it's another comment. Then an amusing thought. Then a joke. Before he can get to the punch line, I tell him he needs to be quiet.

"Okay, dude," he says. "Whatever." And then he goes sulking off, just far enough that I can still hear him muttering about how no one appreciates his humor.

I can't help but smile. And it occurs to me that some of my fondest memories of not only the past few months but of my entire existence have been with Rita and Jerry—the night we met Ray, going hunting for Breather, staging my parents' deaths. I never had friends like this in my previous life. And I realize that getting killed in that car accident was the best thing that could have ever happened to me.

I can't wait to share this revelation with Helen and the

rest of the group. My guess is that everyone else feels the same way. Or at least I hope they do.

Rita and I walk for a while in silence, just enjoying each other's company, lost in our own thoughts, watching our shadows on the ground in front of us. I don't know how much time passes, but at some point the silence strikes me as wrong.

I suddenly realize I don't hear Jerry anymore.

I stop and turn around, searching through the moonlit graveyard, but Jerry is nowhere to be seen.

"Hey, Jerry?" I say.

"What's wrong?" asks Rita.

On the ground, a third shadow joins those belonging to Rita and me. I start to turn around, expecting to see Jerry sneaking up on us. Instead, someone slams into me, separating my hand from Rita's. The next instant I'm hitting the ground, pinned beneath a huge, sweaty body.

"Get his hands!" a male voice hisses above me. "Get his hands! Get his hands!"

"Hold on!" says another voice. "Stay away from his mouth!"

I can't move and I can't breathe. I try to shout out but the weight pressing down on my chest is crushing my lungs. The next thing I know, my ankles are bound with zip ties, then the same is done to my wrists behind my back.

I don't hear Rita at all.

"Okay, okay," says a voice. "He's good. Let's go."

Before I can snap my teeth and bite into human flesh, the weight lifts off of me and I can finally breathe, but I still don't have enough air to shout out. So I growl.

"Shut him up!" someone whispers.

A boot kicks me in the back, then another in the kidneys. I roll over and try to curl up into a ball to block the blows, which is when I see Rita on the ground just a few feet away, unconscious. Two figures stand between us.

"Come on," says the one who'd been kicking me, stepping away. He's short with blond hair and he's holding a baseball bat. "Let's finish this and get out of here."

"Hold on," says another one, wearing a knit beanie and army fatigues. He leans over Rita and reaches down and grabs her left ear. A few seconds later, he's holding something in his hand and Rita's earlobe is ragged and bleeding.

That's when I smell the gasoline.

A guy the size of Martha Stewart's ego approaches us with a three-gallon can of unleaded in one hand and what looks like an unlit emergency flare in the other.

I'm beginning to think that World Death Tours aren't such a good idea.

The other two back away as the big guy reaches Rita, puts the flare in his pocket, and unscrews the gasoline cap. I try to get up, try to let out a cry for help, try to do anything to stop him, but I'm tied up and can't catch my breath.

Somehow I manage to get to my knees, but before I can lunge forward and try to bite anyone, the blond kid takes a swing at me with the baseball bat, catching me along the side of my head. I fall to the ground, the world momentarily blacking out. When I blink my eyes open, Martha Stewart's ego is standing above Rita, pouring gasoline over her.

I hear the sound of approaching footsteps in the grass, fast and determined.

The big guy looks up.

"Shit . . ."

Jerry hits him high and hard before he can react, knocking Martha off his feet. The gas can falls to the ground a few feet away, spilling its contents out on the grass.

"Fuck!" shouts the kid with the bat.

The one in the army fatigues turns in circles, searching the darkness, his eyes wide. "Nick, let's get out of here!"

He turns and runs off.

"Fuck!" says Nick again.

Martha Stewart is screaming.

Jerry has Martha on the ground, biting at his throat, but the big guy is putting up a fight, pushing Jerry away. I'm not sure, but I think Jerry is laughing.

Instead of running away, Nick starts walking toward Jerry, the bat held out in front of him. I want to warn Jerry but I can only watch as Nick creeps up behind Jerry and cocks the bat over his right shoulder, his hands shaking. Just as he's about to take a swing, Jerry turns around, his cheeks and chin covered with gore, glistening in the moonlight.

Nick freezes.

"Jesus," he gasps.

"Sorry, dude," says Jerry, standing up, leaving Martha gasping and groaning on the ground. "He couldn't make it."

The smell of blood and gasoline fills the air.

Jerry steps forward but instead of swinging the bat, Nick starts to back away, then turns to run and trips over the gas can and goes sprawling, the bat tumbling from his hands.

Jerry laughs. Not in a mean or malicious way. He just thinks it's funny and starts laughing, like he's out in the cemetery clowning around with his buddies.

Nick scrambles to his feet and turns around, looking for the bat, but the nearest weapon is the gas can, so he picks it up and shakes it at Jerry, which only makes Jerry laugh harder. So Nick throws the gas can at Jerry, who's still laughing when the can hits him in the head and splashes gasoline in his face before falling to the ground at his feet.

"Oww! Shit, dude," says Jerry, wiping at his eyes. "That's not cool."

But that's the extent of Nick's courage. After throwing the gas can, he turns and flees, racing off in the direction of his accomplice, leaving his other friend to die.

I roll over to check on Rita. She's still unconscious, her face and hair wet with gasoline that glistens in the moonlight. Next to her, Martha Stewart lies on his back, barely moving, though he appears to be fumbling with something. It takes me a few seconds before I realize he's got the emergency flare in his hand and he's twisting off the plastic cap.

I try to warn Jerry, but all that comes out is a gasp.

In the darkness I hear Naomi's and Tom's voices, but I can't tell where they are.

Martha has the cap off, exposing the igniter button.

Jerry is still facing away from me, trying to rub the gasoline out of his eyes. He's standing right next to the gas can in a puddle of regular unleaded.

A few feet from me, Martha has rolled over onto his side and ignited the flare.

"Jerry," I finally manage to say.

Jerry turns around, still rubbing his eyes, then opens them just as Martha tosses the ignited flare onto the grass.

"Dude."

The flare hits the ground. An instant later, Rita is on fire. Before Jerry can move, the flames race across the gasoline-soaked grass until they reach the gas can, which explodes directly beneath him.

Jerry staggers away, engulfed in flames, then falls to the ground and rolls around, trying to put out the fire, all the while screaming in pain, screaming in fear, screaming for someone to help him. A few feet from me, her pale face no longer visible behind the flames, Rita burns in silence. I can smell her hair burning, her flesh cooking, melting from the bone. I open my mouth to call her name, but all that comes out is a sob.

I struggle to free my hands but it's no use. I can't move. I can't call out for help. I can't even cover my eyes. All I can do is watch and cry as Jerry and Rita and my unborn child burn to death, two in silence and one in agony. In the end, it's more than I can bear, so I close my eyes and listen to Jerry's screams.

Chapter 56

I'm in the back of Helen's minivan sitting next to Rita's charred remains. I keep trying to hold her hand, but I can't find anything that looks familiar so I just cry harder. What was left of Jerry is wrapped up in Naomi's leather jacket on the floor behind us.

When the others showed up, Jerry had stopped screaming and moving but he was still on fire, so they used Naomi's leather jacket to put him out. Rita, who never regained consciousness, laid smoldering until Carl threw his overcoat on top of her.

We hoped Rita and Jerry could be force fed enough to reverse the damage, but all that was left of them was flesh melted to bone. Even if they could have reanimated, their mouths and throats were gone, so there was no way for either of them to consume any Breather.

My own face is blistered, my eyebrows and hair singed. At some point, I crawled over to Rita while she was still burning and laid down next to her. I don't remember doing it. I just remember opening my eyes and seeing Rita less than a foot away, an indistinguishable, black lump in a scorched bed of grass.

I can still see her face, her pale flesh and dark eyes and sweet lips adorned in one of her dozens of colors. It doesn't seem possible that she's gone, that she's been destroyed beyond all recognition. But then I look down and see this mass of bone and melted tissue and I'm flooded with an anger that can't be denied.

There was no sign of either of the two attackers who ran off, and by the time we got to him, Martha Stewart had died from his injuries, so we couldn't find out where they came from. Then I remembered how the one in the fatigues had torn something from Rita's earlobe. The letters on Martha Stewart's T-shirt confirmed my suspicions.

Nobody has said a word since we left the cemetery. We've just been driving in silence, none of us wanting to talk about what happened but all of us knowing what has to be done.

First we have to take Rita and Jerry's remains someplace safe. We'd prefer to bury them ourselves, take them to a spot out in the woods and give them a proper sendoff, but that's not possible. We don't have the time. Not tonight. And I don't know if there will be a tomorrow.

Once we drop off their bodies, we'll swing by my place to see if Zack and Luke want to come along. I wouldn't hold it against them if they didn't, but I'm pretty sure they'd want to make that choice for themselves.

After that, there's only one more stop.

Chapter 57

"Trick or treat!"

True, we're two months late, but it's the spirit that counts.

The member of Sigma Chi who answers the door stands in the doorway with a beer in his hand and looks at us as if he's trying to figure out the punch line.

"Who are you?"

"We're friends of Nick," I say, then grab him by the shirt and shove him against the door before biting into his throat. He's still twitching when I let him go and he falls to the floor, blood pooling around him in the doorway, his beer still clutched in one hand.

Two young co-eds standing in the foyer near the foot of the stairs scream and drop their drinks, then run upstairs. Zack and Luke take off after them like greyhounds, then the rest of us storm inside and lock the front door.

The winter quarter doesn't begin until Tuesday and it's nearly two in the morning so we didn't expect a full house, but the music's still thumping and the booze is still flowing so chances are we're going to be busy. Which is good. Dad always said, "Idle hands are the devil's tools."

Helen and Carl take the downstairs, while I follow Zack and Luke's lead to the bedrooms upstairs. Tom and Naomi remain inside at the front door to prevent anyone from leaving. It's admittedly indiscriminate and a few innocent people might end up paying for the actions of the three who attacked us tonight, but we've had enough.

Shouts of surprise and screams of terror are already filtering down the stairwell, accompanied by the building sounds of general chaos and hysteria, which means Zack and Luke are doing their job.

I really need to give them a raise.

Halfway up the first flight, I encounter a kid wearing only a pair of boxers and a partial erection.

"Run!" he says, trying to get past me. "There's someone upstairs eating—"

That's when he notices my blistered face and the blood running down my chin and splattered across my shirt.

He turns to flee but Zack takes him down in a way that almost makes me jealous. He has so much passion. I leave him to finish the job and continue to the second floor.

The first two rooms I check are empty, but in the third room I find a naked guy with a hairy ass trying to escape one leg at a time out the window. Before he can get his second leg through, I bite into his thigh, puncturing the femoral artery, then grab him and yank him, screaming, back inside.

At first I don't recognize who it is, then I see the army fatigues on the floor. For some weird reason, he's still wearing his knit beanie.

"No!" he screams. "No! No!"

His arms flail as he tries to grab something to hit me with, then he starts beating on me with his fists. I grab his balls and squeeze to stop him, then bite into his arm and start chewing, tearing off chunks of flesh and spitting them out until I hit bone. Mom always told me not to waste food, but I don't really have much of an appetite. I just want this one to suffer.

Between his leg and his arm, he's lost a lot of blood, but he's still breathing. And conscious. But he won't be for long.

I lean over him, his own blood dripping from my lips onto his, and I look into his eyes. I don't know if he recognizes me. I don't know if he recognizes anything. But I want my face to be the last thing he sees before he dies.

"This is for Jerry," I say before sinking my teeth into his throat.

Once his pulse stops I get up to leave, but stop when I hear the sound of muffled crying. When I open the closet door, I find a naked girl curled up on the floor, shivering in a pile of dirty clothes. She stares up at me, her eyes filled with tears.

I stare back at her, at her pale face and her dark hair, and for a moment I imagine she's Rita. Then the moment passes.

"Hey," she says.

Either she's in shock or she recognizes me from *The Daily Show.*

I realize how I must look covered in her boyfriend's blood. Or maybe he was just a one-night stand. Doesn't matter. She's better off.

I pull a blanket from the bed and cover her up, then put a finger to my lips and close the closet door.

When I come out of the room, Luke is standing there with another fraternity member dead and bleeding at his feet. Down the hallway, Zack chases a screaming brunette into one of the bedrooms. By the time I finish checking the remaining two rooms on the second floor, her screaming stops.

From downstairs comes more screaming and shouting, only not all of it is in agony or terror. Some of the fraternity members are fighting back, calling out to each other, trying to rally some courage. Above it all, I can hear Naomi, whooping and hollering, exhorting Tom to "Rip that bitch apart!" and challenging any and all comers, "Bring it on, dead meat! Bring that weak ass shit on!"

And I was worried she wouldn't have a good time.

I don't hear any voices that sound like Carl or Helen, but they're more subtle than Naomi, so I just have to hope they have the back door secured. I don't hear any sirens yet, which means we still have time.

On the third-floor landing, Luke is feeding on a petite blonde with bad fashion sense. I remind him that there'll be plenty of time for snacking later and that he needs to remain focused on the task at hand.

Luke leaves the blonde and takes off down the hallway, while I open the first door on my left and discover two young kids sitting on a couch. One is slouched on the couch grinning while the other is leaned over a bong. Neither one is Nick and both are completely stoned. They look up at me and start laughing, a lungful of smoke exploding from the second one's mouth.

I walk over to the second one, grab him by the hair, slam his face into the coffee table, then pull him to his feet and bite off his nose before launching him through the window and out into the night.

Somewhere in the middle of all this, the other one stops laughing.

He gets up and tries to put up a fight, but it ends quickly when I pin him against the couch and chew open his carotid artery.

While the wholesale massacre of the Sigma Chi members is, in itself, gratifying and addictive, it won't feel complete unless I get who I came for.

If you've never raided a fraternity to exact mortal revenge for the immolation of the woman you love, your unborn child, and your best friend, then you probably wouldn't understand.

In the bedroom across the hall, I find a girl passed out with her panties around her ankles and a used condom on the bed next to her.

Honestly, someone should have killed the members of this fraternity a long time ago.

Back out in the hallway, some kid who looks like Jerry Seinfeld is holding up a fire extinguisher, threatening to empty it at Luke. Zack, meanwhile, has his hands full with a feisty, six-foot-tall redhead who rakes her fingernails across his face.

In the distance, I hear a familiar wailing.

Prior to entering the fraternity, we all agreed that once the sirens started, everyone would scatter. But I'm not going anywhere until I find Nick, and from the look and sound of it, neither is anyone else.

Maybe we can't stop.

Maybe we know running would be pointless.

Or maybe it's just too much damn fun.

Luke is laughing as he closes the gap on Seinfeld's twin, who depresses the nozzle on the fire extinguisher. When nothing happens, he throws the fire extinguisher at Luke, then runs down the hallway past a short kid with blond hair who has stepped out of a room with a can of Lysol and a lighter. Luke sees him and rushes forward, but the kid aims the can of Lysol at him, depresses the nozzle, and sprays a jet of flame directly into Luke's face.

Luke screams and falls to the ground as the kid turns toward Zack, the can held up, the flame of the lighter flickering.

"Zack!" I yell.

He ducks out of the way before the flame shoots out, but the six-foot redhead isn't as agile. Her synthetic sweater catches on fire and she starts screaming, trying to slither out of it until she finally goes running off down the hallway, smoke and flames trailing out behind her.

The sirens are getting closer. And there are more of them. More than I've ever heard.

Luke is on the floor, being checked by his brother. I can't tell how badly he's burned, but I can't concentrate on Luke. I've found my mark.

Nick is standing less than ten feet from me, the Lysol and Bic held up in front of him like a crucifix. His hands are trembling, but at least he's fighting back. You have to admire that in a Breather. Most of them are just pussies.

"Hey, Nick," I say.

He seems stunned that I know his name. But then recognition dawns in his eyes as I start to walk toward him and whatever courage drove Nick out into the hallway abandons him.

"Stay back," he says, his voice uneven, his hands starting to shake. "S-s-stay back."

When I pass Luke and glance down, I see that his face is blistered worse than mine and his eyebrows are gone.

"Get him out of here," I say to Zack.

Zack turns and lets out a growl that chases Nick back inside his room, then he helps Luke to his feet. As they start to descend the stairs, I hear the first sirens coming down the street.

Nick closes and locks his door, but that doesn't keep me out. I'm inside and cornering him against his bar in seconds. He tries to shoot me with his Lysol flame but his fingers are shaking and he can't get the lighter to work, so he gives up and throws them at me.

"Fuck you!" he says. "Fuck you, you freak!"

Those aren't his last words, but when a zombie is devouring you while you're still alive, you tend to speak in gibberish.

When I've eaten enough of him so that he's hovering on the edge of consciousness, I grab a bottle of Bacardi 151 from his bar and dump it across Nick's ravaged body, then I pick up the can of Lysol, hold the lighter up in front of it, and spin the wheel.

From downstairs comes the sound of wood splintering and windows breaking, followed by authoritative voices barking commands. Outside, sirens continue to wail and red lights flash through the bedroom windows.

I think about Rita. I think about my unborn child. I think about Jerry. I think about the plans I had, the hopes and dreams, the love and friendship. I think about all that I endured for the past five months and how none of it can compare to the amount I've suffered this evening. To what I've lost.

"This is for Rita," I say, then I depress the nozzle on the can of Lysol, turning Nick's body into an instant inferno.

At least he's still conscious enough to scream.

Chapter **58**

arl and Tom are on one side of me, while Helen is across from us next to Naomi. It reminds me of high school dances—boys on one side, girls on the other. Only without the music or the nervous anticipation of awkward, adolescent sex.

The five of us are in the Animal Control van, our ankles and wrists restrained and secured to one another and to the sides of the van, our mouths strapped and muzzled with leather harnesses. We're like the Hannibal Lecter quintet.

Being bound and muzzled isn't as bad as you might think. The restraints are actually nylon and the muzzles are soft and have that new-car smell. The worst part was all the TV cameras and reporters waiting for us outside. How embarrassing. Talk about an awkward moment.

At least Zack and Luke got away. Or that's what we hope. No one saw them after the Santa Cruz County SWAT team arrived and no one heard any gunfire or sounds of pursuit. My guess is they'll disappear into the mountains until things die down. Maybe Ian will take them in, though he's probably going to try to distance himself from us as much as possible. I wouldn't blame him. After all he did to help us, after all the work he did to bring our plight into the national spotlight, we probably killed the civil rights movement in less than an hour.

Sooner or later something like this was bound to happen, either in retaliation or for the simple pleasure of human flesh. We're zombies. We eat Breathers. It's in our nature to feed. And while you can suppress that nature for a period of time, eventually it's going to clamor for attention. And the more you feed it, the hungrier it's going to get.

No one has said much since the more than two dozen cops, sheriff's deputies, and Animal Control officers captured us, restrained us, and led us out of the fraternity and into the van. We didn't put up much resistance. Killing and partially devouring Breathers takes a lot out of you and when you're done, you just want to relax with a good book and a mug of peppermint tea. Helps with the digestion.

But for the most part, no one has said anything because there's nothing to say. We all knew the consequences of our actions. We all knew how this would turn out.

Even for celebrities, there are certain transgressions that society won't tolerate. Like shoplifting in Beverly Hills. Or having sex with a minor. Or slaughtering everyone at a fraternity New Year's party.

You don't do what we did and expect to spend the night in a posh cage at the SPCA next to Bandit or Tigger. And white-collar prisons don't exist for the undead. We're going to the county, to the laboratory, to the donation station—to Dr. Frankenstein or Cadaver College or whatever euphemism you want to give it.

A couple of us will likely end up getting farmed for organs or used for vehicle impact tests. Maybe one or two of us will get decapitated, our heads used to help the future plastic surgeons of the world. And at least one of us will probably spend the rest of our existence in restraints on the side of a hill at a field research facility for human decay, left out to rot to help with the study of criminal forensics. In the end, it amounts to the same thing.

We're all going to be destroyed.

"Well," says Carl, breaking the silence, his voice muffled behind his leather muzzle. "I don't know about the rest of you, but that was definitely worth the price of admission."

Tom voices his agreement. Across from me, Helen and Naomi nod their heads. Although there's no sense of joy, there's a definite sense of satisfaction, of having done what we needed to do.

I look around the van at my four remaining friends and I'm reminded of the dream I had where we were all in the limo. Except we're in an Animal Control van.

And Jerry and Rita are dead.

And Carl's not barbecuing.

Though he did tend the grill at the dinner party, so there's that.

I just wish Rita and Jerry were here to share this with us. Granted, events probably wouldn't have played out the way they did had Rita and Jerry not been destroyed, but it just doesn't seem complete without them. A piece of us is missing. And for me, that piece is larger than for the others.

I close my eyes and I think about Rita.

I think about her touch and her laugh and the way she made me feel alive.

I think about her taking my hand in the rain and walking with her through Soquel Village and eating my mother's ribs together by candlelight.

I think about all of the things about her that I'm going to miss.

I've never believed in reincarnation or an afterlife or

heaven, but if one of them exists and affords me the opportunity to see Rita again, then I'm willing to take a leap of faith. I'm willing to renounce all of my preconceptions and all of my doubts about God just to be able to see Rita's face one more time, to hold her hand and take one more walk.

Of course, considering all of the Breathers I've killed and barbecued over the past month, I probably wouldn't be on God's short list for having my prayers answered. It's more likely his counterpart would be interested in setting up a meeting. Unless I don't actually have a soul, which would pretty much put the kibosh on the whole afterlife thing.

The Animal Control van comes to a stop. I open my eyes and look across at Helen and Naomi, then turn to Tom and Carl. Outside, voices shout commands and the unmistakable sound of footsteps can be heard coming around the side of the van.

I don't know if this is the end of the road, but it sure feels like where we part.

No one says anything. We all just share glances, though I can see tears in Helen's and Naomi's eyes. Before I realize what's happening, I feel them spilling down my own cheeks.

Outside, the shouting continues. Any moment I expect the back doors to open and for us to be taken to our final destinations by our SWAT team escort armed with Taser batons and flamethrowers. But the doors don't open. And in addition to the commands being given, I hear the sound of vehicles arriving behind us and car doors opening and other voices shouting back in defiance.

The volley of shouting continues to escalate until it's punctuated by the sound of gunfire that echoes through the walls of the van. Silence follows this, stretching out for several moments, thick and heavy. Then, from somewhere off in the distance, comes the sound of laughter.

After that, it's a mixture of voices shouting and weapons firing, the unmistakable *whoosh* of a flamethrower and the howl of someone in agony. Screams seem to come from all around us. More commands are shouted, the voice giving them sounding rushed and rattled. Footsteps race past on either side of us, at least a dozen by the sound of it. Something thumps against the outside of the van. A scream starts up and cuts off. Nearby, a frantic voice is calling for backup. Then it falls silent.

Footsteps come around the van again and the five of us turn our heads. Moments later, the back doors open and headlights from the SWAT truck behind us flood the inside of the van. I can't see anything other than shapes and shadows as several figures climb inside and start to unhook our wall restraints one at a time while several other figures stand guard outside. It's not until he's right in front of me, smiling through the burns and blisters of his already healing face, that I recognize Luke. And right beside him, unlocking Naomi's wrist restraints, is Zack.

I really do need to give them a raise.

Once our restraints are unlocked and our leather harnesses removed, we exit the van to discover that we're about thirty miles north of Santa Cruz on an empty stretch of the Pacific Coast Highway. On one side of the two-lane highway a sheer cliff rises up into the dark winter sky. On the other side, a guard rail is all that stands between the highway and a drop to the Pacific Ocean nearly two hundred feet down.

Behind us, several cars sit with their engines running and their doors open, while up ahead, in the headlights of the Santa Cruz County Sheriff's cruiser and the Animal Control van, a couple of SUVs block both lanes of the highway.

In addition to Zack and Luke and the handful of others who helped free us from the van, more than two dozen members of the undead roam the highway—checking for survivors, high-fiving each other, feeding on fallen Breathers. Intermittent gunfire and the occasional scream of agony comes out of the darkness, and more than a few of the undead have been permanently processed, to use one of Helen's euphemisms, but for the most part the battle here appears over.

Unfortunately, it doesn't look like we'll have much time to savor the victory.

Off in the distance, the flicker of emergency lights appears as vehicles converge on us from both directions along the highway. While the attack Zack and Luke led on our armed escort had the advantage of the living dead outnumbering the Breathers more than two to one, from the looks of it, this time the numbers appear to be significantly in the favor of the living.

Several of the undead, apparently not up to the challenge, leap over the side of the highway, choosing to take their chances on surviving the fall on the rocks below. I look over and recognize one of them, standing atop the guardrail. Tom glances back at me and smiles sheepishly with a shrug, then waves with his shortened, hairy arm before leaping off the guardrail into the darkness.

I look around at the rest of us. At Helen and Naomi and Carl. At Zack and Luke. At the two dozen remaining zombies gathered on the highway on this first day of the New Year.

It's at that moment I realize everyone is looking at me. Everyone is waiting.

Like Ray said, you can't wait around for someone else to solve your problems. Sooner or later, you have to help yourself.

"Zack. Luke," I say. "We've got company."

Without needing any more instruction, they're organizing everyone for the arrival of the enemy. Naomi and Helen both come over and give me a hug before heading off to help the twins. Carl turns to me, shakes my hand, and says, "Andy, it's been a pleasure."

And then he's gone, running to join the others, picking up a discarded flamethrower along the way.

For a moment I'm left alone, standing by the side of the Animal Control van, thinking about how all of this started for me.

How I lived.

How I died.

How I survived.

I look at the column of approaching emergency vehicles, at the procession of lights getting closer, and I realize this is probably where it ends for me. Where it ends for most of us. But at least we'll go down on our own terms and not theirs. We'll go down fighting for our right to exist.

Though, I have to admit, I'm not exactly thrilled about the prospect of being set on fire or having my head chopped off. I can think of better ways to spend a Friday night. But it sure beats spending the rest of my existence at an organ farm, an impact-testing center, or a human decay research facility.

If you've never been dismembered or crushed or allowed to slowly disintegrate until you turn into chicken soup, then you probably wouldn't understand.